MW00943145

E X T A N T

The Coelacanth Project
Book One

Sarah Newland

Books may be purchased in quantity and/or special sales by contacting the author at
SarahNewland@SarahNewlandBooks.com.

Visit the author's website at SarahNewlandBooks.com.

ISBN: 978-1-7333458-0-4

LCCN: 2019910328

First Edition

Hiking Hedgehog Press, LLC is dedicated to promoting thoughtful living and celebrates the right to read.

For Adam, who made it real.
For Lauren, who made it possible.
And for Sir GusGus, who reminded me to take
snack breaks.

WHEN I HEARD THE LEARN'D ASTRONOMER

When I heard the learn'd astronomer,
When the proofs, the figures, were ranged in columns
before me,
When I was shown the charts and diagrams, to add, divide,
and measure them,
When I sitting heard the astronomer where he lectured with
much applause in the lecture-room,
How soon unaccountable I became tired and sick,
Till rising and gliding out I wander'd off by myself,
In the mystical moist night-air, and from time to time,
Look'd up in perfect silence at the stars.

Walt Whitman 1819-1892

EXTANT

CHAPTER 1: NAUTILUS CHAMBERS

She hadn't seen the sun in three days. It had abandoned her in perpetual twilight with nothing to do but wait. Seconds stretched into minutes that slipped into hours. In the shadows, Natalie waited.

Kindling her hope was proving harder than accepting she could—

Don't even think of it.

Seven days had passed since the first bombing, since the night her parents went missing. There was a decent possibility they were trapped, or captured, or killed.

No, she refused to believe that. *Be positive.*

Natalie had not seen her friends since they were taken. She assumed they waited in cells like her own, or they had been moved, or killed.

Stop it.

Natalie rested her head against the cool, chiseled wall. She had conducted the same circular train of thought for days. She was a prisoner to her captors, her cell, and her own mind.

Moonbeams from the barred skylight high above her illuminated the scratches on the door to her cell. She wiggled her naked toes under the coarse blanket to hide them from the chill. A round clock on the wall opposite her obnoxiously ticked away the time. Tick-tock, tick-tock.

There was just enough light to make out the numbers. An ache churned her stomach. It had been thirteen hours since her last meal.

Ha!

Thirteen hours had passed since she ate, but it had been three days since she had seen a meal. She wondered if the ever-silent Chef would offer her any real food before Nautilus killed her.

Surely, Nautilus will kill me. I won't give them what they want.

Mortem ante cladem.

Natalie picked absentmindedly at the scabs on her fingertips. Every second she remained a prisoner put her family at risk.

If they're still alive, and Nautilus doesn't have them, they'll search for me. If my parents find me they'll die, or worse: get caught.

Mom and Dad, Christopher, Enzi...

She glared at the door to her cell while the clock mocked her, ticking away. Tick-tock, tick-tock.

Natalie was restless. When the door to her cell finally opened again, she wouldn't hesitate.

I have to get out.

She traced the intricate white scar swirled across her wrist.

I missed something. I have to get out.

CHAPTER 2

Natalie Morrigan turned off the car and wiggled her feet back into her high-heeled sandals.

"Seventeen years of these dinners and we still can't go casual? Ridiculous."

Natalie let her hair fall forward to hide her grin. Other than a few fleeting seconds of squealing excitement for their night out, Tawney spent the drive complaining about having to wear a dress and any footwear other than sneakers.

"Our parents do love tradition," Natalie emerged from the car. Her squished toes screamed in protest.

"Tradition is one thing," Tawney shook her head, bouncing her ringlet curls. "This is torture." She inspected Natalie's attire and poked her shoulder.

"You don't care because you actually look like a girl! You're blessed with the goods. I look like a stick-bug wrapped in a leaf." Tawney twirled her hips to make the sheer green chiffon of her dress spin. Under five feet tall and skinny as a beanpole, Tawney was tiny.

Natalie grasped Tawney's shoulders.

"You're gorgeous and you can still kick ass in that outfit, which makes you all the more amazing."

Tawney curtsied mockingly at her.

"I'll allow it." She linked her arm with Natalie's and together they met the lantern lit pathway through the woods.

"Ready?" Natalie asked her.

"Ready to skip to dessert," her friend snorted.

Natalie's shoes sank awkwardly in the mulch as the parking lot faded behind them.

"I'll admit, I am excited to see everyone." Tawney pulled Natalie a little faster. "It's going to be terrible when the summer's done and you leave. You can always go to William and Mary with me instead of moving away."

"We're nearly there," Natalie noted, ignoring her comment. Tawney had been lobbying for them to attend the local college together since their sophomore year.

Leaving is going to be hard, but it will be good.

The thought of moving an ocean away from her parents made her head spin; however, the opportunity to study at Oxford was not something she would turn away. She could practically smell the aged oak and ancient books that waited for her.

A faint glow flickered between the thin trunks of the pines, grounding her back on Virginia soil. They rounded the last cluster of trees and a grassy glade spread before them. Natalie took in a deep breath. A mixture of honeydew and charcoal greeted her nose and warmth filled her from the inside out.

The large pavilion occupied most of the clearing, with strings of twinkling lights hanging from its rafters. Rustic lanterns illuminated a lengthy, white-cloaked wooden table laden with steaming hot plates of homemade food and sterling silver ice buckets filled with soda cans. Larger than life photographs of their graduation ceremony covered the single brick wall on the far side of the pavilion. Natalie watched one of the fathers carry a plate of food from the quaint kitchen within the brick structure out to the table.

I am going to miss this.

Tawney left her and ran toward a small group gathered beneath the lights.

"Hey guys!" she shouted, managing to embrace all three boys at once. "I can't believe you're going to your far-off universities this fall! I demand you stay here!"

"Hello to you, too, Tawney," Leo's voice rose from somewhere in the mix.

Owen laughed, his black-framed glasses skewed across his face. Natalie spotted his red hair from across the glade.

Brant whistled as he removed his cap and pushed his mop of brown hair aside to appreciate Tawney's green cocktail dress.

"Oh no," Natalie hurried to them. As always, Tawney was faster.

Her brown eyes cut from gleaming to glaring. There was a green blur and a loud squeal, and in a matter of seconds Tawney had Brant pinned to the ground.

"You couldn't make it five minutes, could you?" she snapped at him, her knee digging between his shoulder blades.

"I was giving you a compliment!" Brant yelled into the ground, his hat a few feet away in the dirt.

Leo pulled out his wallet.

"I really thought they might last longer this time," he said, passing Owen a clump of dollar bills.

Owen pocketed his winnings.

"Statistics thought otherwise," he mused.

"Maybe going to different schools will be good for you two," Natalie rescued Brant's old hat and joined them.

"Nerd!" Owen hugged her, his stubble beard tickling her forehead. Tall and gangly, his embrace enveloped her.

"Hey, nerd," Natalie returned the greeting. "You look nice."

He averted his gaze and sheepishly touched the gel slicking back his ginger locks.

"He's practicing for those college girls," Leo winked at her.

His short brown hair had been brushed back for the occasion. His nose was slightly crooked in the middle, a result of years of competitive soccer, yet it managed to make him appear even more attractive.

"You can't even grow a beard," Owen muttered, patting his own stubble proudly.

Leo pulled Natalie in for a brief hug and she caught the faintest scent of cedar.

"No one wants to help me here? Seriously?" Brant complained at their feet.

Tawney let him up and he brushed the dust off his suit.

"Miss Nat, as lovely as always." Brant, brawny and boisterous, bowed dramatically and kissed her hand.

"Oh thank you, good sir." Natalie relinquished his faded red hat, the sole casual apparel permitted at Formal Fridays. "Fancy meeting you here, at the weekly march of the penguins."

Brant adjusted his bowtie as Leo and Owen pretended to smooth wrinkles out of their black suits.

"We do make an impressive flock," Leo noted, brushing imaginary lint from Owen's chest.

"We sharpen up in a peck," Brant snickered.

"Actually, as penguins we would be referred to as a 'waddle' not a flock," Owen corrected.

"Honestly, Owen," Tawney rolled her eyes. "Will M.I.T. have anything to teach you?"

Owen flushed from his neck to his ears.

"So, my fellow graduates," Brant finger gunned at each of them. "Are we doing the D.o.G. Street Strut and Coaster Crawl tonight?"

"Oooh, free dessert samples and rollercoasters until we vomit!" Tawney gave Brant an enthusiastic high five.

"On a Friday night in the summer?" Natalie frowned. "The park will be packed."

"Coaster Crawl, Nat, not Roller Rush," Leo reminded her.

"Traditions only stay traditions if you're committed," Owen

said, earning himself a celebratory fist bump.

Natalie smiled and gave in.

Living in Williamsburg has its perks; we can always go again tomorrow.

"Are you all done fooling around? We're starving!" Mrs. Elizabeth Merrick, Leo's mom, called out to them from across the clearing.

Tawney pulled them into a tight group hug. Natalie's head pressed between Leo and Brant's shoulders.

"I've missed you all!" Tawney yelled for their parents' benefit before dropping her voice. "Have any of you seen what I've been talking about? They're acting weird."

"Something's definitely going on," Leo agreed. "My parents will barely let me go to the grocery store on my own, and this morning I caught my mom going through my E-mail," he paused and glanced at the table. "Then they insist I drive dad's ride here while they take the car? It's more than just weird."

"Last night my dad asked if anyone odd had been contacting me. Anyone out of the ordinary," Brant snorted. "What kind of a question is that? It's college — no one is ordinary."

"We should do this later. Alone," Natalie suggested, sensing the stares of multiple parents on them now.

This group hug has lasted longer than a presidential handshake.

"Ice cream?" Tawney offered, breaking their embrace. "Before the colonial district and amusement park?" Her bare feet tread silently on the concrete floor of the pavilion as they approached the table. Her shoes swung uselessly at her side.

"Custard."

"Specifics," Tawney waved a pointed heel at Brant.

"Important specifics," Owen noted.

Natalie drifted to the back of their group and braced herself for the onslaught of greetings.

It's not as if we do this every week or anything, she thought sarcastically.

The people blurred together as they passed Natalie from

arm to arm, parent to parent. Mrs. Johnson's perfume burned Natalie's nose, Leo's mom gawked over her dress pockets, and Mrs. Davis talked so fast all Natalie had to do was smile and nod. Despite attending them her entire life, the gatherings were always overwhelming. Too many people with too many questions. It had all the makings of a family reunion, except they weren't family.

How can they work together eight hours a day, five days a week, and still want to socialize on the weekends? I only have to see everyone for an hour and that's exhausting enough.

With some strategic side-stepping, Natalie clutched the back of her usual seat and pulled herself out of the throng of bodies. Relieved, she sat and meticulously folded a navy cloth napkin across her lap as others began to follow her lead.

Eventually, everyone assumed their seats. Owen and his parents, Mr. and Mrs. Johnson, sat at the end closest to Natalie, followed by Mr. and Mrs. Merrick on either side of Leo, Mr. and Mrs. Davis on either side of Tawney, and finally Brant and his father, Mr. Smith, claimed the opposite end of the table. Natalie's mother and father each kissed her head as they settled on either side of her.

Natalie's father winked a green eye as he passed the first dish: garlic-roasted red potatoes. Her mouth watered as she put a generous portion on her plate.

"Save some for the rest of us!" Her mother nudged her and Natalie reluctantly passed the dish on.

Tawney's curls bounced as she swung her feet impatiently beneath the table. When Brant's father finally finished filling his plate with a heap of Mrs. Merrick's homemade macaroni and cheese, he gave the nod to dig in. Natalie ate slowly, savoring each bite of the made-from-scratch meal. Finals, graduation, and advanced placement tests had resulted in fast food for the majority of her weekday meals.

Small talk exploded amongst the large group. All the routine questions she had been fielding for months:

"Are you excited about Oxford?"

Of course.

"Did you make any new friends at orientation?"

Acquaintances, maybe.

"What's your major again?"

Philosophy and Modern Languages. Cue blank stare. It's mostly studying the application of logic and, shockingly, modern languages.

"Meet any cute college boys yet?"

And here comes the uncontrollable blushing. No comment please.

Seated near the end of the table Natalie kept her head low, hoping to avoid the onslaught of conversation filler as much as possible. Eventually, her interviewers moved on to more willing participants. Leo was kind enough to entertain her mother's questions regarding his various soccer scholarship offers. Tawney caught Natalie's eye as she tried to keep pace with the firing squad herself. Natalie did her best to watch and listen as a quiet presence on the fringes.

As plates began to clear and the conversations dwindled, Natalie noticed Mr. Johnson shift in his seat and lean towards her and Leo's fathers.

"Catch the news report this morning?" Mr. Johnson's voice was low and he kept his gaze towards his food.

"There's a bit of a tempest headed our way," Mr. Michael Merrick said from beside Leo.

"Nothing we weren't expecting," Natalie's father brushed away their concern.

"It's said to be much stronger than we were expecting, John. And coming fast."

Natalie pushed her food around her plate. She listened carefully, absorbing every word.

They are not talking about the weather.

Her foot searched for Leo's beneath the table. He sat directly opposite her and was engaged in obnoxious conversation with Brant, who sat further down. Finally, finding what she hoped was the correct foot, she pushed her heel hard onto his dress shoes.

Leo dropped his fork and started on Natalie in alarm.
"Ow!"

Natalie shushed him and nodded towards their fathers. Leo
regained composure. He cleared his throat and helped himself
to more pudding as Natalie continued making abstract art of
her food.

"We are prepared," Natalie's dad insisted. His blonde hair
had begun to show flecks of grey over the years. "We've been
preparing for nearly two decades. Our contact is in position—"

A soft chirp interrupted him and he produced a thin cell
phone from his jacket breast pocket.

"How can we be certain when we've heard nothing from
them in months? Not a word," Mr. Merrick swallowed hard
before continuing. "Thomas and I were thinking...it may be
time to reinstate Coelacanth."

Natalie's dad stared at the screen of his phone; its pale glow
underlined his frown. He shook his head and declined the call.
As he returned the phone to his pocket, Natalie was just able to
make out the name of the caller.

That's odd.

"John?" Michael Merrick tried to salvage her father's focus.
Leo had his athletic build, but his father's face was more
rounded and topped with short, jet black hair. "Your thoughts
on proceeding with Coelacanth?"

"No," John snapped back to the conversation. "Absolutely
not."

"This organization is a democracy, John. You're outvoted,"
Thomas said softly from the corner of the table. His hair was
more auburn than Owen's and curled tight around his head.

"No," her father's fist slammed on the table.

Natalie jumped in alarm, her oblivious charade shattered.
She had never seen him so angry. She looked up from her plate
and accidentally made eye contact with Brant's father, Robert
Smith. He seemed unwell, even more so than usual. His dark
eyes were sunken and his skin appeared nearly translucent.

Like Brant's mom before...

Natalie glanced at the empty chair beside Brant. It had been seven years since her death, but the chair remained at the table. The empty seat stood vigil as a solemn reminder.

"Coelacanth will sacrifice all we've worked for; it will have been for nothing," Robert Smith's voice was monotone and low.

"Maybe this isn't the time," Sam Davis, Tawney's heavy-set, reserved father spoke up.

Natalie realized the table had fallen silent as all other conversations had ceased. The entire table fixated on her father. Though she knew no one focused on her, cold sweat beaded on the back of Natalie's neck from their stares. The silence simply made it worse.

"Honey," her mother's voice was velvet soft as she reached across and touched her father's forearm. Her gaze, on the other hand, was stern.

"They started it," John muttered indignantly.

Natalie gasped as her cool-headed father threw back his chair and paced behind her mother. He pressed two fingers to his temples.

"Why don't you all go have some fun?" Patricia Davis suggested. The excitement in her voice fell short of genuine. Her long blonde hair was a stark contrast to Tawney's head of brown curls.

"Ice cream!" Tawney leapt boldly from her seat.

"Custard!" Brant stood and tossed his cloth napkin onto his plate.

Natalie folded her own napkin and stood to leave. Her farewell to her mother was interrupted by several high-pitched beeps from around the table. Each parent produced a tiny black box with a narrow screen across one end. Natalie's mother rose to stand with her dad.

"You all have pagers?" Owen asked incredulously, adjusting his glasses as though it would change the impossible sight before him.

Mr. Smith hurried to the brick wall of the pavilion and ripped down a black and white photograph of Tawney receiving her diploma. He pushed on the wall and an entire section of brick slid in. A panel floated upwards, filling the vacant space with a wide television.

"We've had a T.V. this whole time?" Tawney's mouth fell open. "I've missed so many football games for these dinners! For no reason!"

"Pagers?" Owen pointed at one of the black boxes in disbelief.

"What is this?" Leo managed to verbalize the question burning through Natalie's mind.

Her stomach knotted on itself until she couldn't move, let alone speak.

"Not sure," Natalie's father loosened his tie. "The pagers inform us if there's an emergency."

"I guess this happens a lot for your job?" Brant probed.

"No," John Morrigan scowled. "This is the first time."

The knot in Natalie's stomach tightened.

The television blinked to life on the local news station. A young woman was reporting on a new therapy to reduce the number of lives claimed annually by lung cancer.

"While no vaccine offers one-hundred percent protection, the immune response produced by this new vaccine could significantly reduce the rate of growth and metastasis of lung—"

An alarm interrupted the report while a red banner across the screen read 'Breaking News.' Images of billowing smoke and fire replaced the tidy, quiet newsroom.

"I'm coming to you from the Naval Station in Norfolk, Virginia, where an explosion occurred moments ago." The reporter yelled over car alarms, screaming, and the sirens of emergency response vehicles. The camera panned over the rubble of a collapsed building.

Natalie moved around her parents to get a better view of the screen.

Smoke filled most of the image. Out of it rose masses of warped metal and crumbled concrete. People stumbled into the street hurt, confused, and covered in blood-streaked soot. Brave souls ran into the smoke, following the screams of victims trapped inside.

"One building has been nearly demolished. Reports of any casualties or injuries have not yet come through. Local Fire and Rescue have arrived on the scene—"

The image on the screen trembled and an enormous roaring sounded through the speakers. The camera captured the ground. A pair of brown sneakers flashed in and out of the screen as the camera operator ran. The image blurred and cut out. Silence rang through the clearing for a moment before the television station returned to the anchor. She stood with her mouth hanging open in shock.

"Another explosion just occurred at the Norfolk Naval Station," her voice trembled as she read off the teleprompter. "According to base police they're…they're being bombed."

CHAPTER 3

M r. Smith clicked off the television and stared at its blank screen.

"Bombs?" Leo asked in disbelief. "Bombs in Virginia? Are they sure?"

"Isn't your office in Norfolk?" Owen asked his parents.

They exchanged a silent look, ignoring his question.

"Who is it?" Tawney's hands balled into fists. "The U.S.S.R, North Korea, Syria, or one of the other countries we constantly bicker with?"

"There's an equal chance it's an extremist from our own country," Mr. Johnson replied, scratching his chin as his mind worked.

"It's actually the Russian Federation now," Owen corrected Tawney quietly. "You're thinking of Stalin."

"Who's Stalin?" Tawney asked, exasperated.

Owen puffed out his cheeks and gawked at Natalie in alarm.

"Humanitarian," Leo snorted, patting Tawney's back to

calm her.

Owen let out a tiny squeak and pulled at his hair.

"Even I know who Stalin is," Brant muttered.

"Hardly the time," Natalie hissed, ending their conversation.

She glanced from parent to parent. Fear was plain on each of their faces. She had never seen her father scared before. His skin blanched and beads of sweat glistened on his forehead. It was more real than the news report, more real than the smoke, more real than the sirens and the people screaming.

The ground suddenly felt unreliable beneath her feet. Natalie gripped the end of the table for support. A lifelong perception shattered; she studied her mother and father as though seeing them for the first time. Her entire life they had stood on a pedestal: invincible, infallible, constant. This bombing wasn't a world away; it was in their backyard. In a second, it changed everything. She could see her parents clearly now. Their fear and their confusion. Their raw humanity.

They're as scared as I am.

"What do you do?" Natalie demanded the truth from her mother. "Why do you get called when bombs go off?"

"You know I can't tell you," Mrs. Morrigan tucked a brown curl behind her ear.

"Because you've sworn not to or because you're scared to?"

"I've found out more in the past hour than I have my entire life," Tawney chimed in, defiantly facing her own parents. "What is going on?"

"It risks your safety to divulge—"

Brant threw back his chair, cutting off Natalie's father.

"Our safety? A bomb goes off, what, an hour away at most? In the same city as your office? And you're called? You, of all people. Are you honestly convinced we feel safe right now?"

"Enough," Mr. Smith gripped Brant's arm with more strength than he appeared capable of. "That is enough."

"All of you go on and get your ice cream—"

"Ice cream?" Leo interrupted Mrs. Davis. "I'm not going

anywhere until you tell us what's going on."

"We deserve the truth," Owen added, his gaze flicking from the pagers to the hidden television screen.

Natalie's father scowled and dark circles shadowed his eyes. She wondered how she had missed it before, the evidence of stress etched into his skin.

I didn't want to see.

After a long moment, he faced Natalie and slowly closed his eyes. When they opened again, they brimmed with tears. The knot twisting in Natalie's abdomen fell into oblivion. She wanted to hold him, to take away his pain, but the thought terrified her.

He's my father. The strongest person I've ever known. I can be strong enough to rise up, to console him.

She couldn't.

She settled for returning the slow blink. When Natalie opened her eyes, his tears were gone. The curtain of fearlessness cloaked him once again, but it was too late. She had seen the truth.

He blinked...he promised.

"We have to call the office," Natalie's mother gave her hand a tight squeeze.

"Good, do it now," Leo offered his own phone.

Natalie saw the silent plea in her mother's stare, the way she barely squinted at her.

He promised.

"Let them do their job," Natalie conceded. "Let's go."

"What?" Owen and Brant cried out, confused. Brant slipped out of reach of his father.

"Now is the time to get answers!" Tawney yelled, standing on her chair.

"No, it's time for them to do their jobs," Natalie corrected her friend quietly. "People were probably just killed, Tawney. Our questions can wait a few more hours."

Leo stayed silent. He leaned forward on the table, his mouth set as he tried to read her.

Tawney unleashed a string of obscenities and jumped down from her perch.

"Come on," Leo said over her foul language. "Dessert is on me."

Mrs. Davis kissed Tawney on her forehead and dismissed them with a wave. A heavy hand fell on Natalie's back. Her father managed a half-hearted smile as he guided her a few paces away from the table.

"We'll be waiting for you," he tucked her hair behind her ears. "Don't be scared, little bilby."

"You blinked," Natalie hissed under her breath. "You blinked, so you promised."

"Yes," he sighed. "I know. Your mother and I will explain when we get home."

"Everything?"

He hesitated.

"Okay. Everything." He slipped away, not giving her the opportunity to press for more information or to ask why he called her a bilby or what a bilby even was.

"Come on, Nat," Tawney pulled her towards the pathway, her shoes slung over her shoulder. "We have tons to discuss already."

Natalie let Tawney convince her to traverse the two blocks to the ice cream parlor on foot while the boys drove separately. It was a silent trek other than Tawney's occasional hissing after stepping on a rock or pinecone. The cobblestone path was interrupted every hundred feet or so by a tall lamppost.

Natalie tried to shake the image of the rubble from her mind. She feared for the people caught in the blast and in the aftermath. She worried for her parents who were, for some reason, called in to help.

Voices drifted to them on a cool breeze.

"Is that coming from the parlor?" Tawney asked.

Natalie groaned when they turned the corner. The typically

desolate ice cream stand was packed.

The parlor was quaint. It was a cement block with purple paint and a single counter for ordering. Giant plastic scoops of custard adorned the corners of the roof and molded sugar cones supported the counter. The surrounding outdoor space was fair game for seating, and almost entirely occupied. People spanned the grounds and the line for orders wrapped around the building.

"Alright, who spread the news about Colonial Custards?" Leo asked as he, Brant, and Owen ran to join them from the parking lot.

"Nothing like a threat to our national security to remind us of what really matters in life," Owen nodded solemnly. "Frozen desserts."

"You know," Brant chimed in, "they say violence increases proportionately to ice cream sales in a given area."

"Yeah, I'm sure it's the sugar high and not the summer heat making everyone irritable," Leo smirked.

Tawney held Natalie's arm to keep from losing each other as they elbowed their way along the crushed oyster shell path to the counter. Every conversation Natalie passed through involved the bombing. Even the two televisions above the counter broadcasted the breaking news report.

Who was behind it? Why did they target Norfolk? How many were injured or dead? Was another attack imminent?

A final strategic shift through the crowd and Tawney claimed the counter. As her friend placed a sampler order for the group, Natalie stared at the T.V., barely able to make out the report over the chatter of the other guests.

"Sixteen reported injuries and climbing...no known fatalities...Naval Station expected to remain closed for several days...essential personnel only."

Someone bumped against her. Leo stood transfixed by the report as well. Brant bumbled past them, desperate to add some final toppings to Tawney's order.

"Let's find seats," Owen shifted uncomfortably in the large

group of people.

As they surveyed the limited seating options, Natalie saw many of the other ice cream goers staring back at them. Her cheeks flushed.

"I guess we're a bit overdressed," Leo observed, casually slipping his jacket over her shoulders as though it would disguise the shimmering purple dress beneath it.

Natalie pulled the jacket tighter and the scent of cedar engulfed her. It was utterly intoxicating. Her cheeks blushed harder.

What in the world?

Owen pointed to a solitary picnic table beneath an old oak tree where a family of four packed their trash to leave.

"On it!" Brant dove into the crowd.

Natalie caught brief glances of his red cap bobbing between tables. Reaching his goal, Brant stood on the seat and thrust his fist in the air in victory.

"The only way out is through," Leo said before squeezing between customers.

"Encouraging," Natalie muttered, tucking in close behind him.

It seemed to take forever to reach Brant. Natalie was elbowed and jostled by people in the crowd and had her hair pulled more than once by bored, hip-riding toddlers.

"That wasn't so bad," Leo noted as he and Brant took their seats.

Natalie sat opposite them and shook her head.

"We have different definitions for what qualifies as 'bad.'"

"Definitions, no. Perceptions, maybe."

Natalie raised her eyebrows.

"This is awesome!" Tawney declared as she plopped the buffet of frozen treats on the table. One of the strangers closest to them shot her a condescending glare.

"I'm talking about the ice cream, honestly," Tawney stuck her tongue out at them.

Owen emerged close behind her and passed out spoons.

"So," Brant spoke through a mouthful of brownie sundae, "hidden televisions and super-secret pagers...definitely spies."

Owen pointed his spoon at him.

"We ruled out spies years ago, Brant. Did you not notice the tech our parents were using? Pagers. No spy is using a pager."

"And no spy can work regular business hours. Our parents are always home for dinner. Don't forget the basics," Tawney cut in.

"Fine," Brant caved. "Maybe they aren't the spies in the field using fancy tech, but every spy organization has a home base! Maybe they're secretaries or something."

"That's idiotic!" Tawney insisted.

"It's much more likely they're with the Department of Defense," Owen reached for a miniature banana split.

"You would agree with her," Brant sneered, grinning around his spoon. Owen's ears burned red.

"Or we could all be wrong," Leo shrugged.

"There's some positivity," Brant chuckled.

"We probably are," Natalie agreed with Leo, pushing away her chocolate custard. Her nerves made her too nauseous to eat.

When she was a child, her parents told her they were whatever she wanted them to be: an astronaut, the President, a firefighter. As she grew older, their responses changed.

"Don't you worry about it dear. We work hard each day like everyone else."

It was not until she started high school that the most recent piece of information had surfaced.

"We don't have clearance to share our duties with you, but trust we are keeping you safe."

It was this statement that solidified the idea their parents were some kind of secret agents. Brant was completely convinced once they discovered all of their parents had fed them the same lines, word for word. However, reality soon dampened the theory.

Our parents work normal business hours and never take any odd leaves of absence.

Most days Natalie didn't bother with the fact she had no idea what her parents did when they left home each morning. She had never known anything different. Even though her parents had never told her the truth about their jobs, she loved them for never actually lying about it. It had always been an open secret, a known unknown. Normally, she didn't have a problem with it.

That was before they were the first point of contact after a bombing.

"Did anyone else hear them talking about the tempest tonight? A tempest refers to a storm and there's been nothing on the weather reports to suggest anything of that magnitude," Leo's question drew Natalie out of her thoughts. "And I doubt they were quoting Shakespeare."

"Could be anything," Brant adopted Natalie's abandoned ice cream.

"Does anyone know what a bilby is? Or Coelacanth?" Natalie asked, digging her phone out of her dress pocket.

"What's this gibberish? Seals can't what? Is the sugar getting to your brain?" Brant placed his palm on her forehead as though to check for a fever.

"Seel-uh-kanth, not 'seals can't'," Natalie pushed him away and focused on her internet search. "A bilby is—" She stopped herself, distracted by the description of the small creature. "Do you guys think I have big ears?" Natalie pulled on a lobe, concerned.

"You've never noticed?" Leo smiled.

"Ha, ha, very funny. I guess I'm as blind to them as you are to deadlines. Have you decided on a college yet?"

Leo shrugged as he spooned chocolate syrup into his mouth.

"I figured it would be easy for you."

"That's what everyone keeps telling me. And yet," Leo

shrugged again.

Concerned she had touched on a sensitive subject, Natalie returned to her original question.

"This says bilbies have extensive tunnel—"

"Nat, please, we're discussing adult things here," Brant cut her off.

"Unfortunately, he's right," Tawney nodded solemnly, as though that fact alone was a sacred occurrence.

Natalie shoved her phone back into her pocket. The tiny marsupial with gigantic ears scampered frantically about her brain, searching for its niche within the precariously stacked shelves of stored information.

"After seventeen years of silence, how are we going to get our parents to suddenly open up?" Owen twisted a particularly long strand of beard hair.

"It has to be something different," Leo said.

"I might have something," Natalie remembered the call her father received moments before their pagers had gone off.

"What's that, dear?" Tawney slid into the seat next to her.

"We ask Uncle Chris."

Silence. After a few awkward seconds, Brant cleared his throat.

"Um...what?"

"No," Tawney crossed her arms. "We haven't heard from him in years, Nat. Years. No visits, no phone calls, no birthday cards. Next option?"

"He tried calling my dad right before the bombing was broadcast."

Tawney's big brown eyes somehow got wider.

"You're lying," she accused.

Natalie scoffed.

"Since when do I lie to you?"

"Let's call him now!" Brant shoveled in the last of his dessert and stood. "We also have to find a new ice cream parlor. The commoners have invaded."

"Yes, God save us from the plebeians," Leo nodded, gathering their trash.

Brant dropped his bowl onto the food tray and the rest of the plastic bowls trembled. Green acorns rained down from the branches of the oak tree above them.

"What the—" Brant backed away from the table in alarm.

The crowd surrounding the ice cream parlor grew eerily silent as a low rumbling filled the air. The trembling continued for a moment, then everything was still.

"Earthquake!" Someone shouted nearby.

A terrified murmur swept through the crowd. Above the tree line, a few streets towards the darkening horizon, a cloud of smoke rose towards the first twinkling stars.

"That wasn't an earthquake," Owen said quietly, pointing to the billowing cloud of ash. "It was an explosion."

CHAPTER 4

The parlor erupted with chaos. People shouted as they abandoned their custard and ran for their vehicles.

"It was an earthquake, Owen," Tawney argued, her voice unsteady. She stared at the rising smoke in the distance.

The television screens flickered. The news report from the Naval Station switched to a man sitting behind a large glass desk. Natalie struggled to catch sound bites over the noise of the crowd.

"Reports are coming...another explosion...Williamsburg..." The man nodded at something beyond the camera before continuing. "Residential...continuation...in Norfolk earlier this evening."

"Explosion," Owen nodded, also fixed on the television.

"How did they get a report so fast?" Natalie asked, watching people flood the parking lot. "It just happened."

That was near instantaneous.

Owen squinted at her. She imagined the gears in his brain

working.

"That was too fast," he agreed.

"We need to get home," Leo said, rising from the table.

Smoke swirled above the trees and dissipated, lost in the night sky.

Home.

Natalie's head spun as she pictured the worst: her house in flames with her mother and father caught in the blast. She took out her phone and tried to call her mother's cell. The call transferred straight to voicemail.

"Residential," Natalie muttered, repeating the newscaster's words. She tried calling her father's phone.

"We need to get home now," Leo insisted. "Natalie, where's your car?"

The call went to voicemail again.

"They aren't answering," Natalie told him.

Leo lifted her chin so she saw nothing but his face.

"Are you with me? Where is your car?" His brown hair fell into his face, but he didn't seem to care.

"The pavilion," Natalie answered. Her mind sank into fog. Her thoughts lost their way from one synapse to the next.

"I'll take you home," Leo insisted. "Brant, take Owen and Tawney home. They're both on your way."

Natalie put her phone away and hugged Tawney tight.

"Call me when you're home."

Tawney nodded and hurried after Brant and Owen. Her shoes laid on the seat of the picnic table, forgotten.

By the time they got moving, the parlor grounds were completely trashed. Trays full of frozen treats laid abandoned in the grass. People cried as they watched the news report, talked loudly on their phones, or scrambled towards their cars.

"Come on," Leo had to shout over the noise. "You're going to have to sit close, and be careful with your legs."

Certain she had misheard him, Natalie followed Leo away from the parlor. People shoved against her in the madness. Leo held her wrist and pulled her behind him as he navigated the panicked mass of bodies. Still strapped in high heels, her feet throbbed by the time they reached the parking lot.

Ridiculously impractical footwear, she thought, cursing Formal Fridays.

Natalie stood patiently next to a four-door sedan, waiting for Leo to unlock the doors. Instead, he tossed her a shiny black helmet.

"What—" Natalie had turned to ask what the helmet was for, but stopped short when she caught sight of him straddling a motorcycle. Every inch of it was flat black: the seats, the handle bars, the bags, even the chrome.

Natalie realized her mouth was hanging open and cleared her throat.

"Leo, I couldn't possibly."

"You can and you will," he offered a hand to help her get on.

She stared at it, hesitating. Natalie adjusted his jacket and pulled the sleeves above her wrists.

Of all the nights…

"Isn't this your dad's?"

"He suggested I take it tonight. Crazy, right?"

Not as crazy as me getting on it.

Natalie awkwardly climbed on behind him, trying to be as ladylike as possible in her dress. She reluctantly slipped the helmet onto her head.

Leo chuckled when he peered back to check on her.

"You look terrified. You're going to be fine."

"Yes, you and your imaginary motorcycle license are so reassuring."

"Hey, I can drive."

"Just because you can doesn't mean you should."

"I thought that was the goal of humanity: push the envelope, do the impossible."

Natalie frowned at him.

"Okay, okay," he conceded. "I'll take you to your car."

The motorcycle rumbled to life. Though quieter than most bikes, she still jumped at the sound. Natalie stared back at the now abandoned ice cream parlor. Two employees in powder blue shirts stood in the clearing, surrounded by a sea of strewn cups, spoons, and half-eaten waffle cones.

My car is two blocks in the wrong direction, a complete waste of time. Smoke continued to rise against the blackening sky.

I want to see my parents.

"Take me home."

"You sure?" he asked, flipping down the faceguard on his helmet.

Natalie hesitantly held on to his shoulders to brace herself.

"Positive," she replied, not positive at all. She tried to imagine the motorcycle equated to riding a rollercoaster, but the logic won out.

No tracks, no safety checks, no control. Natalie chewed her lip. *Oh, and no license.*

"Okay then," he sounded surprised. "The pipes on this bike don't get as hot as most, but still be mindful where your legs are. I don't want you to get burned. Keep your calves on mine."

Natalie was suddenly grateful for the helmet as her entire face flushed pink.

"And hold on," Leo wrapped her arms tight around his waist.

Thankfully, he did not wait for her to respond. He pulled smoothly away from the curb and confronted a long line of cars waiting to get out of the parking lot. Natalie tapped her toes impatiently on the foot stand. It would take ages to get home through the traffic.

Without warning, Natalie lurched backwards as Leo popped the front end of the bike onto the sidewalk. She yelped and squeezed him tighter to keep from falling off. They leveled out as the back wheel cleared the curb, and then they were racing along the cobblestone path.

"This is so illegal," Natalie said as she buried her head into Leo's back. Trees blurred past them, streaks of brown and green. A few moments later she yelped again as they dropped back onto the road.

Leo gained speed on the pavement. They bobbed in and out between cars and cruised through stop signs. Natalie tried to focus instead on how the wind whipped Leo's white dress shirt into rippling waves across his back.

Sooner than she expected, they began to slow. Natalie summoned enough courage to watch the familiar houses flitting past them. Brick ranchers on spacious, manicured lawns lined either side of the road, each with a lit lamppost at the end of the driveway.

"Doing okay?" he called back.

Natalie hit his arm and pointed ahead of them. She lived in one of the few two-story houses in the neighborhood, and its windows glowed bright a few lots ahead.

"They're home!" Natalie said, relief flowing through her.

They're home. They're safe.

She felt Leo relax beneath her grip.

"I'm going to drop you off at the door and head home to my folks," he explained as they rolled off the asphalt and into the gravel driveway.

They reached the narrow cement path leading to the front door and Leo flipped up his faceguard. His mouth was set in a thin line as he surveyed the lot. Natalie was pondering how best to dismount when Leo interrupted her thoughts.

"Where is your parents' car?"

Natalie examined the yard. The driveway was empty, but light spilled from every window of the house. The front door swung back and forth a few inches with the breeze.

"The door's open…"

Natalie heard the concern in his voice. A shadow moved across one of the windows on the second floor.

"They are home!" she exclaimed. "My dad promised to tell me the truth. I'll fill you in after."

"When did he say that?" Leo asked, skeptical.

"Right after the bombing; he gave me a slow blink."

"Slow blink?" Leo shook his head. "Is that a millennial form of winking?"

Natalie shifted impatiently.

"No. It's rumored animals can communicate their intent through eye contact and blinking speed. Staring suggests they're asserting dominance. A slow blink is them saying 'trust me, I come in peace.'"

"You truly believe that?" Leo arched an eyebrow.

"Of course not, Leo," Natalie shook her head. "It's something we discussed years ago, but he knew I would remember."

"So you expect your dad to divulge our parents' deepest secret because he slowly blinked at you?"

"Yes."

Leo stared at her for a long moment.

"Uh-huh. Nat, this doesn't feel right. We're leaving," Leo snapped his faceguard down and whipped the bike around, flinging gravel into the yard.

"What are you doing?" Natalie yelled at him, barely able to stay on.

"You're coming home with me. Something's off."

He had nearly reached the end of the driveway when Natalie made up her mind. She let go of Leo's waist, put her arms around her face, and rolled off the back of the bike. The ground rose up around her much faster than she expected. She cried out as searing pain exploded where she landed on her shoulder. Her head bounced off the ground hard as she rolled to a stop.

Natalie lay stunned for a moment. Her body quickly gave her an itemized summary of her injuries and she groaned. Her shoulder burned as though someone pushed an iron poker into it and her legs stung where the gravel cut into her exposed skin. Every muscle protested as she pushed off the cracked helmet and forced herself to her feet.

She took a few uneasy steps towards the house, holding her left shoulder gingerly. The helmet and Leo's jacket had saved her a lot of damage. She scratched a tickle on her leg and her fingers came away wet with blood. Long, shallow cuts wrapped around her thighs and calves. Somehow, the abrasions began to sting more after she saw them.

"Nat!" Leo called out. He spun the bike around and sped next to her. "What the hell!"

Natalie strode stronger with every step, determined to get inside.

Leo's helmet hit the ground and the motorcycle fell silent.

"You're insane!" he said incredulously. "You jumped off a freaking motorcycle!" Leo skirted around to confront her.

"They're here, Leo."

"I don't think so."

"What if you're wrong?"

"Then I'm wrong," Leo shrugged. "But process what you're seeing, Nat."

She tried.

She saw her home. She saw the dark painted shutters that merely framed the windows for aesthetics. She drank in the scent of the freshly mulched flower bed and watched its garden flag, embroidered with a cursive 'M' for Morrigan, sway in the warm breeze. She saw Leo with his thin black tie hanging loose around his neck, standing between her and the porch.

His athleticism showed. Soccer had made him strong; his shirt fit snug around his shoulders and biceps. Soccer had made him analytical; his brown-green eyes focused intensely on hers, flicking briefly to her arms and feet, waiting for movement. However, most inconveniently, soccer had made Leo fast.

I'll never make it around him to the door.

Natalie watched a shadow move across the glowing window

above them.

I have to get inside.

She advanced towards Leo. Before she took another step, he cleared the distance between them and took hold of her wrist. Natalie winced and gasped. He dropped his hold and she gingerly clutched her wrist against her side.

"I'm so sorry! Did you hurt it on the gravel?" He frowned with genuine concern, giving Natalie the slightest twinge of guilt. While he fussed over her feigned injury, she took two strategic steps and positioned herself between Leo and her house.

"No, Leo, I'm sorry."

She saw his confusion before she turned and ran. Her pointed heels sank awkwardly in the grass on her first step, but her second landed on the solid stone sidewalk. She pushed off hard. He had speed and training on his side. All she had was surprise.

Natalie leapt over the porch stairs and ran through the open door.

Home.

She had lived her entire life in the one house. The foyer opened to the living room and kitchen, and reached up high to a balcony on the second floor. An ornate atom-structured chandelier hung from the ceiling, illuminating the family photographs adorning the walls. Despite having bookcases in nearly every room, stacks of novels spilled onto end tables and windowsills. Hanging green plants crept their way across the ceiling to the tall French doors that led to the back yard. The kitchen shone with stainless steel appliances and black granite countertops. A large white lantern sheltered three pillar candles on the center island. In the evening, their flickering glow would find the mirrored flecks in the granite and make them sparkle. Aside from the occasional change in paint color, the house had remained the same her entire life.

Natalie stopped short a few paces into the foyer. It looked as though a tornado had blown through her home. Mail littered the floor and stuffing cascaded out from the brown couches, forming snowdrifts in her living room. Photographs that normally hung on the walls were smashed, reduced to glass shards that crunched under Natalie's feet. The kitchen cabinets had been emptied and their contents strewn across the floor. Broken china made the kitchen practically impossible to navigate.

"We should leave," Leo glowered at her from the doorway.

The floor above them creaked.

Natalie's head whipped around to the stairs. Bloody paw prints trailed down them, through the wrecked kitchen, and out the back door.

Enzi.

"Someone is here," Leo hissed.

"Yes, my parents."

"Or maybe someone else. There's no way they didn't hear the bike. We need to—"

Darkness engulfed them. Natalie stood frozen, incapable of movement, incapable of breathing. Her mind struggled to adapt to the sudden absence of light. It invented ominous shapes in her vision, setting her imagination on fire.

Don't move. Your eyes will adjust, she told herself.

Trying to compensate for the sudden blindness, her ears amplified every sound. Her shallow breaths seemed to reverberate off the walls. Her heart bellowed its beats like a gong. After an eternity, she made out the faint outline of the front door.

Natalie jumped as a soft touch traced her arm until it found her fingers. Leo led her towards the door. She was nearly there when glass shattered in the kitchen.

We're not alone.

Abandoning all attempts of hiding, Leo ran full pelt for the door. Natalie scrambled desperately behind him. She slipped on a pile of glass and fell. Every time she tried to stand, her ankle rolled or more glass slipped out from under her. Leo continued to pull her as she struggled to find her feet.

The stranger grumbled loudly, his voice much closer than Natalie expected. Two burly hands took hold of her waist. She screamed as she rose into the air, plucked from Leo's grasp.

CHAPTER 5: NAUTILUS CHAMBERS

Despite their narcotic concoction, Natalie was certain she remembered more than her captors intended her to.

Kidnap Palooza, Natalie thought bitterly. *They ambushed us. They had us in seconds. We missed something. They wouldn't hunt us simply because we can —*

No. Focus on the facts. How did Nautilus find us so fast?

Natalie closed her eyes and tried to recall the events of her capture as clearly as possible. Natalie had offered herself up. She promised to go willingly if Nautilus let her friends go.

What a joke.

She remembered a sharp pinch in her neck as they injected something into her. Nearly instantaneously, the world fell away. Brief glimpses of consciousness interrupted her sleep. A hard bump in the road jolted her in a van and she recalled the loud engines of a plane. It was not until she had been poked again Natalie truly started to wake.

A painful prick on the inside of each elbow told her they were drawing blood. Her head was heavy and her thoughts traveled agonizingly slow. Peering through her eyelashes, she saw her wrists were bound to a chair by thick leather straps. She tried to pull against the restraints, but her body refused to listen. Her left pinky managed a single pitiful twitch. Avoiding the vials of blood, Natalie listed her head to the side to locate her friends.

She found herself in a white, circular room lit with long fluorescent bulbs humming on the ceiling. White tile floors reflected the light off stainless steel lamps and tables strategically arranged around several padded reclining chairs. The effect was blinding.

Natalie squinted at the petite figure strapped in the chair to her right.

A sharp beeping blared in her ears and unfamiliar faces in white surgical masks swam before her. They spoke quickly to each other and one shone an annoying penlight in her face.

The beeping is my heart rate!

They're going to drug me again.

Closing her eyes, Natalie rested her head against the padded chair and forced herself to remain calm.

Deep breath in…long breath out.

Don't panic.

The beeping slowed and the penlight faded away.

Regain control.

Finally, the needles were removed from her arms and a bandage applied to each puncture. Her bindings were undone and two people pulled her into a slumped standing position. Natalie wondered if it was the drugs or the loss of blood making her head swim. She tried to search for her friends, but the room was dancing and morphing in a blur of white and light.

Natalie's captors adjusted their grip and dragged her between them. Their fingers dug painfully into her biceps, sending blood trickling down her forearms around the bandages they had placed. She looked up in time to see her friends being taken away from her. Their heads hung heavy on their chests, still sedated.

Natalie yelled for them. She screamed so loud her throat threatened to rip apart. She took in the deepest breath possible and bellowed until her chest ached, but what escaped her mouth was barely louder than a whisper.

The blinding white room faded away as they dragged her into a dim passageway. Her bare feet bumped along the cool, unfinished floor. Even her escorts tripped occasionally, dropping her roughly into the dirt. Soon the glow of the clinic was gone. Instead of fluorescent bulbs, red beacons illuminated the floor every few hundred feet. They ascended a gentle upwards slope with several turns and countless branching passages. Natalie would never remember the way.

They may have lugged me around in circles and I would never know.

Unexpectedly, her captors dropped their hold on her and she sank to the floor. She was able to push herself onto one of her elbows as a huge wooden door closed off the passageway. It slid left out of the wall, sealing her in.

Natalie collapsed in the dead-end where they left her. A soft ticking alerted her to the clock. She stared at it. A quarter after three. She assumed it was three fifteen in the morning, since the skylight high above her showed a twinkling starry sky.

Natalie let the exhaustion take her and rested her cheek in the dirt.

When she woke later that day, the fog of the sedative had gone. Natalie got to her feet as panic hit her hard, making cold sweat bead on her forehead.

I'm trapped.

She traced along each wall of the cell. Solid, cold stone. She traced the seam of the door to find it was flush with the wall. Natalie clawed at the wood, scratching and screaming until she lost the ability to speak. She opened her mouth and no sound came out. Blood dripped from her fingertips, staining everything she touched.

There has to be another way out.

The cot on the far wall did not move no matter how hard she pulled or kicked. She stood on the mattress and reached stupidly for the skylight still at least ten feet above her. The night sky glowed with a rare ribbon of color.

It's still dark?

Natalie scowled at the clock on the wall. It was exactly six. Whether it was six at night or six in the morning, there must be daylight at some point.

Where am I?

Defeated, Natalie slumped against the wall and sank to the cot.

I have to get out.

She stared around her cell, working the problem in her mind. Four stone walls, a door without hinges, an unreachable skylight, a loathsome ticking clock, a thin cot with a thin blanket, and a cold dirt floor. That's all she had. After hours of analyzing the same variables, she reached the simple, crushing truth.

The only way out is through that door.

After establishing that the door to her cell was the sole way in and out, it was by far the most interesting part of her room. It opened at least twice a day, sliding left into the wall itself, revealing a short dark passageway to a bathroom with a frigid shower. More interesting still, was the door could also slide to the right, leading to a much longer passageway. The passageway that brought her to the cell. The passageway that lead to freedom.

She sat in purgatory, tending the door, willing it to slide to the right.

I have to get out.

When she became tired of sitting, Natalie paced restlessly. Convinced she had missed something, something important.

Nautilus must have figured out how to find them beyond tracking tacking signatures. She touched the shining white scar on her right arm and scoffed at herself.

We were reckless.

Natalie had finally grown accustomed to the silence when a metallic grinding made her leap off the cot in alarm. She held her fists high in front of her and faced the door, prepared to fight whatever stood between her and freedom. Her heartbeat pounded in her ears as she waited. The screeching continued, but the door had yet to budge.

A blur of movement caught her eye along the baseboard beside her cot. Natalie watched apprehensively as a square of wall revolved and a bowl of soup and a cup of water appeared. The panel shuddered to a stop and silence enveloped her again, thicker than before.

"Hello?" Natalie croaked, still hoarse from her screaming. "Who's there? What are you going to do with me?"

Silence.

She stared at the food, her stomach grumbling. Steam swirled up from the soup, carrying a mixture of spices that made Natalie's mouth water. She tried to lift the bowl, but it was stuck to the revolving panel.

Natalie had briefly entertained the idea it was poisoned. She shook her head at the thought. It made no sense to go through the trouble of kidnapping her simply to poison her. The fact she was imprisoned meant they knew who she was. What she was.

No, definitely not poisoned.

Her internal debate lasted too long and the offering revolved back beyond the wall, untouched. Natalie cramped with hunger as she slumped against the cot.

She nearly lost her mind that first day. She was certain Nautilus would come to question her, but no one came. Ever.

The next food offering arrived several hours later and she devoured it without question.

Officially not poisoned.

"Thanks Chef," Natalie had said to the panel half-sarcastic, half-serious.

It had been three days since she was dragged into her cell. Three days of darkness and silence. Natalie never saw her nicknamed 'Chef' who brought her rations of food, and there was never any sound of their approach. She was not sure anyone brought it at all. For all Natalie knew, Chef didn't exist. Perhaps the panel connected to a magical, automated food dispenser and her rations materialized with the push of a button. If there was one thing she had learned in the past few days, it was that anything is possible.

Question everything.

Natalie stared at the purple and green bands of light flickering far beyond the window. She feared for her friends. If their captors were not torturing her, they must have started with one of the others. The idea made her cringe. She wished they would take her out and get whatever they were going to do over with. She wondered if she was strong enough to endure torture and not tell what little information she had managed to gather between the bombing and their capture. She touched the healing scabs on her legs.

Probably not.

For what was probably the millionth time, Natalie kicked the cot and flung the tattered blanket to the ground.

Then there were the bombings.

How are we supposed to protect the world if we can't even manage to free ourselves?

The question mocked her as the hours continued to tick by. Tick-tock, tick-tock.

Her stomach grumbled, but she ignored its complaints. She began to go through her capture again. She must have missed something.

I have to get out.

CHAPTER 6

The man draped Natalie easily over his shoulder and carried her deeper into the house. Each second took her farther away from the door and farther away from Leo. She kicked and scratched and slammed her fists against his back, but all of her blows reverberated off him. Her captor bounced slightly and Natalie winced as his shoulder dug into her stomach. He bounced again, and again.

Oh no.

"Leo!" Natalie cried out.

The man jostled her. The bouncing continued. Steady, rhythmic.

He's going upstairs!

Natalie threw her weight around, hoping to catch him off balance, but he continued his climb.

"Stairs!" Natalie screamed to Leo. "Stairs!"

Something collided into the man from behind, sending him stumbling up against the rising stairwell.

"Natalie, run!" It sounded as though Leo was right next to her.

The man grunted as she hit him repeatedly, desperate to get away. Still in his grasp, Natalie just barely touched a solid stair beneath the toe of her right foot. She tried to kick off, but it was too far. The man restrained her firmly. He was so large she couldn't reach the ground to get off him.

"Ugh!"

Something tumbled down the stairs, landing at the bottom with a solid thud. Her captor rose and resumed his march.

"Leo?"

Silence.

"Leo!"

"Got her!" the man barked.

"What about the boy?" a woman asked from the shadows, her voice squeaky.

Natalie choked back a sob. There were more of them. And the man was absolutely correct: he had her. Her captor shrugged, rocking Natalie up and down on his shoulder.

"What about him? I got one, didn't I?"

The bouncing ceased when they reached the top of the stairs. Natalie attempted to stifle her fear so she could think clearly.

They're going to kill me. They're going to use me as bait to draw out my parents. Maybe torture me? I don't know anything!

"Natalie!" Leo's voice came to her from far away. Muffled, but definitely him.

"Leo!" her scream broke into a sob. She kicked harder.

"Hey now. Stop that, little one," he shook her.

"Hold on, Nat! Kick, scream, bite. Give 'em hell!"

Give 'em hell?!

I'm going to die.

Leo's shouts continued to drift to her from somewhere below, but she hardly heard him. A low growl sounded from the shadows in front of her, near the staircase. The man tensed beneath her.

"Did you hear that?" he whispered.

The growl rumbled louder, closer. Natalie's captor squeezed her so hard she struggled to breathe. Whatever the creature was, it wasn't with him.

Snarling jaws snapped as the creature lunged for them. Fur brushed against her face and the man howled. He let go of Natalie to defend himself and she fell to the floor. The pitch-black hallway echoed with terrifying roars and the man's horrific screaming.

Natalie pushed herself to her feet only to tumble again. The adrenaline was making her shake, making her clumsy. She stumbled towards the stairwell, guiding herself along the balcony rail. She caught Leo's jacket on something in the darkness. When she tried to pull away, it squeezed her arm.

"You come with us, sweetie," a woman whispered in her ear.

The fierce beast snarled and its jaws smacked shut. There was a nauseating splatter of liquid against the walls. The man shrieked. Distracted by the attack on her partner, the woman's hold on Natalie's jacket softened. Natalie yanked herself free and ran. Her mind was sluggish and foggy, but her muscles knew the way. She made it back to the staircase and collided with something solid.

It grunted.

Natalie pushed the stranger and tried to rush past, but they stopped her.

"No, no, please no," Natalie begged.

"Nat?"

"Leo," she breathed.

"Go, go," he pushed her ahead of him as the man's deafening howling resumed.

Natalie hurried down the stairs, clutching her dress above her knees. She cleared the last stair and Leo flew past, taking hold of her. He pulled her faster towards the door.

"Come, Enzi!" Natalie called as she emerged through the front door. She jumped the four brick stairs leading off the porch and fell to her knees in the grass.

Leo pulled her to her feet.

"Enzi!"

"He'll catch up. Come on," Leo pulled her towards the bike. Moonlight shone through the trees. Natalie was relieved to be able to see again. Leo reached the motorcycle first. He slid on his helmet and revved the bike to life.

Fur barreled past Natalie. A massive white Shepherd bowed before her, his tail wagging high in the air. His bright blue eyes gazed up at her with pride. He licked her neck and cheek before growling at the house. With his hackles raised, Enzi appeared twice his normal size.

The woman Natalie had heard inside pursued them, hunched as she ran. Natalie caught sight of an embroidered design on the shoulder of her navy blue jumpsuit. Her grey hair stuck out wildly and a brown birthmark covered her forehead and right cheek. She stopped short when confronted with Enzi.

His gleaming white fur shone with blood. It dripped freely from his muzzle and chest. She stomped her foot in frustration and pulled a slender rod from the middle of her back. The staff expanded outwards and both ends shone silver as she methodically passed it back and forth. She smiled at Natalie. It wasn't malicious or vindictive, but disturbingly genuine.

Enzi snarled and bared his teeth.

She slunk off the porch, inspecting Enzi warily. One hand beckoned Natalie to her while the other continually rotated the steely grey pole. Natalie thought she heard a quiet humming sound coming from the device.

"Come now, dear. Call off your hound."

Not a chance.

Natalie got to her feet and ran for the motorcycle. Leo tossed her the helmet as she approached. She slammed it onto her head and climbed on behind him, all ladylike concern long forgotten.

"Enzi!" Natalie called him as they tore out of the driveway with gravel flying out behind them. The canine abandoned his charge and sprinted after her. His tongue flapped in the wind and his pointed ears flattened against his head.

Leo pressed a button on his dashboard depicting a green phone.

"Brant," he spoke into his helmet. "Hey, playground in two minutes. Yeah, same here."

Natalie couldn't stop herself from looking back. Her house shrank in the distance as they raced down the street. Enzi ran hard but fell farther and farther behind them. So far, he was the only thing following them.

Leo pulled off onto a dirt road. They rolled into a simple neighborhood playground. Natalie had spent many of her childhood summers on the basic swing set and green jungle gym. Normally teeming with local kids, she was not expecting to find the playground deserted.

Of course no one is here, Natalie chided herself. *No sane parent is letting their child go for a jaunt across the monkey bars when bombs are going off.*

A lonely lamppost stood guard over the four typically coveted parking spaces. Relief washed over Natalie when she spotted Brant's black truck waiting for them. Leo parked beside Brant and promptly dismounted. Their friends rushed to them with an onslaught of questions.

Natalie's ears were buzzing as Leo took off her helmet. A purple bruise was blooming on his left cheek and a thin cut on his forehead oozed a trickle of blood. She wiped it away and noticed her hands were trembling. His eyebrows furrowed and her helmet fell from his hands as they moved to palpate her neck and jaw. The summer humidity hung thick in the air, but his touch was still warm against her skin.

"What happened to you?" Tawney's mouth twisted with a mixture of shock and disgust.

Leo filled Natalie's vision. His brown-green eyes met hers every few seconds and it made her insides swim.

Uh-oh.

Natalie closed her eyes, fighting waves of nausea.

"Why's she so pale?" Brant asked over Tawney's shoulder.

"Shock or blood loss," Owen suggested.

"Or both," Leo added. "I can't find where she's bleeding."

Someone pressed against her back, steadying her.

"Can you talk to us, nerd?" Owen asked. "Does anything hurt?"

Leo's touch left her. Natalie looked up as he wiped his blood-soaked fingers on his white dress shirt.

Uh-oh.

The bile rose quickly from her stomach as she slid off the bike. Owen tried to stop her, but she shoved him away. She made it to the tree line and emptied what was left of her dinner and dessert into an unfortunate clump of ferns.

When she had finished, she trudged back to her friends. Brant passed her a bottle of water from his truck. She took it gratefully. Owen covered Leo's cut with a bandage, but he hardly noticed. His attention was fixed on her.

Natalie's gut flipped again, but this time it was empty.

Enzi trotted into the parking lot to join them. He paced next to Natalie, panting but proud, with his pearly white fur caked in blood. Her friends looked from Enzi to Natalie in horror.

"It's not my blood," Natalie explained quickly, realizing their assumption. "Enzi bit him, then licked me, so it's not—"

She stopped. The thought of that man's blood on her made her insides churn.

"Enzi bit someone?" Tawney asked in disbelief. "Who?"

"They were just—just waiting for us, and my house…"

"Who was in your house?" Brant asked.

Tawney dug around in the back of Brant's truck for a silicone pet bowl. She propped it up at Natalie's feet to share her water with Enzi. He lapped it up nearly as fast as Natalie poured it.

"One large guy and an old lady," Leo pushed back his hair. "Maybe more. The man took Natalie…I couldn't get her back by myself, I had to get Enzi from the backyard."

Natalie remembered hearing the man's blood splatter the

wall in her house after Enzi attacked him.

"He's probably dead," Natalie murmured, feeling unsteady on her feet.

"Well, thank goodness," Tawney scratched Enzi lovingly behind the ears. "What a good boy, Enzi!"

Having just been attacked in her own home, Natalie thought she should have agreed with Tawney, but she didn't. She was thankful Enzi helped rescue her, but the thought of him killing someone was unsettling.

"My house was trashed," Natalie bit the inside of her cheek to quell the tears fighting to overflow. "Everything's destroyed."

Not only our photographs and keepsakes, Natalie thought bitterly. *Our home is broken.*

She would never be able to set foot in the house again without seeing their life shattered across the floorboards. She wouldn't be able to climb the stairs without feeling herself hoisted up them. She couldn't traverse the hall to her bedroom without hearing the burly man's blood splatter her walls.

It won't feel safe again.

"Tawney's house was trashed, too, and Owen's was in flames," Brant explained. "We were already on our way to you when Leo called."

"In flames?" Leo repeated.

Owen nodded, staring off into the woods at nothing in particular.

"That was the explosion we saw at Colonial Custards," he said quietly.

"I'm so sorry, Owen."

He clenched his jaw and nodded.

My home is broken, but his home is gone.

"Were people waiting at your place, too?" Natalie asked Tawney.

"No idea," Tawney poked her in the chest. "I wasn't stupid enough to wander around inside and find out."

Natalie huffed once and nodded.

"Fair enough." She lifted her skirt slightly to clean some of the cuts with the water Brant had given her.

"Woah," Brant gasped. "Is that from the guy grabbing you?"

"Uh, no," Natalie blushed.

Leo shook his head at the sky as though still struggling to believe what she had done.

"I kind of hopped off the back of the motorcycle because I thought my parents were inside the house," she confessed.

"No," Leo pointed at her. "You threw yourself off the bike onto your gravel driveway as I was accelerating. After you saw the door was ajar!"

"I couldn't just leave!" Natalie argued.

"Woah, woah," Brant interrupted. "We can deal with adrenaline junkie here later." He had produced a towel from his truck and was trying to clean Enzi, but the result was more of a burgundy dog than a white dog. Enzi rolled onto his back as Brant rubbed his belly with the towel.

"Yeah, where are our parents?" Tawney asked. "If those people were waiting for you…"

"Whoever they are, I don't think they have our parents," Natalie leaned against Brant's truck to keep herself vertical. "My dad said something weird to me at dinner. He called me a 'bilby.'"

"A what?" Owen asked.

"Exactly," Natalie nodded, "so I researched it at Colonial Custards and apparently a bilby is…well, it resembles a rat crossed with a kangaroo. It's adorable actually, giant ears, long nose. Anyway, it makes several burrows so it can move between them to hide from predators. It's also described as endangered, but still surviving."

"So, you think our parents have made burrows?" Brant scowled.

"Not so literally, but yes. They may have a safe house. Or multiple. And the message was supposed to be they are in danger, but okay."

We'll be waiting for you, Natalie remembered her father's words. She imagined him standing in front of her, still smiling. *We'll be waiting.*

"That doesn't make sense," Leo shook his head. "Why would they go into hiding and leave us exposed if they knew they were in danger? What if the message was for us to go into hiding until they say it's safe?"

"Do you have any burrows we don't know about?" Brant taunted.

"We have Christopher," Natalie said bluntly.

"No, we don't," Tawney dismissed her. "What about that other word you mentioned? Coleanthea or something?"

"Coelacanth," Natalie nodded. "I'm not sure. Coelacanth is an order of fishes once deemed extinct but actually aren't. That one didn't make sense."

"Fish," Brant corrected her.

"Fishes," Owen corrected Brant.

A rumble shook the ground and Tawney clutched Natalie's bad shoulder. She groaned in protest and pulled away. Bright flames rose above the trees in the direction of Natalie's house.

She gaped at the gathering clouds of smoke, the pain in her shoulder forgotten. Her house was gone. Her family photographs, her stuffed animals, her childhood artwork, her history: it was all burning.

It was suddenly difficult to catch her breath. Her vision blurred.

Gone. It's all gone. My life is gone. My home, my parents, my books. My life happened in those walls. My house. Broken and then gone. Violated and then gone.

Natalie was vaguely aware of Tawney rubbing her back. Owen spun her away from the flames and hugged her tightly.

"It's okay, nerd; we're going to be okay. It's just a house."

Natalie pressed her cheek against Owen's chest.

It's not just a house. It's my home.

She struggled to breathe. Her lungs heaved faster and faster, but it wasn't enough; there wasn't enough oxygen. She was suffocating.

Leo took her chin with his thumb and forefinger and forced her to focus on him. Black spots left behind by the glare of the flames danced in her vision when she blinked.

"We've got you," he told her sternly. "You saved the most important thing."

"You got him out," Natalie whispered, her bottom lip quivering.

"No," Leo put her hand on Enzi's head. "I got him to you; you made sure he got out. You saved him."

She brushed the tears away from her cheeks and hugged Enzi, bloodstains and all. He was all she had left, her last tangible piece of home.

"Let's move," Leo announced. "If they've finished with the house, I imagine they will be after us next. They were trying to take Natalie, even chased after her."

"They wanted you, too," Natalie said, her strength returning to her voice. "The woman was irritated he didn't get us both. And she had a strange metallic staff."

"I think you all were smart not going into Tawney's place," Leo nodded towards Brant.

"Why would they want us?" Tawney asked.

"Probably to get to our parents," Owen suggested. "Leo's right though. Let's get out of here."

"Uncle Christopher," Natalie suggested again, wiping her face dry on the sleeve of Leo's jacket.

"He's not going to help us," Tawney protested.

"Natalie's right," Brant strategically utilized Owen as a buffer between himself and Tawney as he spoke. "Christopher tried calling her dad today; maybe he knows where our parents are."

"Agreed," Leo nodded.

Owen took a thin cell phone from his pocket.

"You have his number?" Leo asked, surprised.

Owen flipped the device over. Without answering Leo, he put his phone on the ground and stomped on it. The black screen shattered. Owen removed the battery, and threw both pieces into the woods beside the playground.

"What are you doing?" Tawney yelled at him.

"Phones can be tracked. Let's assume our parents are with the DoD; let's assume they're spies. If people are trying to find us to get to them, the first thing they will do is track our phones. Come on," Owen gestured to the pavement. "Get rid of them."

Leo promptly took out and smashed his own phone. Tawney slammed hers onto the ground before throwing it into the woods with a jump.

"What if they call us?" Brant asked, hesitating.

"They won't." Natalie placed her phone on the pavement and pressed hard with the heel of her shoe. The screen splintered as she stabbed through the device to the battery.

"If people are after them, our parents aren't going to put us in more danger by calling us," Owen explained.

Frowning, Brant crushed his phone and tossed it into the nearest trash can.

"Enzi, up," Natalie hit the back of Brant's truck until Enzi leapt in. She hooked his collar to a safety lead to keep him confined to the bed of the truck. Natalie made to retrieve her helmet, but Brant stopped her.

"Woah there, you're definitely riding with me."

The truck was cool, quiet, and peaceful. It would give her time to think. Natalie did not want time to think.

"No, I want to ride on the bike," Natalie insisted. "It's not so far." She clambered on behind Leo.

"Wave if you want to hop in," Tawney rubbed her arm. "I'll watch out for you."

"As always," Natalie tried to smile, but it faltered.

Brant, Owen, and Tawney filed into the truck. Tawney

opened the back window and Enzi happily put his filthy front paws and head in. Brant led the way out of the playground to the main road. Natalie watched the flames rising above the trees in Leo's side mirror.

Two fire trucks screeched past as they left the neighborhood. Natalie glimpsed a flicker of hope.

Maybe they can save something...anything.

Leo turned the corner and they abandoned her broken, burning house behind them.

CHAPTER 7

The ride passed faster than Natalie remembered; however, her body was beginning to protest. The summer heat followed the sun below the horizon and Natalie trembled as the wind chilled her. Despite the goosebumps on his arms, Leo insisted she keep his jacket. Her legs cramped from shivering and holding onto Leo for dear life. Natalie repeatedly reminded herself to relax.

He doesn't have a motorcycle license, but so what? He knows enough...

Despite the risks, Natalie was thankful someone else was driving. On a normal day, she may have remembered the way, but the farther they got from home the more the highways blurred together.

Her body slid forward against Leo's back as they slowed. Natalie peered over his shoulder as the toll plaza sign passed above their heads. The attendant working the station eyed the motorcycle with concern.

"It's windy tonight," she warned. "You may want to wait until morning."

Leo passed her a twenty-dollar bill from a compartment

between the handlebars.

"We'll be alright," he assured her.

She frowned. Her red lipstick faded in the corners of her mouth.

"You would not be the first to die on this bridge," she scanned Natalie up and down.

She must think we're a couple of dumb kids, Natalie realized. *Two daredevil teens dressed to the nines for a midnight joyride across the Chesapeake Bay Bridge-Tunnel.*

Along with being a man-made marvel, the Bay-Bridge Tunnel was also known for its deadly traffic accidents. It was not uncommon for a gust of wind to blow a tired truck driver over the side, and very few survived the fall. Natalie didn't blame the attendant for attempting to stop them.

"We'll be careful," Natalie told her.

The woman shook her head and passed Leo his two dollars of change.

"Just don't want to catch you on the morning news."

"Only if we win the lottery," Leo nodded in appreciation and sped out of the terminal.

The bridge curved away into the distance, a glowing serpent traversing the mouth of the bay. Natalie stretched tall in her seat, straining to see over the barricade separating them from the seventy-five foot drop to the water. Pushing on Leo's shoulders, she saw where the starlit horizon met the black sea. It didn't take long for the shore to disappear behind them, and then there was only water. It was unnerving to trust a two-lane bridge into the seemingly infinite stretch of waves with your life.

Sea spray filled the air as waves crashed against the pylons supporting the bridge. For an instant, Natalie worried the waves would crash right over the guardrail. She knew the bridge stood too high for that to happen; her dad had assured her of this many times on their trips to the Eastern Shore.

The last time she had traversed the Bay Bridge-Tunnel at night had been with her father. She had woken in the car, still in her pajamas, as they were clearing the second tunnel.

"Are we going to Uncle Christopher's?" she had asked him with a yawn.

"Not quite." His skin was smooth and his blonde hair still thick. He held a metal ring with a single key and a rainbow-striped anchor-shaped float.

Natalie perched on her knees and watched out the window. Calm, flat water flowed far beneath them.

"But it's so cold out." She remembered being confused, wondering what madness had gotten into her father. *"Why are we going boating when it's cold?"*

"Look! Flurries," he pointed at tiny flakes of snow blurring past them. *"They're good luck. Go back to sleep, princess. I'll wake you when we're there."*

A gust of wind bullied the motorcycle into the other lane. Natalie held tight around Leo's waist as he fought to regain control. Headlights flashed bright behind them. She turned to see Brant's truck straddling the two lanes to block anyone from passing them, giving Leo the entire width of the northbound bridge to drive. Natalie pressed her helmet between Leo's shoulder blades as another gust rocked them.

Only 17 miles of bridge to go.

The drive took a half hour to complete and Natalie spent nearly the entire time with her teeth clenched and her abdomen tight. She found brief spells of relief in the two tunnels. Walls rose up around them as they sped to the bottom of the bay, sheltered by the thick concrete channel. However, the moment they emerged they were again at the mercy of the wind.

She had never resented a ride across the Bay Bridge-Tunnel before this. Natalie leaned back in relief when the wheels bumped over the connection linking the bridge to the Eastern Shore.

Dry land. We're nearly there.

A few minutes later, they leaned right, turning onto a winding gravel drive. She wondered if Christopher's house was the same as she remembered.

Ahead of them rose a colossal aluminum building. A single flood lamp illuminated the side facing the driveway, revealing two massive floor-to-ceiling doors latched shut. Faded yellow paint adorned both doors so when they closed, the painting formed a radiant yellow sun. Natalie knew behind those doors stretched rows and rows of dry-docked boats, all silently waiting for their propellers to dip into the bay. Under the ridge of the aluminum roof, blue letters named the building Morning Sun Marina.

Leo rolled past the large boathouse and stopped in front of a cabin that was miniscule in comparison. White siding, blue shutters, and two potted plants made the cement cube a touch homier. A swinging wooden sign on the porch read Office Closed.

The bike fell silent as Brant parked next to them. Natalie took off her helmet and basked in the serenity around her. Three piers jutted out into the cove from the marina. A few boats docked for the night creaked periodically against the wooden pillars. Salty water lapped at the shore, providing a rhythmic melody for the crickets to sing to. Moonlight reflected off the calm water in the cove, accompanied by the steady red and green beacons that safely guide captains through the inlet. Lightning bugs courted between the reeds; their yellow-green bioluminescence made the shoreline sparkle.

Everything was exactly as she remembered it: the marina, the cabin, the water, the lingering smell of seafood and charcoal. It felt so normal.

He's never going to believe us. Natalie began to worry. *I wouldn't believe us. After six years of silence, we just show up at his home? 'Hey there, Christopher, been a while. Our parents are missing and my house burned down. Can we crash on your couch? Yes, all five of us, please.'*

Natalie bit the inside of her cheek.

We don't have any other options; there's no point in getting cold feet.

Unleashed from the truck, Enzi pushed his head into Natalie's palm, eager for a scratch behind the ears.

"You remember this place, bud?"

Enzi's ears stood at attention. A rustling had disturbed the stems of some nearby sea oats. He stood on his hind feet and pounced his front paws into the bush. An alarmed blue crab took off for the water, leaving needlepoint tracks in the sand. Having lost the sidewinding crustacean, Enzi dutifully inspected each of the docked boats.

"Think he's awake?" Brant asked quietly, nodding towards the cabin. Soft light glowed from a square window, but the house was quiet.

"He will be once we wake him," Leo said, dismounting the bike. Natalie slid off after him.

"Hmph," Tawney huffed.

Leo leapt onto the porch and knocked on the door. They waited. Natalie fiddled anxiously with the end of Leo's jacket sleeves. It was hopeless to stop them from slipping past her fingers. After a minute of silence, Leo approached the door again and knocked harder.

"If you're out of gas, you had better pump it yourself or find an open slip and wait 'til mornin'," a voice boomed from inside.

Tawney shouldered past Leo and banged both of her fists on the door.

"You get out here right now, you worthless, deserting, piece of—"

The door flew open and Tawney nearly fell inside. She scrambled backwards as a squat man with black hair filled the doorframe. He was heavier than Natalie remembered, and more weathered.

"I said, you had better pump—" He caught sight of Leo and stopped short. The color drained from behind his salt and pepper beard.

"Hi Christopher."

Christopher opened his mouth to speak simply to shut it again. He paled as though he had seen a ghost. He scrunched his bare toes as he looked at each of them in turn, his gaze always returning to Leo. After a long minute, he retreated into his cottage and slammed the door shut.

Natalie stared at the door in shock.

"No," she said, shaking her head. "No, he can't do this."

"I told you!" Tawney yelled, silencing the crickets. "I told you he wouldn't do a damn thing!"

"Give him a minute," Leo said.

"Where do we go now?" Brant asked, his voice a little higher than normal. He wouldn't lift his gaze from the gravel.

Tawney obtained a large rock from the driveway and chucked it at the house, hitting the door dead center.

"Ugh!" she yelled as she threw another, and another.

A fifth rock soared through the air as the door swung back open. It bounced off Christopher's side.

"Hey now," he dropped a suitcase and raised his arms in surrender. "If you hurt me, who's gonna be drivin' the boat?"

"You're going to help us?" Brant asked in disbelief.

"Kid, I'm startin' to believe I was born to help y'all," Christopher lifted his suitcase and an ankle-high ball of fluff darted out of his house, headed straight for Enzi. Enzi bowed playfully and put a large paw gently on the miniature dog's head. The black mound of fuzz barked at him and Enzi rolled submissively onto his back.

"Is the yippy thing coming, too?" Tawney pinched the bridge of her nose.

"If I'm goin', Angie's goin'," he nodded towards the two dogs. "Enzi might like a friend, eh?" Christopher turned to Natalie for confirmation and gasped.

"Oy!" he cried out, pointing at Natalie. "What have y'all done to her?"

"Technically, she did it to herself," Owen clarified.

"People may be following us, Chris," Leo glanced back towards the entrance to the marina. "We need to get somewhere safe."

"Not that you care anyway," Tawney spat.

"If I didn't care, I wouldn't have been sittin' here for six years waitin' for you," he brushed a patch of dirt off the knee of his jeans. "I saw this whole arrangement was about to go to Hell, but your parents are a stubborn lot."

"Do you know where they are?" Natalie asked hopefully. "Are they at a safe house?"

"Alright now, hold your horses," Christopher waved his hands. "We shouldn't talk about this now."

"You don't know where they are," Tawney said plainly.

"No," he admitted. "But right now we need to get y'all safe."

"Who is going to keep them safe?" Owen asked.

"You," Christopher scooped Angie up in his free hand. "By not bein' stupid and gettin' caught. Now, I reckon you put your vehicles in the boathouse, all the way in the back."

"Where are we going?" Leo asked.

"Lemme surprise you."

Natalie shared loaded looks with her friends. It didn't matter in the slightest where he was taking them.

We have nowhere else to go.

Christopher pulled open one of the massive boat motel doors, splitting the peeling yellow sun down its center. Brant drove in his truck as Leo rolled the motorcycle along behind him. Once they had emerged, Uncle Chris latched the doors shut and headed for the dock.

Natalie and her friends trailed after Christopher like ants. Enzi weaved in and out between them, his nose to the ground. At the dock, Natalie slipped off her shoes and pressed the damp, worn wood against the blisters forming on her feet.

"Gimme those dumb things," Christopher said to her.

She relinquished the heels without a second thought.

Christopher stopped at the last docked boat and gestured for them to hop in. Natalie traced along its white side, her fingers sliding down shining black letters.

Learn'd Astronomer.

At least thirty feet long from bow to stern, the boat was large enough for everyone to rest comfortably on cushioned seats. Christopher plopped Angie onto the floor and she scampered into the cabin.

"You changed her name," Natalie tapped the vinyl letters as her friends climbed aboard.

"It was time. Thought it appropriate."

"I didn't say I was opposed."

Angie emerged from the cabin dragging a bright orange square alongside her. She leapt into Tawney's lap and gazed at her expectantly.

"Do you mind puttin' on her life jacket?"

Tawney picked up the tiny life preserver and frowned.

"Well, that's kind of adorable."

Christopher jumped on board and tossed Natalie's shoes into the cabin. Natalie followed and took a seat along the side of the boat. She sank into the cushions as her mind relaxed, switching to autopilot. Whatever was going on, Christopher would get them through it.

He'll take care of us.

Christopher swung a ring around his finger with a single key and a faded anchor-shaped float attached. Natalie fixated on it as the rainbow anchor appeared to move in slow motion through the air.

"Wake up," her father said, shaking her shoulder. "Natalie, come and see!"

Natalie yawned and rubbed her face. The bitter cold wind whipped her hair about wildly and smelled of salt. She stood and the floor rocked beneath her feet, sending her to the ground. The white textured floor dug into her palms as she caught herself. She began to cry.

"Aw, princess," her father picked her up from under her arms. He lifted her high until she sat on his hip, her arms looped lazily around his neck.

"We're on the boat?" Natalie asked, her mind struggling to understand how she had gotten from her cozy bed at home to the winter

chill of the sea.

He pulled the hood of her jacket over her head and pointed out towards a string of lampposts stretched across the water, opposite the brightening horizon.

"There's the Bay Bridge-Tunnel," he explained. "Look there now, between us and where the bridge dips beneath the bay. Watch close."

Natalie watched. The frigid wind stung her eyes and made them overflow with tears. She swayed on her father's hip as the waves rocked their boat back and forth.

"Daddy, I don't see —" She gasped.

A jet of water streamed high into the air with a loud gust. Behind it rose a gigantic tail fluke, which quickly disappeared beneath the waves.

"A dolphin?" she asked, bouncing eagerly to get down.

Her father grinned and held her high above his head.

"Think bigger!"

He set her down and she kneeled expectantly on one of the seats, hanging on tight to a metal rail.

A massive grey creature rose straight out of the water. It's beak and pectoral fins were flecked with white and black spots. Golden drops of water rained down from it in the blaze of the rising sun. As it turned and began to descend, half of its large fluke peaked out from the water's surface. The animal was nearly horizontal when it hit the waves. A large smack sounded from its impact and golden sea spray splashed high into the air.

"Whales," Natalie giggled. "Whales!"

"Humpback whales," her dad clarified. "They breach out of the water to communicate with their pod and knock barnacles off their bodies."

"It was beautiful," Natalie let him slip warm mittens over her fingers. He laughed.

"That's just a lucky coincidence."

"There are life jackets in the cabin if we sink," Uncle Christopher's informal PSA pulled Natalie away from her memories. "It will be about an hour ride, for sure."

The engines behind her rumbled to life. Enzi hopped onto the seat cushion beside Natalie and laid the front half of his body on her lap. Angie tilted her head to the side.

"He insists he's a lap dog," Natalie shrugged.

Christopher pulled smoothly away from the dock. Leo and Brant made their way to the bow while Owen sat still as a statue with his eyes squeezed shut.

He's a bit green...

"Tawney," Uncle Christopher called, "drive for a bit?"

Tawney jumped from her seat and eagerly took the wheel. Angie followed her and settled for laying at her feet.

"Keep the red signs on your right, green signs on your left, and head for the lighthouse at the tip of the cape there. Watch—"

"Watch out for crab pots. It's easier than riding a bike," Tawney had to stand to see beyond the bow as she drove. "I'm still mad at you," she added after a moment.

Christopher knelt in front of Natalie and produced a square tackle box from beneath her seat.

"Now, we're gonna tend to those wounds, hmm?" He produced a children's wet wipe from the box and gave it to Natalie. "You're a mess, kid."

Natalie nearly emptied the entire container of wipes before they were coming away from her skin without traces of dried blood. He gave her some lidocaine cream to numb any sore cuts and a triple antibiotic ointment.

"Nothin' requires stitchin'," he concluded after assessing most of her scratches. "They're all pretty superficial."

"Do you have tweezers in there?" Natalie asked, peeking over the lid of the makeshift first aid kit.

"For sure," he passed the instrument to her.

Natalie smeared a generous portion of numbing cream on the two white and red paws resting in her lap. Enzi grumbled in irritation and his ears flattened back on his head, but he did not move away.

"I'm worried Enzi has glass in his paws," she explained.

"How'd he manage that?"

"There was glass everywhere in the house—" Natalie

stopped herself. The house was gone, the photographs were gone, and her parents were gone. Tears stung her eyes. She focused on Enzi's feet.

After wiping the cream away, Natalie saw shards of glass glinting in his paw pads. She picked them out and blood flowed freely from the holes left behind. Christopher took cotton balls from the first aid kit and applied pressure where Enzi bled.

"Well," Christopher began as Natalie moved on to the next paw. "Do you want to talk about it?"

"No," Natalie rubbed her forehead. "But we need to. People were in my house, Uncle Chris. They tried to take me."

"Did you get a good look at them?"

"One," Natalie stared at Enzi's paws without focusing on them. "The man I didn't see, but the woman was older and had an odd metal pole."

"A bolt. Don't ever let it touch you. What was she wearing?"

"Navy blue spandex." Natalie could still picture her perfectly in the front yard, beckoning her to go with them. "She had a silver shell embroidered on the shoulder."

"Nautilus," Christopher growled. "I've heard whispers, but I had hoped they were wrong. Fates be damned."

"What's Nautilus?"

"Later," he waved her question away.

"You don't seem surprised by any of this," Natalie said bluntly. "We have no clue where our parents are, people broke into my house, and I showed up on your doorstep after six years dressed like a zombie prom queen on Halloween."

Christopher squeezed her hand.

"Later, I promise."

Natalie fell quiet, watching a drop of blood escape the ointment on her dog's injured paws.

"I think Enzi saved my life."

"As he was trained to," Uncle Christopher gently rubbed the back of her head and returned to the wheel.

Tawney bounced into the seat next to Owen. She took one look at him and scooted next to Natalie instead.

"He's totally going to vomit," Tawney told her.

Owen covered his face.

"There are nausea tabs in the box, too. Fish him out some?"

Tawney dug in the box and passed Owen an orange tablet. He shook his head.

"Come on, Owen, it's orange flavored! Yum!"

"If you choose to hurl, do it out of the boat, yeah?"

Owen snatched the pill from Tawney, put it in his mouth, and laid his head on the side of the boat. Angie settled again in Tawney's lap. Tawney tried to be annoyed, but resorted to petting the small creature.

After a while of riding, they passed the lighthouse at the cape's point and continued along the wooded coast. A line of beautiful houses dotted the shore and the boat veered for one in particular. Its concrete foundation jutted out into the water.

"Is that where we're going?" Brant called from the bow, pointing at the house half in the sea.

Uncle Chris nodded.

Natalie was able to make out more of the house as they got closer. It rose three stories tall with powder blue siding and enormous windows facing the sea. An orange plaque hung below the roof.

ANCORA

"Is this your house?" Leo asked as they approached the foundation.

"Technically, yes."

Natalie shared a look of surprise with Tawney.

"You're getting a little close up here," Brant warned. The mass of concrete was fast approaching. "Hey, you're really close!"

Natalie gripped tight to her seat, preparing for impact.

"You're going to hit the—" Leo's shouts stopped short as the boat passed straight through the concrete foundation.

"Woah."

Christopher chuckled.

"Never gets old."

They floated into in a covered boat slip. A U-shaped dock wrapped around the cement cave, just large enough to accommodate the *Learn'd Astronomer*. Wooden stairs led off the dock directly into the house. Beacons atop each of the dock pylons cast warm circles of light every few feet. Natalie spun in her seat. The wall they had passed through stood behind them: tall, grey, and seemingly solid.

Owen's curiosity overpowered his nausea. He scanned the stone ceiling of the boat garage and pointed upwards.

"Hologram?" He asked, his skin still tinted green.

Uncle Christopher nodded.

Natalie followed Owen's gaze and noticed several black spheres mounted on the ceiling. Wayward specks of dust refracted the beams emitted from the projectors.

"So cool," Owen gave a weak thumbs up. "Much better than pagers. Off, please."

Owen crawled off the boat and sat on the dry, still dock with his head between his knees. He clutched his glasses and groaned.

"Where are we?" Brant asked, investigating the cavern.

"Ancora, duh. Didn't you read the sign?" Tawney joined Owen on the dock.

"Which is?" Brant pressed.

"A safe house," Natalie carried Angie off the boat with Enzi at her heels. She welcomed the stillness of the cavern. After hours of riding on the motorcycle and then the *Learn'd Astronomer*, Natalie was thankful for the solid ground beneath her feet.

"A safe house for our parents," Leo added.

"No," Christopher led them to the door, his single suitcase in tow. "It was built for you. And it may do you good to consider it more of a rabbit hole."

Natalie hesitated as they passed through the door; the reference made her uneasy. She had never cared for Wonderland.

CHAPTER 8

nzi led Natalie inside Ancora. After clearing the last
stair, she let Angie go and the two dogs scampered
away.

"Not so fast, Enzi!" Christopher yelled after them. "You
need a bath, somethin' fierce!"

Enzi barked defiantly from the end of the hall and ran after
Angie. The tile floor chilled Natalie's bare feet as she followed
Tawney deeper inside the house. The narrow hallway opened to
a spacious, stainless steel kitchen that seemed to sparkle. The
countertops actually did sparkle. Natalie touched the smooth
black and opal surface that refracted the track lighting across
the ceiling.

Exactly like the one at home.

"Your mom designed the kitchen," Uncle Chris said to her,
knocking twice on the granite.

"It's all new," Tawney noted.

"A few years old, but never been used."

The kitchen met a wide sitting room with three oversized
white couches, a recliner, and a bowl chair in the corner. Two

floor-to-ceiling bookcases framed large windows overlooking the sea while another waist-high bookcase separated the kitchen from the living room. Ocean themed decorations adorned the walls: driftwood, seascape paintings, antique maps, and shadow boxes filled with shells. A low coffee table supported a fish bowl filled with brightly colored candies sealed in translucent paper.

Christopher unwrapped an orange piece of the salt water taffy and popped it into his mouth.

"There's a room for each of you upstairs," he pointed to a carpeted staircase on the far end of the living room. "With a bathroom, shower, everything you need. There's a library and gym on the third floor."

"A library?" Natalie confirmed.

"Easy there, bookworm," Tawney poked at her.

"The freezer is full of food. Y'all want crab cakes? Made them myself."

The thought of a meal repulsed her. Her parents were gone, her home was destroyed; food was the last thing on her mind. She watched out the window to avoid meeting anyone's gaze. To her surprise, the horizon had a faint bluish hue.

We've been awake all night.

A clock above the stove read four fifteen.

"Crab cakes sound great," Brant answered.

Christopher must have heard Tawney's mouth open and promptly cut her off.

"I realize y'all must have a thousand questions and we'll get to them," he rubbed his tired face. "Been a hell of a night. If you go upstairs, you'll find fresh clothes waitin', and for goodness' sake take a shower. If not for your benefit, then for mine. By the time y'all have finished, crab cakes will be ready. Then we can talk. And you," he pointed a yellow tin of local seafood seasoning at Natalie. "Bathe your bloody dog."

Natalie made her way up the stairs to the second floor with her friends. The first room she passed had a four-poster bed with blue-stenciled letters on the wall that read TAWNEY.

"I wonder whose room this is?" Tawney mused as she pulled open the top drawer of a large wooden dresser. "Ah! Bless you, dad," she hugged a piece of torn, blue clothing. "Jeans!"

Natalie smiled at her. It felt like a weird thing to do so she quickly stopped. The boys readily found their own rooms and Natalie soon realized Enzi no longer padded along by her feet.

"Enzi?" she called as she approached the last room on the hall. Enzi sat at attention, fixated on a thin cardboard box atop her dresser. He managed to ogle her and the box of treats without moving his muzzle.

"You've definitely earned them."

Natalie worked on opening the dog biscuits as she surveyed the room. It was nearly identical to Tawney's. A sea blue comforter cloaked the bed, two gigantic windows gave a panoramic view of the ocean, and a full-length mirror stood propped against the far wall. Painted letters over her headboard read NAT & ENZI. Beside the bed stood a chestnut nightstand with a decorative metal lantern and a single book: a copy of Natalie's favorite novel.

Jurassic Park.

She caressed the binding and fanned through its pages.

This isn't just a copy, she realized. Tears brimmed her eyes. *This is mine.*

It had the same creases in the binding, the same curled page corners, the same stain on the inside cover from the stray drips of a purple ice pop. She fanned the book from back cover to front. It smelled like home.

Home is gone.

Natalie carefully put the book back on the nightstand and forced herself to focus on finding some fresh clothes from the drawers. After a brief search, she settled on jeans, a t-shirt, a comforting hoodie, and thick fuzzy socks for her blistered feet.

Pristine clean subway tiles spread along the bathroom floor and walls. Natalie was reluctant to put her blood-and-dirt-caked-once-purple dress on the floor, but it had nowhere else to go.

She ran the shower until the water was steaming hot and slid in, her cuts burning in protest. Natalie whined and bit her cheek, waiting for the pain to subside. She distracted herself, focusing on the shower itself instead. She was surprised to find all of the same items she had had at home. The same shampoo and conditioner, even the same brand of soap. She washed as fast as her injuries allowed and called Enzi over to her. He sulked by the bathroom door with his ears flat against his head and his tail between his legs.

"Oh, you're getting in," she told him sternly.

He sat stubbornly in the doorway and refused to meet her gaze. Natalie left the shower, naked and soaking wet, and led Enzi in by his scruff. He sat staring at the wall in defeat as the water drenched his fur. Natalie lathered canine shampoo and covered him with it. The draining water ran reddish brown from all of the blood caked in his fur.

"This is gross, Enzi," Natalie muttered as she rinsed him.

Finally, both clean, Natalie cut off the shower and slipped out, shutting Enzi alone in the stall. He shook violently and water whipped against the shower door. Natalie dried herself off and flinched when she accidentally caught sight of herself in the mirror.

Ouch.

Her shoulder boldly painted its pain across her skin. Deep purple and yellow bruising extended from the middle of her neck down her left bicep. Disturbed, she turned away from the mirror and relied heavily on her right arm to get dressed. Enzi nosed open the shower door and Natalie draped her towel over his back, buffing him dry before allowing him to run free. She followed him out of their room and down to join the others, Michael Crichton's *Jurassic Park* in hand.

"He's wet!" Tawney groaned in disgust as Enzi made his grand entrance.

"Better than a bloody mess," Christopher patted the damp dog approvingly on the head.

Natalie was the last one to make it back downstairs; her friends had spread out in the living room with their food. The smell of deep fried blue crab and Old Bay seasoning made her mouth water. Her stomach growled adamantly.

Maybe some food wouldn't be so bad.

Crab cakes were a genius idea on Christopher's part: a heavy dash of protein to fuel their bodies accompanied by a whopping side of comfort.

And they're delicious.

Natalie filled her plate with two golden mounds of crab and a piece of French bread. She settled herself on one of the couches and let the cushions absorb her aching body.

"So we're all here and clean—"

"My question first," Tawney interrupted Christopher. "If the kitchen has never been used, why was there food in the freezer?"

"Seriously?" Owen squinted at her. His cheeks had lost their greenish hue and his mind seemed sharp again.

"It was my job to keep the kitchen and other rooms stocked in case they were needed," Christopher answered her. "Next?"

"Did our parents go to a safe house?" Natalie asked.

"For sure."

"Are they safe?" Leo chimed in.

"Probably. They were supposed to send word if they reached their rendezvous. It's possible they reached the safe house and can't send word, but it's impossible to know for sure."

"I've got another," Tawney raised her hand. "Why'd you ditch us?"

Brant chucked the crust of his baguette at her.

"What? It's a valid question."

Angie reached the crust before Enzi and dove under one of the couches, beyond his reach. He laid with his head beneath the couch watching her eat her prize.

"Now what y'all have to understand about that is,"

Christopher shifted uncomfortably in his seat. "There was a disagreement between me and your parents. They thought it best if I stayed away from your families for a while and, well, legally I didn't have a leg to stand on. A lousy oversight on my part."

"What did you do?" Brant asked suspiciously, peering through the wet brown curls covering his forehead.

"I told the truth, and I wanted you to have the truth, too, but your parents disagreed. They made sure I stayed away."

"The truth about what they do?" Natalie asked, leaning in.

"Yes, but more importantly, the truth about y'all," he breathed a deep sigh and focused on Enzi as he moved from person to person, begging for leftovers. "Staying away was...I never wanted..." He stopped and scanned the ceiling, as though suddenly fascinated by its textured surface.

"You're here now," Owen said, offering an olive branch.

Uncle Christopher gave him a nod.

"What's Coelacanth?" All of Natalie's questions came bubbling to the surface. The word had been tickling the back of her mind since dinner.

"You know Nat, I always thought it ironic that was your favorite story," he pointed a stout finger to the book supporting her empty plate. "The themes are...instructive. Such a wonderful demonstration of how the purest, most innocent of ideas can grow out of control. Can become destructive."

Natalie caught the reflection of the brightening sky in his eyes. Leo sat frozen with a piece of bread suspended halfway to his mouth.

"Did our parents make dinosaurs?" Brant whispered.

Owen smacked him with a couch pillow.

"No kid, it's a bit worse. Uh," he scratched his head. "I'm not sure where to start."

"The beginning?" Leo suggested.

"No, no, definitely not," Christopher snorted. "I'm not even entirely sure where that would be."

"What's Nautilus?" Natalie recalled their conversation on the boat.

"Yes, Nautilus rose from the fracturing of Coelacanth. They're an organization after your parents' life work. They're real cult-like," Christopher shook his head in disgust. "When I heard rumors of their development, I had nearly all of the Coelacanth documents destroyed."

"So now Nautilus is after our parents for information lost in the documents," Brant inferred. "And after us to get them to come forward."

"And what's our parents' life work?" Owen chimed in.

"Well," Christopher anxiously bounced his knee. "You see…"

"How about you just give us the gist," Tawney suggested.

Uncle Chris pointed a finger at her and nodded.

"Yeah, let's try the gist. Ok so," he clasped his hands in front of his nose. "Your parents are involved in a privately funded program called the Coelacanth Project. The project is dedicated to the protection of a group of individuals entrusted with the prevention of nuclear war and other catastrophic events," he slapped his knee triumphantly. "Ha! Gist!"

Natalie stared at him.

"Hmm. No seals, huh?" Brant rubbed his chin.

"What? No," Christopher frowned, confused. "No seals."

"The last 'project' the government funded resulted in the death of thousands," Leo said grimly, resting his elbows on his knees. "And has haunted humanity ever since."

Natalie nodded; her mind had wandered to the same somber thought.

The Manhattan Project. The invention of nuclear warfare.

"The Coelacanth Project isn't government run; it's privately sponsored and its reach is quite limited. The Coelacanth Project exists to protect humanity from extinction. If we continue on our current trajectory, humanity will engineer its own devolution."

"Seems logical," Brant shrugged.

"No, it doesn't," Owen argued. "How do you save life itself from a catastrophic event?"

"Why call it Coelacanth? Aren't they some un-extinct fish?" Natalie furrowed her eyebrows.

"That's where y'all come in," Christopher spoke carefully, as though terrified of his own words. "No one thought the existence of the Coelacanth fishes was possible. They hadn't been seen in centuries, but they're not average fish. And you're not average kids. You're special."

"All parents tell their kids that," Tawney said pointedly.

"I'm not your parent. I'm not tellin' you you're special to make you feel good or important. I'm tellin' you you're special because it's the truth, and the world needs you to know it."

Natalie had a sinking feeling she knew what was coming next.

"We're the Coelacanth Project."

Uncle Christopher's black eyes bore into her and what she saw scared her far more than his words: regret.

"Yes, Nat. You're the Coelacanth Project."

No one spoke. Natalie noticed her friends exchanging confused looks out of the corner of her eye. A thick, molten anger woke inside her.

"I'm about to push you to challenge everythin' you think you know, everythin' you've been taught. All of it. You're goin' to question everythin'. That's exactly what I want you to do. Question everythin'.

"The atom bomb changed the course of history. Its creation was a scientific marvel, but its use seared a scar on the history of humanity. It became apparent if we didn't do somethin', humanity's advancement would result in its own destruction. Our species won't survive a nuclear war.

"So," he gestured to them. "What do we do? Information can't be rebottled once it's out. Nuclear bombs are part of the system now. Every global power has at least one. So, we created a plan. We came up with you.

"You are biochemically unique. You can travel from one point to another in an instant, so long as you're joined with the sea and your spark."

Natalie pulled her knees to her chin. The lava within her bubbled and rose.

We made a mistake.

Leo raised an eyebrow.

"You're saying we can teleport."

"I tried to tell you guys this was a bad idea," Tawney folded her arms and sank into the cushions of the couch.

"Biochemically unique," Brant repeated. "By design?"

Christopher hung his head in shame.

"I wish I could change what's been done, but I can't. We thought we were doing the right thing."

"I don't understand," Owen pulled at his hair in frustration. "What you're saying isn't possible. The science doesn't exist. It's teleporting! It's fiction! How are we supposed to pop from one place to another?"

"With this." Christopher reached into his pocket and produced a narrow, five-sided stone. It was approximately two inches long with raw, unpolished ends.

"There's a connection between you, this stone, and the sea. When the three contact each other, there are three simultaneous reactions: a biological one, a physical one, and an electrical one. Together, they transport you to your intended seaside destination. You need each piece to complete the circuit."

Natalie chewed the inside of her lip and shook her head.

No wonder our parents made him leave. He's lost all sanity.

"Explain," Leo demanded. "Tell us how."

"It's complicated."

"Try me," Owen challenged, glaring at him.

Uncle Christopher sighed.

"Okay well, biochemically speaking you have an additional cellular receptor that interacts with the rare metal alloy aurichalcum. The same alloy is found in this spark," he held up the stone, "and in minute concentrations in seawater. The presence of aurichalcum activates your unique receptors, elevating the atoms that make up your body to an excited state. Swimming with dissolved ions, seawater naturally carries a charge, making it a fair electrical conductor. When you approach the water with your receptors and atoms activated by the presence of the aurichalcum, the tiny wave of electricity traveling between your thought synapses transmits out to the water, like lightning from the ground to the clouds. It creates a quite visible spark of light. Hence," Uncle Chris presented the stone again, "its name.

"It's the electricity and activation of your receptors and atoms by the aurichalcum that allows you to travel instantaneously through space via the electrical conduction of the water. It's the thought, the intent, that specifies your destination," Christopher waved a finger at them. "That's very important. If you aren't focused, you could end up lost or worse. It's officially known as Temporal Associated Conditional Kinesis. T.A.C.K. But we just call it 'tackin'."

Natalie shifted in her seat. She hated conflict. She avoided disagreements and confrontation at all costs, but she was reaching her breaking point. The swell of lava building within her was about to erupt.

Tawney's mouth hung open.

"You're crazy," she whispered, nodding slowly.

Brant stared at Christopher like a wide-eyed child meeting Santa Claus, while Leo squinted at him like the same child perceiving the truth for the first time.

"Well," Leo said, not taking his gaze off Uncle Chris. "Owen?"

Owen seemed transfixed by the floor, but Natalie knew better. His brain didn't perceive the floor. He was visualizing the problem, poking holes in the equation, proving Christopher had gone off the deep end.

"You said we're different by design," Owen said after a long silence. "Are you suggesting our parents biologically altered us?"

It was Christopher's turn to stare at the floor.

"Altered is a strong—"

A sharp smack cut him off. Tawney slapped Uncle Christopher clear across the beard.

"How dare you," she shook with rage. "Our parents are missing, there are bombs going off, and you decide to make jokes? Our parents were right to get rid of you. Go to Hell."

"It's the truth!" he insisted, rubbing his reddening cheek. "You were implemented as a security measure. You can move across the world in an instant; you can prevent so much conflict. The internet revolutionized the ability to communicate, but a computer cannot replace human interaction or human empathy. You could create change in real time. You don't realize your potential! You don't recognize who you are!" He held out five polished grey stones.

Brant studied Tawney, who threatened to spring on Christopher again at any second. The volcano of anger within Natalie finally overflowed.

"I know who I am, Uncle Chris, and now I know you," she stood and called Enzi to her.

"Where are you going?" Tawney asked.

"To bed," Natalie hugged her book to her chest. "This has been a waste of time. I'm sorry I suggested coming here. I'm going to get a few hours of sleep, then search for our parents."

"I'm with you," Leo agreed, standing.

"Fine," Christopher forcefully placed the grey stones on the bookcase. He pushed a button on the top shelf and a large television screen erupted from within the bookcase itself. He tossed a remote to Brant.

"Do what you want. Ignore your purpose; ignore all the people who have died for you already."

"Died for us?" Natalie asked in anger. "You should be committed."

"The bombing, your parents goin' into hidin', Nautilus ransackin' your homes, it's not a coincidence. You were right about your parents goin' to a safe house, but they aren't spies or secret agents or anythin' else you've concocted. They're terrified parents tryin' to protect their gifted children from people who want to use you.

"I guarantee the bombin' in Norfolk was the first of many and Nautilus will escalate until you concede. If you want to work, if you want to help me find out who's behind them and take 'em out so we can bring your parents home, I'm here and I'm ready for you. But if you want to go, then go. Go wander the streets and ferret for your parents without a clue where to start. Go throw all of our work and their lives to waste," he stormed out of the room and slammed the door to the bedroom across the hall.

Natalie stood rooted to the spot in shock. The anger in his voice had upset her but not nearly as much as the fear in his eyes. He truly believed what he was saying.

This is insane. He's insane.

"Remind me to thank our parents for sending him away," Tawney muttered.

"Check the news," Leo instructed Brant. "Maybe there will be something on our homes."

Brant clicked a button on the remote and the T.V. screen glowed to life.

"Although authorities have yet to officially confirm it, yesterday's events are being deemed terrorist attacks," a female voice solemnly spoke over images of the rubble of the Norfolk Naval Station. "So far at the Naval Station, seventeen people have been confirmed dead, twelve injured, and five individuals are still missing."

"Uncle Chris said those people were hurt to draw us out," Tawney's voice sounded small and far away. "Is it our fault they died?"

"No, Tawney," Owen answered, "this has nothing to do with us." Without looking away from the screen, he patted Tawney's shoulder.

"Shortly following the Naval Station bombing," the commentator continued, "the homes of nine of the nation's top scientific researchers were destroyed in a series of fires. The world suffers a great loss tonight, as the nine researchers and their children have all been confirmed dead."

CHAPTER 9

Natalie barely noticed *Jurassic Park* slip from her grasp. Images of her and her friends' homes panned across the screen. Charred foundations, a window frame, half of a roof, all still smoking. Thick, black tendrils rose from the remains into the blue morning sky. The screen filled with family photos, some individual, some of them all together. A photograph of Natalie's mother and father in white lab coats faded into view. Beneath the images read a disturbing message.

John and Mary Morrigan: Confirmed Dead.

Her senior portrait materialized next. Natalie remembered resisting when her mother insisted on taking the traditional image with the black cape and white pearl necklace. Since she paid for the photographs, her mother naturally won out in the end. Natalie wished to do the moment over. She would give her mother whatever she wanted to have her again.

Natalie Morrigan: Confirmed Dead.

"It has yet to be confirmed if the attacks on these researchers' homes and the Norfolk bombings are the work of the same individual or individuals," the reporter continued. "We will keep you posted as we receive more information from the authorities. For now, you are advised to stay alert and report any suspicious activity to the number on your screen."

Brant clicked the remote. The television faded to black, but Natalie continued to stare.

"Confirmed dead," Tawney repeated. For the first time Natalie could remember, Tawney sounded small.

"Means they found bodies," Brant ruffled his brown curls.

"Doesn't mean they were our parents," Leo said firmly, pulling the hood of his sweatshirt over his head. "We were included on their confirmed dead list and here we are."

"This can't be because of us." Natalie shook her head. "Whatever our parents were really working on may have caused this mess, but not us." She retrieved her book from the floor and rubbed the cover tenderly, as though to ease any pain caused by the fall.

"We need to find our parents as soon as possible, but we also need to rest. Leave around lunch?" Leo proposed Natalie's idea again.

"Absolutely," Tawney sprang from her seat, pleased to have a plan of action.

Owen ignored them, staring at one of the stones.

"It's highly improbable," he muttered.

"Then let's put it to rest," Brant snatched one of the stones from the table and marched to the boat slip.

Natalie exchanged glances with her friends before they all grabbed rocks and scrambled down the hall after him. They crowded through the door and she saw Brant standing at the edge of the dock. He tossed the rock repeatedly in the air.

"For the record," he announced. "I think this is incredibly stupid, but it's worth getting soaking wet to prove he's crazy." Without another word, he jumped forward off the dock and fell towards the water. Instead of a splash, a blinding white flash filled the cavern and Brant was gone. The water lapped lazily at the dock pylons, undisturbed.

Ten seconds passed.

Fifteen seconds.

Twenty seconds.

A minute.

There was another flash of dazzling light and Brant pulled himself up from the water on the opposite side of the boat. Nearly twenty feet from where he had disappeared, he was completely dry and white as a ghost. He held the stone out and his mouth dropped open in shock.

"Brant's speechless! It is magic!" Tawney exclaimed.

"It's not magic, it's science," Owen said from behind Natalie. He paced the cavern, unable to contain his excitement.

"Where did you go?" Leo asked Brant.

"Nowhere, I just-just blinked and I was there," Brant pointed at the dock across the water from him. "And then I was...I was," his voice trailed off. Without warning, he stepped off the dock and vanished in a flash of white light. When it faded, Brant was pulling himself onto the wooden planks of the opposite dock, still dry. He clutched the stone wall of the cavern and burst out laughing.

Owen brushed past Natalie's shoulder. She winced and gingerly pressed her palm against the bruises to stop them from throbbing. Pushing his glasses up onto his nose, Owen ran full out off the dock. Tawney followed hardly a second behind him. Natalie squinted against the light as they vanished and nearly simultaneously pulled themselves from the sea on the other side of the cavern. They sat on the wooden planks staring at each other.

"I'm dry," Tawney shook her shirt at them to prove it. "How is that possible?"

"I suppose you never actually contact the water, it's just a medium. You pass through it without touching it," Owen said, staring at the stone.

"It wasn't a real question, nerd," she elbowed him.

Brant high-fived Owen and made to high-five Tawney, but she was already leaping back in. She clambered onto the dock opposite them and triumphantly thrust her fist in the air.

Leo grinned as he strode to join her.

"It tingles," Tawney warned and she shoved Leo hard off the dock.

He flailed for a moment before dissolving promptly into the light. Natalie saw him a second later, climbing up to sit on the opposite dock. He stared across the water to Tawney, slightly paler than normal.

"Woah."

Natalie traced the smooth, five-sided stone. A symbol was etched in black near one end. She ran her finger along the mark. It was simple: a diamond with an upward arrow interjecting from the bottom, perfectly symmetrical.

Spark, he called it?

"It's as easy as walking," Brant told her confidently.

Tawney led Natalie by her good arm to the dock's edge, Enzi on her heels. She held onto Natalie as she put her back to the water. Tawney leaned backwards until Natalie was holding her up to keep them from falling in.

"Let go, Nat!"

Tawney pulled hard on Natalie's arm and she let herself fall towards the water. She instinctively held her breath, preparing to be submerged, but the water never came. Natalie focused on the opposite side of the cavern, where her friends were waiting. She let herself feel something incredibly dangerous: hope.

Maybe Chris isn't crazy. Maybe I'm going to end up on that dock, exactly where I'm supposed to be. Or maybe I'm crazy, too.

A sharp tingling traveled through her body and she felt as though her hair was standing on end. There was a moment, a half of a half of a second, where she was floating. Then the light was gone and she grasped at aged, splintered wood.

Owen and Leo pulled her up to sit on the dock, the dock opposite the one she had fallen from. Twenty feet across from her, Enzi sat with his head cocked.

Speechless, she examined the rock between her fingers. Her

head was spinning. Enzi bounded over and shoved his furry face against hers.

"I need to do this at least five more times," Tawney demanded, one foot already off the dock.

Brant ran around to head her off.

Tawney departed in a flash and popped onto the other pier as Brant rounded the corner. She playfully dodged him for a second and waved as she dove headfirst towards the water. Another flash of bright white and she pulled herself to sit next to Natalie. Leo jumped as though to grab her, but Tawney slinked away. Owen snuck up from behind and hugged her around the waist, lifting her kicking into the air.

"I'm not done!"

"We need to figure this out, Tawney," Owen laughed at her.

Natalie caught Brant wiggle his eyebrows at Owen. His cheeks flushed nearly as red as his hair.

"Let's go get Christopher for more answers," Owen made to leave the cavern, but Brant caught him by the collar of his shirt.

"Woah there, snitch."

"Don't you want to enjoy this for a minute?" Leo asked.

Natalie kept running her fingers over the stone. Her heart raced to match the speed of her thoughts.

Incredible. This is going to change everything. Communication, trade, travel...

"So," Natalie held the spark before her friends. "Where to?"

"Oh! Me! Let me pick first, please!" Tawney stood high on one of the dock pylons, waving her spark in the air.

"It might not be physically sound. We have no idea how far this ranges. I imagine our anatomic structure will be compromised if something goes wrong," Owen scratched his chin thoughtfully.

"You mean...we could be rearranged?" Tawney asked, hesitation in her voice. She did a brief pat down, checking that her arms and legs were still in their proper order.

"Rearranged, split, atomically dissolved into the physical

matrix around us," Owen shrugged. "It's impossible to say. I vote we talk to Christopher first."

"I kindly ask the voice of reason to dismount and take a back seat," Brant teased. "You just lit up this cavern brighter than the Fourth of July, but now you're getting cold feet?"

Leo stood and wiped some sand off of his jeans.

"We just made history. Personally, I don't see how we can entertain the possibility of staying trapped in this cavern."

"Magical things are happening," Brant shook Tawney by her shoulders. "You in or out?"

"Science is happening," Owen muttered, mostly to himself.

"In!" Tawney bounced off her perch and linked arms with Brant. "I'm still picking first," she added.

Owen stood next to Tawney.

"I suppose I wouldn't be the first to give my life to science," he said proudly.

Leo clasped Brant's forearm and held his hand out to Natalie. He gave her a sly smile. It made her brain feel fuzzy.

"I could say we won't go without you, but I would hate to lie to you."

"It was my idea!" she said, despite every instinct of self-preservation telling her not to leave the cavern. She remembered being swept up and away into the dusky depths of her home; swaying on the shoulders of the stranger Enzi attacked.

I don't want to be a passenger. I want to be in control. I want to do this.

Natalie took Leo's hand. A fresh wave of nerves made her shift awkwardly next to him.

Friends hold hands all the time. Don't imagine something out of nothing.

Leo ran the tip of his thumb down the side of hers. A shiver ran through her and she bit her lip to clear her head.

What is he doing? Was that something or was that nothing? Should I do something back? What if I do something back, but that was actually nothing?

"Clear your dumb brains, I'm leading!" Tawney threw herself forward off the dock with Brant and Owen jumping after her.

As Natalie was pulled down, Leo interlaced his fingers with hers. Her heart leapt into her throat.

Now THAT was something.

An intense white light filled the cavern. An instant later, the sensation of falling came and went and she stepped out of the water onto rough concrete.

CHAPTER 10

It was pitch-black. Natalie heard cars beeping and people talking loudly beyond their confined space. Leo gave her fingers a reassuring squeeze, but did not let go.

"Tawney," Brant said nervously. "Where have you taken us? You're fired from choosing. Let's move on."

"No, we just have to get out of this shed...there!" Tawney cracked open a door and fading orange sunbeams spilled in. "Lady and mini-men, I present to you," Tawney made an impressive drumroll sound with her mouth and pushed the door fully open. "Oita!"

"Oita?" Brant and Leo repeated together, puzzled.

"Oita...Japan?" Owen's voice was higher than normal. "That's on the other side of the world."

Tawney nodded so fast Natalie worried she might give herself whiplash.

"Isn't it great?" She ran out into the street, leaving them behind.

"Wait!" Natalie yelled, running after her friend.

She emerged from the cramped boat slip onto a pier. The

sun had just sank beneath the horizon, projecting its final burst of orange and red into the sky. Pale blue lamps shone from high poles, illuminating the sparkling clear water. Gigantic purple sea urchins clung to the pylons and dotted the tan sand on the ocean floor. Resorts and hotels littered the beach, with shining neon shop signs and eateries mixed in between them. Tall skyscrapers rose in the distance with shining red beacons flashing on their rooftops. Beyond them, high mountains cast black shadows against the darkening sky. The city's radiance smothered all but the brightest stars. Above her, the strongest flickered in the twilight, refusing to be extinguished.

Tawney's wild brown curls bobbed between pedestrians on the crowded street. Natalie struggled to keep pace, her friend always just slipping out of sight. Someone caught the back of Natalie's shirt, slowing her.

"It's okay," Owen said, "I'm following her."

A whole head and a half taller than Natalie, Owen towered above most of the crowd. He followed Tawney's petite figure as she made her way through the street. Still occasionally peeking to make sure Owen had a visual on Tawney, Natalie allowed herself to take in her surroundings.

Brightly colored signs with black Japanese script adorned all of the storefronts she passed. Despite the language barrier, it was not hard to tell what was what. Most of the shops were tourist driven, with shining windows full of Oita themed t-shirts. Others leaked glittering smoke trails of burning incense, while more had artists actively painting and sculpting on the sidewalk. The mix of culture was overwhelming and incredibly refreshing. People of every race and color flooded the street, conversing and commuting. Bathing suits, flowing white and tan cotton clothes, jeans, and bright kimonos blurred past her, a harmonious blend of color and culture.

"This is beautiful," Natalie whispered, spinning in a circle as she walked.

"Found one!" Tawney stopped in front of an ornately decorated parlor.

"What is it?" Brant asked, investigating the shop's sign.

"Ramen," Tawney inhaled deeply. "Delicious, authentic ramen."

Two employees stood behind a counter laden with bowls of seasoned noodles. One greeted them with a steady stream of Japanese.

"Konbanwa! Okonomi wa arimasu ka?"

To Natalie's shock, Tawney returned the greeting and proceeded to order.

"Konbanwa! Go ramen onegaishimasu." Tawney tried to give the man behind the counter a twenty-dollar bill. He waved her away.

"Īe, īe. Yen."

Tawney bowed and pleaded with the staff member.

"Onegaishimasu! Īe yen. Honmono no Nihon no ramen o taberu no ga watashinoyumedesu!"

The man stared at her for a moment and then smiled.

"Hai."

"Arigatogozaimas!" Tawney passed him the twenty-dollar bill and he delivered her a tray filled with five heaping plates of noodles. Tawney carried it to a nearby table and opened her chopsticks. She navigated the ceramic utensils deftly around her plate.

"I had no idea you spoke Japanese," Natalie nudged her, helping herself to one of the noodle dishes. She ate slowly, captivated by the people passing them on the street. A warm breeze blew off the sea, carrying the scent of salt water mixed with the spices of the food stands and incense of the traditional shops.

"Enough to order us some ramen," Tawney managed between mouthfuls.

Owen fumbled with his chopsticks and they clattered to the table.

"The genius never learned how to use chopsticks?" Tawney asked in disbelief. "Here." She reached across the table and set

Owen's utensils back into his hand, arranging his fingers appropriately. "Now move these," she moved his fingers and the chopsticks clicked together. "There! Why are you blushing? Now you know. You're welcome."

Owen's ears glowed scarlet. He used the chopsticks to push up his glasses and studied his noodles as though they were the most fascinating thing on the planet.

"Thanks," he stuttered.

Brant grinned devilishly at him, obnoxiously slurping a noodle into his mouth.

"Where to next?" Leo asked.

"I might have an idea," Owen pointed a chopstick in the air to nominate himself.

"Let's go!" Tawney pushed back her chair and carried her half-eaten plate to the tray return.

"But I haven't finished!" Brant whined as she pulled his plate out from beneath him.

Natalie placed her practically full plate of food on top of Tawney's and followed her friends into the street.

"Where are we going?" Natalie asked as she joined Leo and Owen.

Tawney was nearly an entire block ahead of them already. Brant skipped gleefully after her.

Leo scratched his chin.

"We're going on an adventure. I thought you noticed."

"Are you guys seriously walking?" Tawney yelled from the covered boathouse. She was bouncing on the balls of her feet when Natalie reached her. "Finally," she took Natalie's hand. "Lead the way, Owen!"

Natalie entered the tiny boathouse, leaving the colorful streets behind.

"We're going somewhere nerdy, aren't we?" Brant grimaced.

"Guaranteed," Leo nodded.

Natalie's stomach clamped into knots, but it wasn't nerves. It was excitement. She took Owen's arm and closed her eyes as he walked down the concrete slab into the water. White light shone beyond her eyelids, a tingling shock flowed through her body, and the concrete faded to nothing beneath her feet.

A moment later, moonlight beckoned her forward. A salty wind whipped her hair and shells dug into her feet. Natalie found herself on a starlit beach littered with shadowed lumps as high as her knees. Curious, she approached one. It grew and shrank rhythmically. When she was nearly upon it, the lump snorted and rolled.

She gasped and leapt back, laughing.

"Sea lions," she chided herself for not realizing it sooner.

A much smaller creature darted out from a nearby bush and ran for the sea in short spurts of speed. Its scaled tail flowed out far behind the rest of its body.

"Is that...an iguana?" Natalie asked, pointing to the creature. As she spoke, it met the crashing surf head on and was swallowed by the sea. "A marine iguana," Natalie clarified, her jaw falling open. "Owen, are we in the Galápagos?"

Owen clutched his glasses tightly at his side as he pinched the bridge of his nose. "Bienvenidos," he welcomed her, his voice cracking.

"Galápagos?" Tawney asked, boldly poking the bulging belly of a resting sea lion. "Sounds familiar."

"Seriously?" Leo asked, taking a seat in the sand. "Darwin? The finches? The turtles?"

"Tortoises," Owen corrected, gazing wide-eyed at the sleeping volcano that towered before them.

"Semantics," Leo shrugged.

"Species," Owen looked higher and stared at the starry sky. "You can appreciate constellations from both the northern and southern hemispheres here. There are billions of stars we are seeing for the first time."

Natalie put her spark into the pocket of her jeans. The soft sand spread between her toes as a wave rolled gently up the shore. It slipped over her feet to her ankles, colder than she expected.

"Next!" Brant shouted from a pile of rocks nearby.

A few sea lions growled angrily in response. The one Tawney had been poking spun on her with a toothy roar. Tawney tripped on her own feet and scooted away in the sand.

"Yep, next," she agreed.

"You're up," Leo gripped Brant's shoulder and gave him an encouraging squeeze.

Brant stared at the ground.

"Yeah, alright, let's go."

He held out both of his hands for them to catch onto and strode forward into the sea without waiting. Natalie seized Brant's forearm and Owen's shirt at the same time. A flare and gentle shock swiftly swept her away. She opened her eyes to a blood red sky as the sun breached the horizon. A cement sidewalk and wrought iron fence separated the waters of a wide bay from a field of rolling hills with trimmed grass and an assortment of flower bouquets.

"Uh-oh," Owen said.

Natalie glanced around them and grimaced.

"Where are Tawney and Leo?" Owen asked, scanning the deserted embankment.

"It's okay," she told him, fighting the panic building within her. "If they got left behind, they'll go back to Ancora. We'll go meet them there, right Brant?"

Brant didn't answer. He was too busy scaling the metal fence towards the rows of flowers.

"I'll be right back," he told them as he dropped down on the opposite side.

"Brant!" Natalie pressed against the fence. "Brant, where are you going?"

Brant cleared the top of the hill and disappeared over the other side without another word.

What is he thinking?

If Christopher would disapprove of them traversing the planet in a night, he would kill them for getting separated.

Owen rubbed his neck anxiously.

"And then there were two."

CHAPTER 11

A white flash popped next to them and Tawney emerged from the sea with her fists on her hips.

"That was rude."

"How did you guys find us?" Natalie asked, impressed. "Did he tell you where he was going? I don't even know where we are."

"We're at Trinity Cemetery," Leo said, peering through the bars of the fence.

Natalie examined the hillside again and saw the groomed rows of flowers for what they truly were: gravestone offerings.

Tawney shuffled her feet awkwardly.

"I haven't been here since the day of the funeral," Natalie admitted.

"Neither has he," Leo leaned against the fence. "His dad forbids it."

"Ouch," Owen shook his head. "I would have come anyway."

"You don't know. He's torn. He misses his mom but wants to please the family he has left. You can't know what you would do."

Natalie wrapped her arms across her abdomen. It pained her to realize Brant had still been suffering. The passing of time had eased Natalie's sorrow in losing Mrs. Smith, but she didn't live in their home. She didn't have to see her clothes still in the closet and her favorite coffee mug in the sink. She didn't have to face the past seven years without her mother. Brant had carried the pain of his mother's death all this time, yet she never saw him shed a tear outside of the funeral.

But that's him, Natalie scolded herself. *It's impossible to see anything beneath his jovial facade. I should have known better. Leo did.*

"We need to find our parents," Natalie said aloud.

"We do," Leo agreed as Brant came back into sight, hurrying over the hill.

He pulled himself back over the fence and dropped beside Leo. Leo slapped Brant on the back as he stood. Brant returned the gesture and pulled his red cap tight over his head.

His mother made that cap for him, Natalie remembered.

"Well, this has been a downer," Tawney clicked her tongue. "Next?"

"Please," Brant grinned at her, keeping any somber thoughts far beneath the surface.

"I'll go," Leo spoke up.

He took Natalie's hand as she took Tawney's. Leo glanced to either side, checking everyone was accounted for. Satisfied, he strode off the concrete walkway into the water. Natalie followed and the tingling glow faithfully swept her away.

She squinted against the rays of the midday sun. Red and gold banners hung above the crowded city street before them. Music played from a band on the corner and the scent of sweet fried pastries filled the air. Men and women in red and yellow clothes danced in the street. Full skirts flashed back and forth as they entertained the square. Recognizing some of the words printed on the storefronts around them, Natalie figured they must have landed in a Spanish speaking country.

A soccer ball rolled out of the crowd towards their feet. It was yellow in the middle with red caps painted on either side. Leo ran forward and kicked the ball back into the throng of people.

Natalie realized they weren't in a Spanish speaking country, but the Spanish speaking country.

"Spain?" she had to yell over the music and chatter.

"Barcelona!" Leo announced.

Tawney took off after the ball and joined a group of kids playing a pick-up game down the street. Owen hurried after her, shouting something about sticking together. Leo led Brant to a girl in a flowing white and red dress.

"Have you met, Brant?" he asked the girl, who giggled in response.

Brant winked at Leo as the girl led him to the circle of people dancing in the street.

"Let's dance!" Leo guided Natalie towards the music.

She rolled away.

"No, no," she shook her head defiantly. "You're not leading me out there," Natalie pointed towards the dancers.

"You can lead if you'd prefer, I don't mind."

"Ha," Natalie played with her shirt nervously. "Do you even know how to dance?"

"Do you know how to have fun?"

"There are too many people," Natalie hissed.

"And there's about to be two more. Come on, Nat," Leo moved behind her and pushed her by her waist. "You're not missing this."

She reluctantly let him lead her into the crowd. The music played loudly behind them and the ornate dresses of the Spanish women flooded the street. Leo spun her where she stood. Natalie felt ridiculous, her sweatshirt and jeans were a stark contrast to the intricate gowns.

"Stop thinking," Leo instructed. He took both of her hands in his and twisted her from side to side. She tried to ignore how her fingertips tingled where his skin met hers.

Without warning, Leo kicked her calf and caught her back in a quick dip. The sudden rush of adrenaline caught Natalie off guard and she laughed aloud.

"There's a smile."

He pulled Natalie to her feet and took to dancing wildly around her. The maracas set the beat and she spun, clapping. Eventually, the drums faded as the band slipped into a slower rhythm. Natalie's chest heaved as Leo guided her out of the street. He patted her back, pleased.

"Now, when you remember today, it won't be all bad."

"Woo!" Tawney emerged between them with her arms raised high in victory. "I whooped those Spanish brats!"

"Want to play me next?" Leo offered.

Tawney squinted at him.

"I'd prefer to end the day on a high, thank you."

"Ah yes, your soccer victory against a group of kids is certainly the highlight of the evening."

Tawney playfully punched him in the arm.

"Watch yourself," she warned.

Owen arrived behind her, gasping. Sweat ran down his forehead.

"She made you play?" Leo laughed.

Owen nodded. He doubled over, catching his breath.

"Let's round up lover boy," Tawney pointed at Brant, who squished himself between two girls as they danced.

"Got him," Owen heaved. "My awkwardness...thwarts any...romantic endeavor."

Natalie watched Owen drag Brant out from his exotic European sandwich.

"Alright," Leo crossed his arms as Owen returned to them with a pouting Brant in tow. "Take us away, Natalie."

She dug her spark out of her pocket.

"Okay," Natalie held onto Tawney and the boys followed suit beside them. "I'm not sure where to take you."

"Isn't there somewhere you've always wanted to go?" Owen asked.

"The bookstore," Tawney whispered to her.

"Of course," Natalie agreed with them both. "But it's not by the sea."

"Try it," Leo shrugged. "What's the worst that could happen?"

"We don't know," Owen scrunched his nose.

Natalie thought for a moment.

"Okay."

She closed her eyes and focused her mind on the storefront. Though she had never seen it in person, she pictured it clearly: the peeling green paint and yellow sign, the wooden bins overflowing with books outside in the square. A café tucked to the left of the store filled the stone street with the scent of espresso and lemon cake. The tail of a tabby cat flicked out of sight, lost in the maze of bookshelves and reading nooks.

Natalie glided into the sea. Even behind her eyelids, the white light shone so bright she had to squint against it. A tingling traveled from her toes to her fingertips and then it was gone.

She opened her eyes to waves crashing a few feet ahead of her. Music from a street band drifted on the wind. She caught a few notes above the roar of the ocean. Brightly colored fabric swirled in mosaic patterns in the street.

"It was worth a shot," Tawney said, admiring the Barcelona women swinging their colorful skirts around in a circle.

"Pick somewhere else," Leo insisted.

Natalie closed her eyes again and thought about where she wanted to be.

With my parents, she thought first. *We don't know where they are.* She thought about Christopher, the sparks, and the news report. It didn't seem real.

I've traversed half the planet in the span of a few hours. I've felt the light come and take me away. I've seen iguanas, eaten ramen, stood in a cemetery, and danced in Barcelona, and it still doesn't feel real.

"Okay," she said after a moment. "I'm ready."

Natalie pictured her destination in her mind and entered the water. The white brilliance shone again, bringing her its thousand tiny shocks. The ground fell away beneath her feet and she landed on a solid incline. Natalie opened her eyes as the flash receded.

The sun scaled the horizon, its radiant yellow beams fighting to cut through thick morning fog. The few rays that reached the shore were refracted through clouds of smoke and dust rising from the rubble around them. Boats perched precariously on their sides beside the ramp Natalie stood on. One large propeller spun slowly, the lone source of movement as far as she could see.

The buildings on either side of the boat yard had been reduced to a few surviving vertical support beams. Massive pieces of wall and cement foundation jutted haphazardly from the ground. Natalie coughed and covered her nose and mouth with her sleeve. The air reeked of sulfur and smoke. She had been to the Naval Base a few times in her childhood, yet she failed to recognize a single structure in the debris. Her eyes filled with tears and it had nothing to do with the smoke.

Someone pulled twice on the back of her shirt.

"Wha—"

Leo covered her mouth and pulled her against him. He pointed across the cement-paved shoreline. Two boat ramps down from where they stood, the rising sun outlined a lone figure. He wandered lazily atop the cracked wall separating the boat ramps, passing a cylindrical staff back and forth in front of him. He hadn't spotted them.

And we won't give him the opportunity.

She pulled Leo's hand off her mouth and pointed at the water. Holding tight to Leo and Tawney, Natalie crept back into the ocean with Ancora in the forefront of her mind. A second of white light later, Natalie was pulling herself onto the pier in the sheltered cavern. She rolled onto her back.

"Why'd you take us there?" Brant asked quietly.

"I needed to see it," Natalie confessed, letting her arms fall to her side. "None of this seems real. Our parents, the sparks, Christopher, the bombing." She paused as images of the rubble flooded her mind, replacing Brant's face in her vision. "It feels real now."

"It feels like we need answers," Leo rose and pulled Owen to his feet.

"We need to find our parents," Natalie sat up.

"How much trouble do you think we'll be in if Christopher finds out we left?" Owen asked.

"He'll be pissed, but then he'll be fine," Leo answered.

"Chris can never decide if he's lecturing us or enabling us," Brant smiled. "It's nice to have him back."

"I bet five dollars he's passed out asleep," Tawney waved a paper bill in the air.

"You're on," Brant nodded in agreement.

As though on cue, a yipping bark sounded from the doorway to Ancora.

"It's about damn time," Christopher crossed his arms and leaned against the doorframe. "I expected you to try it, but I didn't expect you to leave. Do you realize the danger you put yourselves in?"

Natalie stared at the planks of the dock in shame. *We weren't thinking.*

"Are you sorry?" he asked.

"To be completely honest, no, not really," Brant said.

"I've been worried bloody sick!"

"We're sorry about that, of course," Tawney offered, nodding seriously.

"Well, you're back safe. Y'all get inside now. You need sleep and we got work to do." Christopher made to head inside Ancora then turned back to them with a wide grin. "It's a hell of a thing, isn't it? Amazin' what you can do, amazin'."

"It's incredible," Leo agreed. "So why didn't our parents

want us to learn about it? They supposedly help in this program and made our ability to teleport possible, and then they change their minds? Why?"

"First of all, you're tackin', not teleportin': Temporal Associated Conditional Kinesis. T.A.C.K. And, well," Christopher thought for a moment. "Love affects us all differently. For your parents, it compels them to keep you as safe as possible. For me, I want you to experience all this world has to offer. And it's offerin' you more than it offers most.

"Your parents wanted out of the Coelacanth Project some years ago. They didn't want this responsibility on you. They didn't want the risk of losin' y'all, but it was far too late. Y'all are the fish no one knows exist."

"Well," Brant scuffed his shoe on the dock. "Someone knows."

"Nautilus," Christopher nodded. "I won't let them take you. Don't you worry about that." He went inside and Angie shuffled in behind him.

Natalie stared after him. Some things he said made sense, but there were pieces to their puzzle that didn't fit...

"Pay up," Brant rubbed his thumb and forefinger together in front of Tawney.

Tawney reluctantly relinquished the five-dollar bill.

"I'll get you next time, Brant Smith."

Enzi rubbed against Natalie's knees and put his paws on her shoulders, nearly sending her toppling into the water.

"Yes, I missed you, too, buddy," she rubbed Enzi's ears and followed Christopher inside.

"What work are we going to do?" Natalie asked as they entered the living room.

"Nothin' now. As I said, you need sleep. How long have you been awake?"

The question stumped her. Natalie struggled to remember the last time she had slept. Certainly not since the day before, or was it the day before that?

100

"We aren't tired," Tawney yawned.

"Off to bed," Uncle Christopher commanded as he retreated to his bedroom. "I'll wake you in a few."

Owen stretched, his gangly arms coming dangerously close to the ceiling fan.

"Sleep might be good."

"No, wait!"

Before anyone questioned her, Tawney sprinted to the second floor. She returned a minute later, hidden completely beneath a mountain of blankets. She dropped them in the center of the living room floor and stared at the pile.

"I can't sleep in that room alone," she pointed upstairs and Natalie understood what she meant.

Parents missing, their homes burned to the ground, and their genetic makeup called into question all in one day had been overwhelming to say the least. She did not want to be alone either.

Natalie plucked a blanket out of the pile.

"Share a couch with me?" she suggested, draping the blanket over Tawney.

Tawney nodded and collapsed onto the couch closest to them. Tawney laid with her head on one armrest and Natalie put her head on the other. The couch was so large their feet barely touched in the middle. Enzi climbed up and padded around on top of them before finally settling in behind Natalie's knees.

Owen and Leo each took one of the remaining couches and Brant passed out on the oversized ottoman. Despite the radiant sunlight shining in from the windows, Natalie found it difficult to stay awake. She fought sleep for as long as she could. She worried what she would find when she woke, scared it would all be real.

CHAPTER 12: NAUTILUS CHAMBERS

Natalie sat bolt upright in her cot. A metallic scraping reverberated in her normally silent cell. Her breath caught in her chest as she willed her heart to beat quietly so she could hear. The large door to her cell slid to the right until it had been completely absorbed by the wall.

It's open.

Frozen with fear, she stared into the pitch-black passageway. A red beacon flickered to life on the floor, illuminating the uneven dirt path. It was empty. This was the way out.

Natalie balled her hands into fists to keep them from shaking. She had waited through three days of twilight, stone walls, rations, and silence. Now the door was open and she was terrified. It took everything she had to stand. The brief sound of the door opening had left the silence heavier and more fragile than before.

She forced her face into what she hoped was a placid expression and took a moment to push out the wrinkles on her shirt. Her reaction was the only control she had over the situation and she was going to use it.

The flickering red lantern beckoned her into the tunnel. She took a tentative step into the corridor. The damp earth was cold and soft on the soles of her bare feet. Holding her breath, she took another step. Then another, and another. Her left hand followed the wall, letting it guide her path in the darkness. A few paces in, it slipped into empty air.

Another passage...

Natalie glanced from one passage to the other, torn. If she took the unlit passageway to her left, she would be blindly hoping it led somewhere useful. Remembering all of the passages she had noticed in her drugged state the day she was kidnapped, it was highly improbable this particular one led to freedom.

As though hearing her thoughts, another red beacon flickered to life ahead of her. She could not risk getting lost or punished when there was an opportunity to learn how much Nautilus knew. Natalie continued on her guided path, fighting the fear tempting her to hide in her cell.

The fifteenth red beacon illuminated a white tile floor stained with mud. It was cold and slippery, and she nearly lost her footing more than once. As the passage widened, a new glow came from up ahead: white instead of red. Having seen nothing but moonlight for days, the intensity of fluorescent bulbs made her eyes water. Natalie shuffled forward as they adjusted. Within a few minutes, she had gone from the dim red passageway to the blazing white room.

The clinic.

Natalie realized she was in the same room where Nautilus had strapped her down and drawn her blood, but it had been transformed. A lone table with a television replaced the reclining chairs and instrument stands that once occupied the makeshift clinic. Natalie spun slowly as she moved towards the table. Seven passages branched off from the circular white room. Each appeared identical to the one she had emerged from, which was still glowing faintly red behind her. The domed ceiling shone with fluorescent rods. There were four visible cameras hanging from the ceiling and each of them focused on her.

Natalie reached the table and grimaced at her reflection in the screen of the television. Her hair hung in tangled waves to her back, her clothes were caked with soil and worn thin, and there was dirt smudged on her chin and arms and, well, everywhere.

The screen flicked on with an audible hum and she faced away from the blinding light.

"Good evening, Ms. Morrigan," a man's voice echoed from the television.

She remained where she was. It was the first voice besides her own she had heard in days. She subtly bit the inside of her lip to keep it from quivering. Natalie let her emotions rock her for a minute, a full sixty seconds, and then forced herself back.

I know you.

"Good evening, Ms. Morrigan," the voice repeated, as even as before. "My name is Amir Amani. It is truly an honor to formally meet you and welcome you to Nautilus."

She confronted the screen. He looked as he had before. Smooth olive skin and soulless black eyes. His thin lips broke into a dazzling smile.

Rage bubbled within her.

"Is it?" Natalie said curtly. "I've lost track of my days and nights." Venom dripped off her words.

"Such anger brews in you, sweet child," Amir Amani clicked his tongue. "I do apologize for the actions of my disciples. Their passion for our mission drove them to extreme measures that were not authorized, I assure you."

"Your mission to drive the world to another war?" Natalie challenged. "Did Nautilus detonate the bomb after you captured us?"

"What bomb, child?" Amir frowned at her, his eyebrows cinched with concern.

The sight made Natalie sick to her stomach.

"The bomb. Your mission for peace brought down the city of Norfolk. Did Nautilus detonate another bomb after we were captured?"

"What?" He physically recoiled from her accusation. "Ms. Morrigan, Nautilus exists solely to create and conserve peace and prosperity for all. You and your friends hold the key to unlocking this future for all peoples in all nations. We sought you out to help us avoid war."

Natalie shifted her weight from her heels to her toes and bit her cheek. Amir spoke with such feverish passion it didn't make sense. The bomb threat was real and Nautilus was there.

"No," she said, her certainty faltering. "Nautilus has been hunting us for days. You bombed a navy base!"

"I understand you are upset," Amir nodded sympathetically, his index fingers pinched together against his lips. "But this has all been a large misunderstanding. Nautilus is not behind any bombings. And as I said, my disciples were a touch overzealous in their attempts to gain your ear so our cause may gain you as an ally."

Overzealous? Is he mad?

"Your people destroyed my house, attacked my friends, and kidnapped us. I've been detained in a cell for days! Is that how you treat an ally?"

"Our attempts to speak with you and your gifted friends were repeatedly met with violence. Your power...you can evoke such positive change for humanity, ease so much pain. Yes, we crave for you to align with us and work for peace for all. However, your actions carry weight and we cannot risk the possibility you might strike out against our cause."

"Any actions taken by my friends and I were provoked," Natalie replied sternly, but Amir seemed so sure of himself she questioned her memory.

Had Nautilus ever fired the first shot? Had they outright started a fight? Was there any proof beyond Uncle Christopher's words that Nautilus was behind the bombings?

"Every moment, unspeakable acts take place on this planet. Humans are crueler to each other than any other species."

"So you intend to punish everyone for their own humanity? Guilty until proven innocent? Until proven Nautilus?"

"For the average human, no," Amir spoke softly as though he empathized with her, as though he cared. "You, however, are far beyond the average human, Ms. Morrigan. As I said, your power will facilitate a peace greater than any known to history. We can rid the world of war and disease. In contrast, you could use your ability to realize more power than any ruler to have ever existed, even threatening the rule of God himself."

Natalie ran her fingers through her hair in frustration. Amir's tone and story conflicted entirely with what she had experienced. Bombings, murder, shootings, propaganda, arson, kidnapping.

Is tacking worth this? How are we supposed to rid the world of disease?

"You have potential to evoke change on an unlimited scale. Whether or not that change is for the worse or for the better is entirely up to you. So far, you have welcomed our attempts at conversation with gunshots and violent attacks. So yes, please forgive us for proceeding cautiously."

"Unbelievable," Natalie huffed, yet his words took root in her mind. She only had Christopher's word that Nautilus sought the ability to tack to collect power.

What if they truly do want to use our power to achieve peace? Are we doing the right thing, keeping tacking a secret from the world?

"Voice your thoughts, child. I simply desire to ease your mind so you may join our cause."

"Where are my friends?"

"In their chambers." Amir faded away off the screen. His image was replaced with four all too familiar cells.

Natalie's legs gave way beneath her. She clutched the table as she traced each figure with her scabbed fingertips. Tawney flipped restlessly in her room, using the cot as a launch pad.

Brant sat on the floor, his head between his knees. Owen was drawing some sort of diagram on the wall with dirt from the floor, his glasses reflecting the moonlight. Leo laid in his cot, vacantly staring through the skylight above him.

They're okay. They're here.

An ominous thought tainted her swell of relief.

"Question everything," Natalie whispered.

"Hmm?"

"Can you prove this is a live feed?"

"Of course, child."

A piercing alarm reverberated around her. She dropped to the floor, covering her ears. Panicked, Natalie scanned the room. The inability to hear anything but the alarm set her on edge; she expected Nautilus to converge on her from the passages. After a second, her eyes landed back on the screen. Tawney had fallen flat on her back to the floor, Brant covered his ears, Leo stood on his cot, and Owen stared at the door to his cell.

The siren stopped and the room fell dead quiet. Then the yelling started.

"Hello? Let me out!"

Natalie touched the screen. Tawney banged on the door to her cell, screaming, but Natalie didn't just hear her through the speakers.

"Let me out of this damned hole!"

I can actually hear her.

Natalie's head swiveled until she identified the right passage.

"Tawney!" Natalie called, sprinting towards one of the unlit passageways.

"Nat! NAT! I'm here!"

Natalie was sure now, definitely the passage directly ahead. She was close. A large wooden door descended from the ceiling, not only on Tawney's passageway, but on all of them. Natalie ran harder. Her bare feet smacked against the tile floor and a cramp stabbed into her side as she gasped for air. The wooden guillotine was falling too fast and she was running too hard to stop. The door met the ground with a solid thud, muting Tawney's screams. Natalie collided against the rough wood and pounded her fist against it.

"No," she said breathlessly. "No, let me see her." She rested her head on the door, letting her hair veil her face from the cameras. Natalie tried to quell the relief swelling through her, but she couldn't help it. She smiled.

They're alive, and they're all here. We're all here.

She gasped for air and absentmindedly rubbed the swirled scar on her wrist.

We might have a 0.01% chance of getting out of here.

"Let me see her," Natalie said louder, leaning her back against the door.

"I will, Ms. Morrigan, I promise you," Amir once again filled the screen across the room. "I'm going to talk to each of your friends and then you will be able to see them. It is important we clear this terrible misconception you all have developed concerning Nautilus's purpose and the role each of you have to play in achieving prosperity and peace."

I want you to outsmart them. Uncle Christopher's words rang clear in her mind.

One of the wooden doors beside her rose into the ceiling. Red beacons illuminated the pathway awaiting her.

"What would it take for you to release my friends?" Natalie asked, Tawney's screaming still ringing in her ears.

"What do you offer?"

"Myself," Natalie opened her palms at her sides. "I'll help Nautilus; I'll tack to help you. Please, let them go."

"Tack?" Amir squinted at her. "You'll tack for us?"

"Yeah," Natalie bit the inside of her cheek hard to keep herself composed. "Temporal Associated Conditional Kinesis..."

Isn't that what you want?

Amir's index fingers pressed against his lips in thought.

After a long silence, the screen went black.

"Amir?"

Nothing.

"Amir Amani!" Natalie yelled. She hurried to the screen and shook it. She fumbled desperately along the sides for a power button, an outlet, anything.

"Let them go!" Natalie screamed at the black screen.

Fingers dug into her bad shoulder and spun her around. She cried out and tried to pull away, but Amir only held her tighter.

"Stop," Natalie cried.

"You should be more concerned with your own safety, Ms. Morrigan," Amir sneered. "Your friends are tucked away in their cells, while you, you're here with me."

Natalie clutched at his arm with both hands, pulling desperately to separate herself from his grasp. Her shoulder was on fire. Black spots swam in her vision. She sank to her knees and Amir stood over her. His shining black shoes and pleated suit dampened the glow of the white room. The nautilus shell on his arm reflected the fluorescent glare. He gripped her right forearm and ran his thumb roughly over her peculiar scar.

"I see you understand exactly how much danger you're in."

"Please stop," Natalie begged. "I'll help, I'll help Nautilus."

"I am so pleased to hear you will assist Nautilus on our path to procure peace," Amir Amani loosened his grip and held Natalie out before him.

She caught her breath, refusing to look into his pointed face.

"However," Amir continued. "Peace blossoms under the boughs of allegiance, deference, and cooperation. Nautilus would be best served through the combined efforts of your gifted companions. Might they listen to your guidance?"

"My friends will follow me," Natalie nodded. "They may not understand at first, but in time they will learn."

Learn that lying with the enemy is the fastest way out of this pit. The faster Amir trusts us, the faster we get out of here.

"Ah, yes. Time is the most powerful weapon of all," Amir

paced around her. "Time heals our greatest wounds by helping us forget. Time takes life to make way for new life. Perhaps with time, even you will learn."

Without warning, Amir slapped Natalie hard across her face. The stinging pain on her cheek brought bitter tears to her eyes. She furiously wiped them away.

"What do you want from me?" Natalie asked through gritted teeth.

"Your allegiance, deference, and cooperation."

"I said I will help you!"

"And I said I wanted allegiance, Ms. Morrigan, not weakness. Deference, not fear."

"I'm not afraid."

Amir bent down until his thin nose was an inch from hers. He smelled like pines.

"Cooperation, Ms. Morrigan, not lies."

Outsmart them.

Natalie stood, holding her shoulder gingerly. Amir rose with her, frowning in disappointment.

"I said I will serve you."

Amir leaned closer until his sharp cheekbone brushed against her stinging skin as he whispered in her ear.

"Maybe, with time, you'll mean that." Amir turned his back on her and strode towards one of the sealed passageways, his hands resting casually in his pockets.

Natalie resisted the urge to attack him from behind. She wasn't a strong fighter. He would overpower her easily and destroy what fragile groundwork she had managed to establish. Her jaw clenched as she forced herself to remain still.

"I will speak to your friends," Mr. Amani called back to her. "Then we will meet again, Ms. Morrigan. I hope by then you speak the truth, for both of our sakes." A barricade closing off one of the passages opened as Amir reached the wall. He passed through the archway and the barrier fell behind him, leaving her alone.

A low grinding sound reverberated around the white room. Natalie's own red passageway opened to her. She trudged towards it. Her shoulder throbbed with each beat of her heart and her left cheek smarted terribly. She kicked at the tile in frustration.

That did not go well.

Natalie imagined Tawney's reaction to Amir Amani's speech on allegiance, deference, and cooperation. She smirked.

Maybe they'll take the cost of the television out of his salary.

CHAPTER 13

The sun had begun its descent when Natalie woke. Panic struck her and she leapt off the couch.

Where am I?

Enzi pushed his head into her side as she frantically scanned the room. The day before came flooding back. The bombings, her home, her parents, Ancora, the spark...

Natalie dug into her pocket and touched the modest stone.

The spark.

The realization her nightmare would continue made her lip quiver. Her friends slept soundly; she was the first awake. Natalie pointed to the couch and Enzi claimed the spot she had abandoned, resting his muzzle on Tawney's stomach. She scratched his head and climbed the carpeted stairs alone.

Instead of stopping at the first landing as she had earlier, Natalie continued upwards to the third floor. The staircase ended with a long narrow hallway. She tread the hardwood floor cautiously, careful not to slip in her socks. About halfway down the hall, she came upon two closed doors: one on her left and one on her right.

Natalie opened the door to her right and peeked in. Black rubber mats sprung back beneath her feet. Several treadmills and stationary bikes filled the middle of the room while weights, resistance bands, and yoga mats lined the walls. Uninterested, Natalie left the room untouched.

She opened the door opposite the gym and left the hallway in awe. Thick, soft carpet enveloped her toes. Spacious loungers and couches divided the room, surrounding a square coffee table. The far wall was comprised of wide windows, giving a beautiful view of the sunset over the waves. A red teapot occupied a quaint dining cart in the corner, along with an assortment of eccentric mugs. The walls consisted of floor-to-ceiling bookcases filled with stories she knew and others she had never heard of. The subjects ranged from entertaining fiction to the lineage of Europe's kings and queens. She traced her finger along one of the bookshelf ladders.

"Incredible," Natalie whispered.

She tapped the bindings as she searched through the titles.

16th Century Cartography, Advancements in Oceanography, Tectonic Plates.

Natalie moved a few bookshelves over.

Plato's Complete Works.

She took the soft leather-bound book from the shelf.

"Not what I was after, but thank you," she muttered to the library.

The floor in the hall creaked. Natalie stared at the empty doorway.

Not here. They can't be here.

She envisioned the man carrying her up the stairs in her house, hoisting her easier than a sack of flour, his shoulder digging painfully into her stomach...

"I thought I might find you here." Leo leaned against the doorframe.

Natalie sank against the bookcase. Her heart rate began to slow to normal. Enzi slinked in behind Leo and rubbed against Natalie's knees.

"I didn't mean to scare you."

"I didn't realize anyone else was awake."

"Hard to sleep through Brant's snoring," Leo assessed the book she carried. He raised an eyebrow. "You woke up craving Plato?"

"No," Natalie traced the book's cover. "I was trying to find something else. This will be for fun."

"Interesting idea of fun," he chuckled. "What were you looking for? I'll help."

"Well," Natalie hugged Plato's writings to her chest. "Uncle Chris said the Coelacanth Project was named after the order Coelacanth, because we are something no one thought could exist."

"Okay," Leo nodded.

"But that logic doesn't pan out. Coelacanths did exist. They were thought to have gone extinct and were rediscovered. They're endangered, but very much alive. However, tacking has never existed before. For researchers to title their endeavor the Coelacanth Project when they were creating something entirely new doesn't make sense. I have trouble believing the people who discovered tacking would be content with such an error. Moreover, he said we were given this ability to prevent cataclysmic disaster. How is tacking supposed to do that? We're missing something," Natalie scanned the shelf again. "I need a book on marine biology. Maybe I'm misunderstanding Coelacanth's history."

Leo crossed his arms as he processed what she said.

"Alright, I understand what the problem is."

"You do?" Natalie asked, surprised.

Do I understand what the problem is?

"You're thinking too much."

"Excuse me?" Natalie huffed. "Don't you want to learn

more about what our parents spent our entire lives hiding from us?"

"Don't you want to actually enjoy it for a minute before analyzing it to bits?"

"I want to understand!"

"No book in here is going to tell you what you really want to know, Nat," Leo said bluntly. "You have to speak to your parents. We all do."

Natalie stared at him, his candor taking the fight out of her.

"You know what? You need to buck up."

"Buck up?"

Leo stepped on the ladder and pushed himself along the rack.

"Let's find you a nice, happy read to help you unwind. Ah-ha!" He pulled a novel bound beautifully in green and gold leaf off the shelf and tossed it to her. "This seems cheery."

Natalie flipped the soft pages through her fingers. The inlaid filigree on the binding was gorgeous and begged to be cracked, yearned to share its secrets. She saw why he picked it. Natalie read the cover and smirked.

"*1984* by George Orwell."

"Oh no," Leo snatched the book away. "Not that one."

Natalie laughed. It felt good.

"That's probably the first time *1984* made anyone laugh," Leo put the book back on the shelf.

Natalie's smile faded as she sank back into thought. Enzi's nose stuck straight in the air and he ran from the room, his furry paws slipping as he hit the hallway.

"We'll find you a book later. Right now we should worry more about breakfast."

As soon as he mentioned it, Natalie caught the scent of fresh bacon wafting up from the floors below them. Her mouth started to water. They made their way down the stairs. Natalie stopped briefly on the second floor to tuck Plato safely away on her bedside table for later. Voices drifted to them as they approached the first floor.

Natalie entered the kitchen. Owen sat at the bar while Brant and Tawney stood at either end, blocking in Uncle Chris between them. Christopher stood with his back to the stove and a spatula in each hand, his eyes darting from Brant to Tawney.

"I told you no more! You've had a piglet each and you will turn into piglets if you eat another bite!"

"But Owen has some!" Tawney argued.

Owen crunched happily on a piece of freshly cooked bacon.

"That's his first piece!" Christopher argued. "Ha!" He pointed a spatula at Natalie and Leo as they entered. "Guard your own bacon so I can make the waffles."

Tawney held out her arms to stop Leo from passing. He picked her up under her biceps, spun, and released her when he was on the same side as Christopher.

"Huh," Tawney shrugged. "I'll allow it."

Natalie took a plate and accepted a few pieces of meat over the bar from Leo. She welcomed the comfort food. The bacon was warm, crisp, and slightly salty.

Christopher turned his back to them and focused on cooking. Owen tossed a piece of bacon towards Tawney. She reached out to catch it, but Enzi's jaws snatched the strip of meat right out of the air.

"No, Enzi!" Natalie yelled at him.

He met her stern stare as he swallowed the snack whole. Tawney doubled over laughing.

Christopher passed around a stack of freshly made waffles. Natalie took a seat next to Owen and prepared hers with icing sugar and maple syrup. Christopher produced two dog bowls from the cabinet and poured dry kibble in for Angie and Enzi.

"Last night you said we need to work," Leo prompted, passing around forks.

"First," Christopher pointed at him with a piece of waffle dangling from his fork. "About last night. What you did was dangerous."

"Because we can be anatomically dissolved into the physical makeup of the universe?" Owen asked.

Christopher stared at him.

"No, kid, sheesh," he shook his head. "Because there are people wantin' to use you, use what you can do."

"Even though we can only move as far as the sea? We only go from point A to point B," Tawney pointed from one couch to the other in demonstration.

"It's called tackin', and you're right. Tackin' does have limitations, but don't underestimate your power. People want to use that for their own gains."

Brant nodded.

"Why'd Coelacanth choose us?" Owen asked, helping himself to a second waffle.

"You were all born 'bout the same time and a good age when the program began. Old enough to tolerate the testing, but young enough the memories of it shouldn't be permanent. Your parents consented. That way you could still grow and develop like any other kid, have a normal life. Thought you deserved that much at least."

"I guess that's why our parents are so close," Tawney said, sneaking another piece of bacon.

"They have something in common no one else in the world does," Uncle Christopher agreed. "I've only seen one lot closer."

"So," Natalie knelt with an arm around Enzi's fluff. "Our parents went into hiding for fear someone would use them, or the information they have, to manipulate us."

"They were supposed to get you to me first and then go to their safe house. Something must not have gone accordin' to plan."

"If our parents were captured," Owen adjusted his glasses. "Would we know?"

"Yes," Uncle Chris nodded. "Nautilus would make sure of

it. They would use them to manipulate y'all into doin' whatever Nautilus wants."

"Manipulate us how?" Tawney asked.

"Would you be able to stay here, hidden, if someone threatened to kill your parents?"

No one answered. Natalie's heart threatened to beat out of her chest.

"We need to find them," Natalie said, standing. "They're more at risk out there than here with us. If they're with us, no one can get them, no one can use them."

"No, Nat, you need to stay here and keep your head down and train up. Your parents know how to stay hidden."

"Train up?" Leo asked.

Christopher moved to the living room and stood by the wide ottoman Brant had slept on.

"Of course. You have to get ready to end this. The bombings will escalate until Nautilus gets control of you. The sooner we take the fight to them, the more lives we'll save."

"When you say 'end this' do you mean…" Natalie drifted off, unable to put the thought into words.

"He means killing them," Tawney jumped in. "And I intend to."

"You don't mean that," Natalie told her.

"Why wouldn't she?" Brant crossed his arms. "People have been killed, our parents have been forced into hiding, and our homes are destroyed. Whoever is behind this should die. I'll do it myself."

"It may end up bein' the only way," Christopher shrugged. "We need to be ready. Tack exclusively under covered areas like the cavern. They can track you otherwise."

Natalie exchanged anxious glances with her friends. They had spent hours the day before gallivanting across the globe.

"Track us?" Brant repeated, his voice high.

Owen snapped his fingers.

"Satellites!"

Uncle Chris nodded. "The light and energy set off by tackin' is so immense it can be detected in space if done in the open, but is pretty easily concealed by most physical barriers. So, for example, no satellite can detect you comin' or goin' from the cavern here."

Natalie swallowed hard.

Nautilus wouldn't have been able to trace us back here.

What have our parents signed us up for?

"Well," Christopher kicked the side of the large white couch. "This is what we're workin' towards." He lifted off the top of the ottoman and a multi-leveled storage unit expanded out of it. Black and silver metal glinted on its shelves.

Natalie crossed her arms.

"Are those guns?" Leo gasped.

"I slept on a freaking arsenal," Brant whispered, pulling his old knit cap over his head.

"Is this necessary?" Owen asked, following Tawney as she investigated the stocked shelves.

"Absolutely. We need to make sure you're ready."

"Ready for what, exactly?" Natalie asked.

Uncle Chris took one of the pistols off its shelf and studied the metal as though seeing it for the first time. He looked pained as he forced the weapon into Natalie's grasp. The steel was cold and menacing. She worried it might fire at any moment, regardless of how far her fingers were from the trigger.

"I don't know," Christopher confessed. "But Nautilus is comin' for you. As far as they're concerned, if they can't have you, no one will."

Leo eased the gun away from Natalie and she happily let him have it.

"If Nautilus falls, we can find our parents?" Leo clarified.

"If Nautilus falls, your parents will come to you."

"Then let's train," Brant said, a gun at either side.

Uncle Christopher chuckled and took Brant's weapons away

from him.

"We're not trainin' with these."

"Thank goodness for that; we'd be dead in a day," Tawney muttered.

Natalie watched the shelving unit sink back into the ottoman. Christopher replaced the cover and it became another piece of living room furniture.

Question everything.

"Now, y'all seem to have gotten comfortable with tackin' yesterday, but I want it to become second nature. Practice a bit in the cavern, and then we'll run some self-defense drills."

Tawney led the way with Owen, Leo, and Brant following behind her. Natalie stalled, putting their dishes in the dishwasher and wiping the counter clean.

"Somethin' on your mind, kid?" Christopher sat at the bar across from her.

Natalie didn't answer.

Where do I start?

"They wouldn't want you to sit frettin' about them," Uncle Chris said softly. "Your parents knew there was a chance you would be facin' this alone and the more they tried to fight it, the more likely it became. Now we have years of trainin' to do as fast as we can manage."

"We don't have a chance, Uncle Chris," Natalie said bitterly.

"No, no, we'll get you trained up—"

"We're kids! Nautilus got away with bombing a military base. We can't compete with an organization that extensive, not without a lifetime of training. We're going to die because of what our parents did to us. Then they're going to die, too."

Christopher sat silently, his expression unreadable.

"What?"

"I'm allowin' you a moment of weakness."

"Weakness?" Natalie choked.

"You have no idea what Nautilus is capable of, kid," he said sternly. "Those bombs will be nuclear soon enough. Nautilus will do whatever is necessary to push you to tack for them. They want the power and I forbid you to take the easy way out. I forbid you to die to keep it from them. You will live because of what your parents did for you, what I've done for you. I promised I would keep you safe, no matter what."

Natalie stared at him.

"Fear does not equate to weakness."

"You were expressin' defeat, not fear, and I don't ever want to hear it again. To fear is human," he huffed, "to fear is to be alive."

She stood silent for a long moment, listening to the voices of her friends echo to her from the hall.

"Why did the Coelacanth Project choose us?" Natalie repeated Owen's question, hoping for the real answer.

"It wasn't a choice; there was no one else."

Natalie raised an eyebrow.

"Coelacanth could have used any kids they wanted, but our parents volunteered us, right?"

Christopher watched the white capped waves breaking in the wind outside the window.

"Fate's a wicked beastie. It may decide your destiny, but it doesn't define you. Only you can do that." He nodded towards the cavern. "Get in there."

Natalie hesitated.

"I don't believe in fate, Uncle Chris. I'm not sure I believe in anything anymore."

To her surprise, Christopher chuckled.

"I bet you a nickel and a penny you change your mind."

Natalie left him in the kitchen and followed the echoing shouts of her friends to the cavern.

CHAPTER 14

atalie entered the boat cavern and squinted against near constant bursts of white light. She briefly turned her back to the water and let her eyes adjust.

"Nat!" Tawney squealed from the end of the dock, hiding behind the *Learn'd Astronomer.*

Natalie carefully made her way to her friend. The boys were tacking in and out instantaneously, leaving ghosts of laughter in their wake. The effect was creeping her out.

"Leo has a shell," Tawney explained as Natalie crouched beside her. "We're going to get it from him."

Natalie watched as fleeting images of Brant, Owen, and Leo materialized on the docks. They were all coming and going so quickly, Natalie was sure Brant and Owen were not even trying to get Leo's treasured shell, but just enjoying themselves. Leo surfaced quite close to where she and Tawney were hiding. Natalie watched him fixate briefly on the dock opposite them.

She clutched the spark in her pocket and rolled into the water, envisioning the same spot Leo had stared at. The sea took her and she was alight with energy. It was as though every cell in her body had awakened and the hairs on her arms stood on end. The feeling was over faster than she could blink. She emerged onto the dock opposite of Tawney.

Another flash glowed a second after her. Natalie reached into it, snatched Leo's shirt, and pulled. He lurched forward in surprise. Natalie steadied him and he grinned at her.

"Lucky catch?"

"You gave yourself away."

"Clever," Leo complimented, tossing her the smooth white shell.

"Yes, you clever girl," Brant growled playfully from behind her. He held the hand hiding the scallop shell and twirled her. A sharp pop sounded and Brant's touch fell away. The white shell dropped into the water with a splash. Brant stumbled back from her and doubled over, clutching his side.

"Brant?" Natalie moved between him and the end of the dock to keep Brant from falling in.

He gasped as he pulled his hands away from his abdomen. They shone vividly red.

"I-I've been shot?"

"For sure," Christopher stood in the doorway. A large gun was propped on his hip and several more draped across his back. "Y'all each take one and follow me below. I swear if you fire any in the house, I'll kill you myself."

He tossed a gun to Tawney who caught it right out.

"Paintball guns! Mom has never let me play!"

"Can't imagine why," Owen muttered.

Brant's cheeks flushed crimson. He snatched a paintball gun from Christopher and brushed gruffly past him. Uncle Chris threw Natalie one and it tumbled to the ground.

"Where's Enzi?" she asked as she reluctantly picked up the toy weapon.

Feels real enough.

"I shut the dogs away upstairs with some treats. I don't want either of them gettin' hit." Uncle Christopher gestured to the door opposite the boat cavern. It was open wide, revealing a hanging rope ladder descending far below them. "Down you go," he gave her a rough pat on the back.

Natalie slung the gun across her back and cautiously climbed down. Her shoulder sent aches of protest through her arm with each passing rung, forcing her to rely on her right arm for the descent. Desperate to reach the bottom, she jumped the last few rungs to the polished concrete floor. Waves of dust rushed away from her feet as she landed.

She stood in an expansive room interrupted by square stone pillars supporting the weight of the house above them. An assortment of obstacles broke up the massive space: overturned picnic tables, junk cars, a few rowboats, and even the thick trunk of an old tree. Along one of the walls hung cloth sheets with ringed targets painted on them. Opposite the targets sat a wide wooden chest with an old-fashioned, wrought iron lock.

The anger Natalie had subdued in the kitchen resurfaced full force. Ancora had been designed specifically for them, for five late teens whose parents had kept the true nature of their existence a secret their entire lives. Bedrooms stocked with sentimental bits of home, a living space that doubled as an armory, a covered boat slip to practice their tacking, a library for researching, a gym for building their stamina to stay alive, and a paintball course for developing their tactical skills.

Mom and Dad actively planned for us to learn quickly. They chose to lie. They chose to offer me up as collateral for the human race, volunteered me for genetic mischief, and then doubted my strength to handle the truth. They kept everything hidden.

Natalie emerged from her thoughts as Brant took aim at the target farthest from her. He let off three quick rounds and deep blue paint exploded on the bullseye. He lowered the gun and shook his curls out of his eyes.

"Where'd you learn to do that?" Natalie asked in surprise.

"I considered becoming a police officer. Took a tactical training course to prepare," Brant gestured at the painted bullseye. "Go on, you try."

Natalie took aim at the target hanging on the wall ahead of her. She squinted through the scope for a moment before letting the gun fall to her side.

"I don't want to learn to shoot. I don't want to do this."

"At least do target practice," Leo advised as he and Owen joined them.

Tawney and Christopher descended the ladder last, with Tawney harassing him about which paintball gun she preferred.

"He's right," Owen aligned himself with the target next to Natalie's and let off two shots. Grey paint splattered the concrete wall. He frowned at the clean target.

Brant whistled.

"We need to be able to defend ourselves at the bare minimum."

Tawney skipped by them, letting off a shot at each target she passed. Black paint hit the wall, the target paper, the bullseye, and finally the ceiling.

"There's no point in me doing this," Natalie shrugged. "I won't shoot someone. Even if they were attacking me, I don't think I could do it."

"Don't worry about any of that right now. We're shooting paintballs at some targets, it's no big deal." Leo's calm demeanor fueled Natalie's anger.

"No big deal?" Natalie dropped the gun on the ground and pointed to the elaborate paintball course behind her.

"This isn't a game, Leo. We're trying to defend not only ourselves, but our parents and whoever else gets in Nautilus's way on their march to get to us. People have died already. Died! It's a big deal."

"You're goin' to stop more people from dyin' by shootin' that target than you will complainin' about it," Christopher said pointedly.

"I am not. I don't want to shoot anyone."

Christopher marched over so he was standing directly

before her.

"I don't want you to either. I want you to outsmart them. But I'd hate for you to die while you figure out how to do that," he picked the gun up and shoved it against her. "Now shoot the damned target."

Natalie aimed lazily at the bullseye with the butt of the gun resting on her good shoulder. She pulled the trigger and the recoil reverberated to her bruises. She clenched her jaw against the pain. Purple paint plastered the corners of the sheet, even a few rebellious splatters wandered onto the target.

"Happy now?" she asked Uncle Chris.

He put a green salt water taffy in his mouth and chewed thoroughly before answering her.

"No. Hit the bullseye and we'll talk."

Natalie clenched her jaw and aimed again.

The five of them spent what must have been a half hour taking shots at the target wall. Christopher made them retreat further from the target as their aim improved. It was not long before everyone had progressed except Natalie. She truly couldn't care less.

This is a waste of time. I won't shoot anyone. I won't carry the gun. I refuse.

"Figured after Nautilus attacked your home you might want a weapon," Christopher grumbled from behind her.

"I never said I didn't want a weapon," Natalie snapped. "I don't want a gun."

"Why not? It lets you defend yourself from a distance. They'd never be able to get close to you. They'd never be able to touch you."

Natalie wanted to scream at him. She bit her cheek and let off another aimless round towards the target.

"Gimme that," Uncle Chris yanked the gun away from her. "Stop wastin' my paint."

She expected him to be angry or disappointed, but when she faced him, he smiled.

"I'll make you a deal, hmm? I won't make you do target practice, but in return you have to carry a gun when I tell you to. Just in case."

Doesn't mean I have to use it.

"Deal."

"And," Christopher passed her a cold, metal rectangle, "you're tasked with solvin' this in place of target trainin'."

Natalie studied the device. Millimeters thick and a few inches long, it fit easily in her hand. The brushed nickel surface was flawlessly smooth. It was roughly the same size and weight as her cell phone, but it had to be something else. There was no screen, no speaker, no input jacks or buttons.

"What is it?"

Christopher squeezed the two long sides of the device with his fingers. The flat surface shifted to reveal several rows of tiny black squares. Blue-white light projected from each square, coalescing to form a glowing orb in the air before her. Bands of ornate black filigree covered the sphere. Intricate swirls came together and split apart, and in each of their centers was a different shape. A few of the trails originated from simple shapes: a circle, a square, a triangle. Others burst forth from complex geometries. Some she knew, the triskele and the infinite loop, and some she had never seen before. Natalie reached out to trace one of the countless trails and her fingers passed right through the glittering beams, sending the projection scattering.

"Hover your finger where you want to interact with the projection. You can't feel it, but it will feel you."

The device reset and once again the orb floated before her. She reached out and rested the tip of her index finger above one of the swirls. The surface of the hologram twinkled beneath her simulated touch. She moved her finger and the sphere spun.

"The orb is a logic puzzle. If you refuse to train your tactical skills, I'll at least have you trainin' your brain." Uncle Chris squeezed the two shorter ends of the metal square. A white peg materialized at the top of the glowing ball.

"The pin is trapped within the orb. Move it to this circle," he pressed on the center of one of the many twisted spirals, "and the pin will slide out to you, freed."

"May I try?"

Natalie was so fascinated by the puzzle that she had not noticed Owen join them. He marveled at the rotating orb, his glasses reflecting the hologram's glow.

"No, kid, this is Natalie's task."

"What happens when I get the pin out?" Natalie asked, already studying the wandering, twisted pathways.

Shouldn't take long. Even if I don't see the solution, I'll easily be able to play with the pin until I happen along the right path.

"Then you'll have the pin. Why do you kids expect a reward for every miniscule accomplishment?" Christopher started on another piece of candy and dragged Owen back to his bullseye. Owen fired off several rounds of grey paint, most of which missed the target sheet.

Natalie cradled the metal box as she crossed the room. She took a seat on the wooden chest behind where her friends stood shooting. The hologram rotated steadily at eye level. She hovered a finger above the white peg atop the orb. It glowed at her touch and obediently followed her finger along one of several pathways from the tip of the sphere. Natalie pulled the pin along and reached a dead end.

Huh.

She lifted her finger and the pin retreated to its perch atop the orb. She tried again, taking a different pathway from the pin. Natalie traced her finger in and out of several spirals, none with the circle center, and ended up back at the top of the orb.

Huh.

Natalie abandoned moving the pin and took to studying the hologram itself.

There must be a pattern; I simply need to find it.

But the longer Natalie stared at the filigreed orb, the more chaotic it became. The pathways seemed to start and end at random, forming shadowed lacework against the sphere's glowing center. The orb commanded Natalie's attention so completely that she nearly missed the sound drifting beneath the firing of paintball guns and splattering of paint. She had no idea how long she had been hearing it before it finally registered.

"Stop! Stop shooting!" Natalie yelled.

Her friends did as she said, staring at her. She rose from the wooden chest, listening.

"We get it upsets you but—" Brant was cut off by Natalie holding up her finger.

Silence fell over them. She heard it clearly then. The color drained from her cheeks. Uncle Christopher cocked his head at her.

"Is that…"

Natalie nodded. She wanted to run, but fear rooted her to the spot. Its branches crept up her legs like tentacles from the earth.

Christopher hurried across the paintball course to a beat-up Ford sedan. He opened the back door and climbed in.

"Weird," Tawney said, as the barking grew loud enough for everyone to hear. "I thought Enzi was trained to only bark at intruders and such."

"He is," Natalie breathed.

Christopher emerged from the car with six sleek, very real pistols. He passed one to each of them.

"Brant, Leo, come with me," he instructed. "Owen, take the girls to the cavern and wait there for us. Shoot on sight, not sound. Don't want you to be killin' one of us. If we aren't back in three minutes, tack here." Christopher passed Owen a creased photograph. Natalie peered over and briefly caught sight of a quaint yellow cottage.

"No way, we're going with you!" Tawney complained.

Nautilus is inside.

Natalie stared at the ground, unable to focus on anything but Enzi's relentless barking. Her mind drifted far away to Williamsburg, to being hoisted up the stairs of her home. She swayed, unsteady on her feet. The barking faded in her ears, the edges of her vision began to blur, and cold sweat coated the back of her neck. The steel of the pistol leeched the warmth from her fingers, making them slow and clumsy.

She was slung over his shoulder, swaying as he carried her up the stairs. She beat her fists against his back, but he carried her higher and higher. He took her away: away from the door, away from Leo, into the darkness…

CHAPTER 15

"Nat!" Owen's voice was muffled, as though he was shouting to her through glass.

Natalie pulled away. She didn't want to hear him; she wanted to sleep.

"Nat, please! We don't have time."

Natalie shook her head.

"Gimme that."

Tawney?

Cold water drenched Natalie's head.

"What are you doing?" Natalie gasped. She sat up and scooted away from her friends, drying her face on her shirt.

"You decided to black out and we can't carry you up that stupid ladder. So buck up, buttercup. Let's go," Tawney pulled Natalie to her feet.

"Ugh," Natalie's head throbbed.

If one more person tells me to buck up...

"Thanks for the shower," Natalie said, shaking water out of her hair.

"She had to do something," Owen shrugged. "Now come

on, up the ladder."

Natalie skimmed the paintball arena. Uncle Christopher, Leo, and Brant had gone. Tawney swung from the hanging ladder, already halfway up its rungs.

Natalie fetched the logic puzzle from atop the wooden chest and put it in her back pocket. Enzi's relentless barking echoed to them from the third floor, giving her chills.

She scrambled up after Tawney and Owen. The ladder swayed freely beneath her, making the one-armed ascent even more challenging. Sweating, she reached the top. Owen stood in the archway to the cavern directly across the hall from her. He impatiently waved her over, but she hesitated. It would take two seconds at most to traverse the width of the hall. Two exposed and vulnerable seconds.

Owen peeked out from the shelter of the cavern and snuck a glance towards the living room. He motioned her over again.

Natalie took a deep breath and ran. She cleared the door into Ancora, crossed the hallway in a single bound, and flew into the cavern. She spun around on the tips of her toes to meet Owen and Tawney. Adrenaline surged in her veins, making her pulse echo in her ears. She expected Nautilus to close its hold on her at any moment.

Owen stayed in the doorway with his gun pointed towards the kitchen. He trembled and beads of sweat glistened on his forehead. Tawney stomped her foot on one of the docks.

"This is such bull—"

"Shh!" Natalie interrupted Tawney's complaints. Silence fell over them.

Enzi's barking had stopped. The quiet seemed to crush her as they waited. Owen twitched nervously, constantly adjusting his grip on his pistol. Tawney stood with her arms crossed, facing the doorway.

The floor creaked above them. Seconds dragged into minutes. Owen abandoned his post and ran to the dock. He retched repeatedly into the sea. Natalie rubbed his back, her attention still fixed on the doorway.

"You're so loud!" Tawney hissed, taking his place as guard. "And you wasted all that bacon!"

"Your concern is duly noted," Owen groaned, rocking on his feet.

A large ball of white fur bounded into the room. Natalie sensed Owen raise his gun next to her.

"No!" She threw herself into him.

The blast of the gun echoed in the stone chamber. Shards of rock rained on Tawney's head as the bullet buried into the wall inches above her. Enzi padded to Natalie, oblivious. She threw her arms around him and smothered her face into his fur.

It's okay, he's okay, everyone's okay, she told herself.

Appalled, Owen let the pistol fall to the ground.

"Nat, Nat, I'm so sorry," he collapsed to his knees. "Tawney…"

"Certainly glad I didn't come through the door first," Brant joked from the archway.

Tawney brushed the debris from her ringlet curls. She gave Owen an okay signal with her fingers, but her face blanched.

"It's alright, Owen. They're okay," Leo assured him, following Brant in from the hallway. He cradled Angie like a baby in his arms.

Natalie stood and paced, trying to stifle her anger.

Owen didn't mean any harm. It's Chris's fault we're playing with guns at all! We'll kill ourselves before Nautilus has the chance.

Christopher filed into the cavern last.

"Fancy a swim, did you?" Brant tugged at Natalie's wet hair.

She brushed him away and rounded on Uncle Chris.

"This is why five teenagers shouldn't have guns."

"No, this is why I said shoot on sight, not sound. Figured y'all understood the importance of knowin' what you're shootin' at before pullin' the trigger."

Owen nodded pitifully.

"What was he barking at?" Tawney flopped Enzi's ears over his head as color returned to her cheeks.

"Haven't a clue," Christopher admitted. "He stopped as soon as we entered the library. We cleared the house; not a soul here but us."

Natalie wrapped her arms around her waist to hide the fact she was shaking. Whether it stemmed from rage or fear, she wasn't sure.

"I want Enzi with us while we train," Natalie announced.

"For sure," Uncle Chris consented. "I can leash him while y'all work."

"We've probably had enough target practice for today," Tawney spoke for the group. She picked up Owen's abandoned pistol and tossed it to Christopher.

"You truly believe people are coming to get us?" Owen asked, his freckles burned stark orange against his pale cheeks.

"They're comin'. We need to be as ready as we can," he collected the rest of the guns and nodded to Natalie. "Where's yours?"

"She left it downstairs," Tawney ratted her out.

Natalie cut her a look.

"A deal's a deal," Christopher grumbled. "No weapon, no logic puzzle, so honor your bargain. Y'all follow me upstairs."

Leo dumped a wiggling Angie into Tawney's arms and pulled Owen to his feet.

"You alright?"

Owen nodded, his eyes averted.

"And you?"

Natalie nodded.

"Good. Now hug it out, nerds," Leo squished Natalie against Owen's chest.

She couldn't help it; she laughed. Her arms wrapped around his thin figure as he patted her back.

"That'll do, nerds, that'll do. Now you two." Leo pulled Natalie off Owen and replaced her with Tawney. Owen blushed nearly as red as his hair as Tawney embraced him. Abandoned on the floor, Angie jealously pawed at their calves.

"I'm so sorry," Owen apologized into her curls.

Natalie stared at her feet, feeling as though she was intruding on something private.

"You were brave to pull the trigger."

"Uh, what?" Brant cut in.

"He was," Tawney stood on her tiptoes to hold Owen's shoulders at arm's length. "Just aim a little farther away from my head, okay?"

"Come on, you lot!" Christopher called from inside Ancora.

Natalie filed into the house behind her friends and Uncle Christopher lead the way up the stairs. She kept Enzi close by her side and trekked along beside Tawney. Upon reaching the third floor, Chris turned right into the gym, but Natalie hesitated in the hall with Enzi. He stared at the wall at the end of the hallway with his hackles raised. Uneasy, she flattened the spiked fur.

"There's nothing there, Enzi."

He bounded away into the gym and playfully cornered Angie on a bench. Natalie followed, analyzing his actions.

Something's up. He doesn't bark at nothing or fixate on walls.

"Now, I want to teach you how to defend yourselves. Nothin' too fancy, simply enough to help you get out of an assailant's grasp so you can escape," Christopher wandered onto a thick floor mat and grimaced. "Tawney, you'd be the best to demonstrate."

"Yes!" She thrust a triumphant fist in the air and pushed her sleeves up above her elbows.

"Remember, I'm an old man now."

"Nah, you're...huh. How old are you?" Tawney bounced eagerly.

"Forty," he answered, bending his knees. "And more fragile than I used to be."

"Well then, prepare to take on seventeen years of feisty fury," Tawney warned.

"Pay attention," Uncle Chris addressed those watching. "I'm

goin' to fake attack Tawney and she is going to fake defend herself. Do you hear that girl?" he asked Tawney directly. "Don't actually hit me, now."

Tawney smirked mischievously and Natalie wondered if she understood the rules of the game.

"Let's say I go to grab her," Christopher moved in slow motion, reaching stupidly towards Tawney with outstretched arms.

"If he's far enough away, I'll deflect his blow," Tawney gently pushed his arms away from her. "If he's too close, I can break his nose," she pushed her palm flat against Christopher's forehead. "But obviously, you hit his nose instead."

"Either is good to distract your opponent long enough for you to get away," Christopher spun Tawney around by her shoulders.

"Now, let's say I approached Tawney from behind." Again, he reached out for Tawney, resembling a stout, Southern zombie.

"Capture their wrist as soon as they make contact. Use their own weight and momentum against them to flip them over your shoulder," Tawney made to catch Christopher, but he snatched his arm back. "That one's my favorite," she snickered. "Or you can elbow them in the abdomen. Hard. Like, break-a-rib hard."

"I'm glad all those years of jiu-jitsu were worth the money," Uncle Christopher smiled.

"What if they already have you?" Natalie asked. The memory of the Nautilus thug's grasp clutched hauntingly around her.

"Don't panic and be patient. Wait for an opportunity to attack a weakness," Tawney absentmindedly twirled a curl in her fingers. "All you need is a second, but you have to be ready for it."

"No one's going to get you again, Nat," Brant said from somewhere to her left.

"Don't go makin' promises you can't keep, kid,"

Christopher said sternly. "If the risk wasn't there, we wouldn't be doin' this. Now," he snapped his fingers twice. "Pair up and practice. Tawney, observe and correct as you see fit."

She gave a mock salute and paired them up: Natalie with Owen, Brant with Leo. Despite the fact they were pretending, Natalie found herself hypersensitive. Each time Owen touched her she backed away. She struggled to allow herself to turn her back to him.

"I'm sorry, I realize I'm being stupid," Natalie bit her lip in frustration. "What if I fake attack you instead?"

"Whatever you want is fine with me," Owen said, bending his knees and holding his arms up as though to box her. "And no one is judging you. You suffered a trauma, it'll take time."

"I didn't suffer," Natalie blurted. "It was nothing. I'm fine."

She moved to catch Owen's shoulder and he deflected her easily.

"Good job."

"Well, you haven't sparred with Tawney as frequently as the rest of us," Owen replied as he pushed away her next attack.

"Maybe because I think before I speak, nerd," Natalie joked, moving to capture Owen from behind.

"My words may be more calculated than you perceive." Owen mimed as though he had flipped Natalie over his shoulder.

Natalie smirked at her friend.

"Is that so?"

His ears blushed scarlet.

"We're good here," Owen deflected as he casually smoothed out his shirt.

"Quite," Natalie grinned. She watched Brant land flat on his back as Leo flipped him over his shoulder.

"You're supposed to be fakin' it!" Christopher scolded them.

Brant laughed from the floor and passed Leo a few crumpled dollar bills from his pocket. Leo refused the money.

He pulled Brant up from the floor and made him play defense. He approached Brant swiftly from behind, but Brant was faster. He spun on Leo, deflected his outstretched arm, and pinned him to the ground. Brant stood and laughed.

Leo punched the ground in frustration as he rose.

"Again."

Brant waved triumphantly around the room. He flashed Natalie a quick wink, but she was focused on Leo. His jaw tightened as he clenched and unclenched his fists. He glowered at Brant's back without seeing him, as though he was somewhere else.

This is escalating quickly.

Natalie subtly elbowed Tawney who stood observing the fight. Tawney stepped onto the mat directly in front of Brant.

"If that was so easy, try it on me," she challenged.

Brant's grin faltered. He cleared his throat and submissively put his hands in his pockets.

"Alright, enough," Uncle Christopher scratched his beard and made to leave the room. "I'm goin' to make dinner. Or breakfast," he gazed out the window to the horizon that was just beginning to brighten and shook his head. "Y'all just make your own schedule, don't you?"

"Thanks!" Tawney called after him.

Leo stormed off the sparring mat. Natalie reached out to stop him, but he shrugged her off.

"Let's go to the library," Natalie suggested before Leo could reach the door.

He stopped and stared up at the ceiling.

"Yeah, alright," he stepped to the side and gestured to the hall. "After you."

"But Natalieee," Tawney whined in protest as she followed them.

In the hallway, Enzi snarled towards the back wall. Natalie guided him into the library, attempting to appear nonchalant. Leo looked from the end of the hall to Enzi.

"What's up with that?"

"No idea," Natalie tucked her hair behind her ears, listening to Uncle Chris descend the stairs.

Natalie dug her toes into the thick carpet. The ceiling high bookshelves enveloped her, forming an impenetrable barricade against the impossible truths of her life that were desperate to overwhelm her. Her parents' disappearance, tacking, the bombing in Norfolk, preparing for an attack by Nautilus: the list was impossible and yet she lived it. The shelves full of factual summaries and fantastical tales suppressed her troubles. So long as she could lose herself within its stories, reality had no power within the library's four walls.

"Okay," Brant sat cross-legged on a round rug by the coffee table. "What's the plan?"

Reality has no power until it is invited in, Natalie amended as anxiety clutched at her chest. *Then it becomes an epidemic.*

"Plan?" Natalie prepared the kettle on the dining cart for tea.

"Christopher has no intention of finding our parents, Nat. We have to go get them," Leo explained. Natalie snuck glances at him as she fingered through the assortment of tea bags.

Relaxed, as though nothing just happened. Boys.

"Wait," Owen sat back in one of the loungers. "Chris said it was dangerous to go after our parents. We'd be putting them at risk, and risk getting caught ourselves."

"He also said we're already in danger, they're already at risk, and we might get caught sitting here," Leo pointed out. "So, we might as well try."

"I do want to hear it from them," Natalie admitted. She doubted she would accept it until she heard the truth from her parents' mouths. "Coelacanth, their cover-up. I want to hear them say it. I want them here with us, helping us."

"Then let's go get them," Brant agreed.

"Where are we going to look, hot shot?" Tawney poked his leg with her big toe. "Even Uncle Chris doesn't have a clue where they might be hiding. Nautilus could have them already!"

"Unlikely," Owen scratched his auburn scruff thoughtfully. "It's as Christopher said: if they were already captured, Nautilus would be using them as bait to make us expose ourselves. They had to have made it to a safe house."

"Which, according to the bilby clue dad gave me, may be one of many safe houses," Natalie dropped a few tea bags into the pot of boiling water. She wasn't sure about the idea of leaving Ancora. It was safe, at least for the moment, and they had no idea what they were doing.

There is one place we could start...

"We could scope out our parents' office," Leo voiced her thoughts.

"What?" Tawney plopped herself on the floor between Brant and Leo.

"I don't care to see the aftermath of the bombing again." Owen hugged his knees up to his chest.

"And there's no way our parents made it to Norfolk from Williamsburg in the time it took us to get some ice cream," Brant pointed out.

Natalie put the pot of tea on the table. Thick wafts of steam drifted up from its spout, carrying hints of cinnamon and honey.

We'll be waiting for you. Her father's words echoed in her mind, making her restless.

"No, but why blow up a naval base to get our attention? Maybe because it's right next to where our parents went to work every day? It makes sense to look there," Leo spun a pen between his fingers.

Natalie caressed a mug of steaming tea, letting its warmth spread through her.

"Nat, what do you think?" Tawney asked.

"I don't think it matters much what I think," she said honestly. "I had come to the same conclusion as Leo about searching their offices, but logically we should stay here. Our parents are probably at a safe house, as Owen pointed out."

We'll be waiting.

"We're safe," Natalie continued, "for now, here with Uncle Chris. And we barely have any idea about tacking. We don't know enough to make any moves right now," she watched the tea in her cup sparkle beneath the dim lamps of the library. "As badly as I want to find my mom and dad, we would be wasting time and incurring unnecessary risk."

"I thought you said you wanted them here?" Leo asked.

"Of course I do, more than anything, but logic says to wait."

"Forget logic," Leo said. "What do you want?"

Natalie stared at him.

We'll be waiting.

"I want to find them."

"Okay, then," Leo nodded. "When do we leave?"

"Two days?" Owen proposed.

"Even if we don't learn any more in two days, we'll head to their office," Brant smacked the table to seal the decision.

Natalie drifted off into thought on the rising steam of her tea. No matter when they left it would be risky. Nautilus might swarm on Ancora at any moment.

If what Christopher says is true, the longer we stay hidden the more desperate Nautilus will get.

Eventually, Nautilus would find them, capture their parents, or set off another bomb. The risk of making a move would increase with time, but Natalie wasn't ready to leave.

I have more questions; I need more time.

"Alright," Natalie conceded, scanning the hundreds of books surrounding her. "Two days and we'll go."

Two days to find you, Coelacanth.

CHAPTER 16

"**D**inner's ready," Christopher called up the stairs. "Or, uh, breakfast is ready! Whatever bloody meal y'all care to call it."

The sun peeked above the horizon. Its yellow beams skipped on the crests of the waves to their window. Natalie led the way down the stairs, her stomach grumbling. Waffles and bacon must have been days ago.

"Are we nocturnal now?" Uncle Chris chided them as he dished up a pile of ground beef and potatoes. "We've got to fix the sleep schedule; it's messin' with my meals."

"We'll sleep in a little later tomorrow," Brant paused with a piece of potato on his fork. "Later today?" he corrected after some thought.

"You see my point."

Tawney piled her plate and scurried into the living room.

"Let's see if the news updated since yesterday!" She lifted her plate high in the air away from Enzi's inquisitive muzzle as she turned on the television.

Natalie settled in on the couch with her own plate of food

EXTANT

and Enzi positioned himself at her feet, abandoning his fruitless efforts with Tawney.

"We come to you this morning with exclusive insight on the bombing at the Norfolk Naval Station and the series of arson attacks in Williamsburg, Virginia."

"Guys, get in here," Tawney called to the others who lagged behind in the kitchen. They rushed in, their plates forgotten on the bar.

"Officials have confirmed the two bombs detonated in the naval base and the vicious murders of the nine researchers and their children were orchestrated by the same individual," the newscaster in a pink pantsuit faded away and the image of a middle-aged man filled the screen. A stout figure with short salt and pepper hair and deep laugh lines stood proudly in front of his marina.

Natalie's fork levitated in purgatory, halfway between her plate and her mouth.

That can't be.

"Christopher E. Reyes, now the owner of Morning Sun Marina on the Eastern Shore, used to work on the same independent research team as the nine families he killed two nights ago. According to our sources, a falling out within the organization led to its dissolution, putting Christopher Reyes out of a job. He hasn't been seen since the attack in Norfolk. Police say this man is unstable, dangerous, and potentially heavily armed. If seen, call the hotline below, but do not approach. There's no telling what he is capable of."

"Those bastards," Christopher hit his fists against the coffee table, shaking the bowl of salt water taffy.

"Did you do it?" Tawney's question seeped with anger. "Did you kill those people in Norfolk? Have you killed our parents? So you can have control of us?"

"You sick son of a—" Brant lunged for Uncle Chris, but Leo scooped him in a bear hug from behind and turned him away.

"Easy, Brant!" he told him.

Christopher spun slowly to address them, his mouth set in a deep frown.

"You believe I would do that to y'all?" The question went directly to Natalie.

She couldn't bear the betrayal in his eyes. She looked away, rubbing Enzi's ears.

"I gave up everythin' for you," his voice was low and menacing, thunder from a distant storm. "I gave up my whole life for y'all. My existence has revolved around servin' you! Bein' your friend, lovin' you like you were my own blood," he shook his head in disbelief. "You think I'd do this to you?" he gestured to the television.

"No," Leo said firmly.

"He may have!"

"Stop, Tawney," Natalie fussed. "The news hasn't broadcast the truth since the original bombing."

"You're right. I'm sorry," Brant took off his knit cap and ruffled his flattened curls. "I guess I'm a little strung out."

Owen snorted.

"What's funny?" Uncle Chris asked, subtly dabbing his beard dry.

"It's just...fake news. Who knew?"

The boys chuckled, but Tawney was not convinced.

Natalie nodded towards them.

"They're not wrong," she told Tawney. "Someone is playing the media like a puppet. We're talking about Uncle Chris. He told your mom and dad you were taking ballet lessons when he was actually taking you to jiu-jitsu. He bought a tutu and everything! And you," Natalie rounded on Brant. "Uncle Chris lived at your house for six months after your mom passed so you weren't alone when your dad went back to work.

"He bought you hydrochloric acid and God only knows what else when you wanted to play Mad Scientist that one summer," Natalie pointed to Owen. "And Leo, when you were obsessed with soccer—"

EXTANT

"I'm sorry, when did that stage end?" Brant asked.

"Did we miss it?" Owen mockingly rubbed his chin.

"Sheesh, I don't play that much, do I?"

"Anyway," Natalie interrupted, returning to topic. "He took you from school to soccer practice every single day. No questions asked."

Christopher beamed beneath his tear-shimmering beard.

"Someone is trying to turn us against him," Tawney decided, sinking back into the couch cushions.

"And make it difficult for me to move you," Christopher chimed in with a great sniffle. "It isn't likely the public would recognize y'all, a couple of dead kids from one news broadcastin', but America's Most Wanted? I can't even go to the market like I planned. Throws a great bloody wrench in things."

"We'll go for you," Brant offered.

"Oh no," Tawney muttered under her breath. "Please, anything but grocery shopping."

"You don't have to go," Leo told her. "Actually, why don't you and Owen stay here with Uncle Chris? Brant, Nat, and I will draw less attention as a small group."

Owen's mouth fell open and he shook his head adamantly.

"Thank y'all," Christopher smiled. "I'll give you the boat keys tomorrow afternoon. This afternoon?" He pointed out the window. "When the sun is past high noon."

Tawney let out a large yawn that quickly spread through the group.

"Love you guys, but," Brant scooped up his blanket from the day before. "A real man requires a real bed."

Tawney snorted.

"Real men don't squeal when they're pinned, but I can't do the couch again either. How do you sleep with that cover hog?" Tawney added to Natalie.

"Well, it's normally only the two of us," Natalie admitted.

"Always?" Brant asked.

Natalie couldn't tell from his tone if he was joking or serious.

"I don't want to hear any of this," Christopher shook his head as though to rid his mind of Brant's insinuations. "Good night y'all. Or...good mornin', whatever, I'm goin' to bed." He left them and Angie trotted behind him, a black mop at his ankles.

Natalie retrieved her own blanket and whistled for Enzi to follow her. She made her way up the stairs and bid her friends good night as they retired into their respective rooms. She reached the doorway to her own bedroom and hesitated.

"Hey," Leo leaned casually against the wall beside her, his hoodie covering half of his chestnut hair. "I'm next door if you need anything, okay?"

"Thanks," Natalie wasn't sure how much sleep she would get alone. "I'll be fine."

"Good job in there," he added quietly. "Even if Christopher did do it, we can't afford to turn against each other right now. We're going to be our strongest together."

Natalie physically recoiled in surprise.

"You think he could have done it?"

Leo bounced his hands up and down, weighing out the possibilities.

"It's not impossible. If Coelacanth was as secret as he says, he is one of very few people who know about us. I can't imagine what he would want to use our tacking for, though."

It was as though Natalie had been hit in the chest.

"But you defended him."

Leo nodded.

"I did. We need to remain a team and the fastest way to dismantle a good team is to create doubt. But it is definitely possible Uncle Chris is involved."

"There's no way he bombed the Naval Station. Or threatened our parents."

"I don't want it to be true either, Nat, but we don't have

proof one way or the other. We have to keep the option on the table. Christopher said it himself: question everything. I intend to."

Natalie frowned at him.

"You don't have any facts to support you; it's speculation at most. If you live that way, you'll never trust anyone."

"If I were the only one affected, then sure, I would trust him one-hundred percent, but I'm not. I have to look out for Tawney, Owen, Brant, and you. I can't afford to be caught off guard. Rule one of playing defense: be there. Rule two: be ready." Leo retreated into his bedroom, leaving the door ajar.

Natalie stood rooted to the spot.

What just happened?

How could he say that about Uncle Chris? Obviously, Tawney and Brant share similar doubts. She suspected it stemmed from residual resentment for Christopher vanishing from their lives, but maybe they had a point.

No.

Enzi whined at Natalie from the foot of her bed. The rising sun painted him gold, as though he had been petted by King Midas. She crossed the threshold and laid next to her furry friend.

"They're out of their minds, Enzi," Natalie said. "He's family."

She took the mysterious logic puzzle from her pocket and pressed the cold metal against her sore shoulder. She leaned back and felt something hard beneath her pillow. Reaching under it, she discovered a textbook with a note taped to its cover.

FOR RESEARCH.

Natalie pulled off the note and read the title.

Orders of Marine Fishes.

She fanned through the slick pages; Coelacanth was already bookmarked. Another book, significantly thinner than the marine biology text, was tucked under it. The cover was mostly white with a funnel of pastel colors on the center. A second note was taped to it.

FOR FUN.

Natalie removed the hastily scribbled message and laughed. *Oh, the Places You'll Go!* by Dr. Seuss.

She let Dr. Seuss join Michael Crichton and Plato on her bedside table while the textbook laid open at her side. Natalie put her back to the glistening ocean and subtly kept watch on the door. Still intrigued by the logic puzzle, she pushed on the sides of the silver device. The glistening orb flickered to life before her, suspended in midair. Natalie gave the puzzle a gentle flick with her finger and the orb began to rotate around the vertical peg at its center. She stroked Enzi's ears as she began to read.

The Coelacanth fishes are incredibly unique. With heavily armored bodies that can grow up to six feet long, they occupy deep ocean waters. They utilize electrolocation to sense their surroundings in complete darkness. Whether passively utilizing a naturally occurring electrical field, or generating their own, the ability to manipulate electricity is becoming increasingly recognized in various other species. Formerly believed to be extinct, the Coelacanth fishes had only been described through the fossil record. Then in 1938, the discovery of a surviving species put Coelacanth back on the map. Despite this, they remain critically endangered. It will take drastic conservation measures to preserve Coelacanth's return from extinct to extant.

CHAPTER 17

"N at."

The voice sounded distant. She wanted to keep it that way. Natalie retreated further into her subconscious and pulled the covers up around her chin.

"Nat, wake up."

Someone gripped her bicep and she shot up like a rocket. She kicked and fought to scramble away, but they gripped her tighter.

"Woah, kid, easy!" Uncle Christopher loomed over her. Leo's warning rang clear in her mind.

"Stop it, get away from me!" she cried out.

Christopher let go and backed away in alarm. Tawney popped up by his elbow and Enzi sat next to her, his head cocked in confusion. Natalie realized Christopher was only trying to wake her. She laid her head back against the wall.

"Sorry. Bad dream," she lied.

"That's alright. Didn't want to hurt you," Christopher smiled at her.

Of course you didn't. You would never do anything to hurt us.

Stupid Leo.

Christopher waved a piece of paper and some cash in the air.

"We have cereal for breakfast, but someone is requesting something else," he nodded at Tawney.

She leaned forward onto the bed, her voice serious.

"There's no more bacon, Nat. We need bacon. We need it now."

"Yeah, alright," Natalie rubbed the sleep from her eyes and took the list from Uncle Chris. "I'll be right there."

Tawney poked Christopher's arm.

"Told you she would understand."

"I was just sayin', a good friend may have let her sleep a wink longer."

Natalie stood and stretched as they exited her room. She retrieved a pair of shorts from one of the drawers, but after sliding them on, promptly changed her mind. The cuts on her legs looked horrendous.

I guess I'm tackling the summer heat in khakis.

She changed and made her way to the kitchen. Uncle Christopher stood behind the bar, anxiously fiddling with a set of keys.

"I imagine you remember how to drive her?"

"Like riding a bike," Leo filled the dogs' stainless steel bowls with a cup of kibble.

"Very good," Christopher tossed the boat key into the air towards Leo. Brant jumped between them and caught it.

"I call dibs!" Brant dangled the key and anchor-shaped float in Leo's face.

"What you're goin' to do is go out past the cape, and head straight for the lighthouse off to the right side. Stay fairly close to shore, water's deep on that side. Watch for Lighthouse Market; big sign, lots of docks to choose from. Get in and get out, you hear? I don't like this. I've more than half a mind to call it off."

"No, no, we'll be fine," Brant assured him.

"If you're not back in two hours, I'm comin' after y'all."

"Two hours!" Tawney cried from the living room. "I can't wait two whole hours! Tack there and—"

"No, no, no," Christopher waved a yellow piece of taffy at her. "There's no coverage at the market. You would be exposed. You have to take the boat, for sure."

"Maybe I'll come, too," Owen said from the stairwell.

"Bye bud," Brant waved as he ducked into the cavern.

"You'll be fine," Natalie smiled at him.

She joined Brant and Leo in the cavern and climbed aboard the *Learn'd Astronomer*. Enzi tried to leap in after her, but she pushed him back. He pouted on the dock with his head nestled between his paws in disappointment.

"Aw Nat," Brant came to Enzi's defense. "Why can't he come? He loves boat rides."

"He made quite an impression on Nautilus in Natalie's house," Leo said, patting Enzi on the head. "And you don't see many pure white Shepherds as it is; he would draw extra attention to us."

"I'm sorry, friend. I tried," Brant gave Enzi an apologetic scratch behind the ears before heading to the wheel.

The engine bubbled to life. Leo untied the ropes tethering the boat, tossing them to Natalie as he walked along the dock. After the last rope was untied, he dropped aboard and Natalie helped him push the boat away from the wooden pylons.

He grinned at her.

"Just like old times."

"What was that?" Brant called back to her from the wheel.

"Someone's being sentimental," Natalie said, stashing the ropes beneath a cushioned seat. "Let's go."

Brant pulled smoothly away from the dock and aimed for the holographic wall. Natalie chose not to watch their approach to the deceivingly solid concrete. Enzi wagged his tail at the end of the dock and Angie padded out of the house to sit with him. They made an odd pair: the massive, sleek Shepherd with the wild ball of fluff sitting between his front legs. Her ears did not even brush his belly.

They flickered before her for a moment, caught in the haze of the hologram, and then Ancora's cavern was gone. A wall of rough concrete rose out of the water inches from their propellers. Now that she knew what to look for, Natalie noticed where the calm waves of the sea flowed unhindered through the projection. On either side, where the hologram ended and the foundation of Ancora began, water splashed up against the stone.

Brant opened up the engines and they blasted forward. Natalie flew towards the stern. She managed to catch hold of a steel railing and saved herself from falling overboard. She shot Brant a disapproving scowl.

"Woohoo!" Leo yelled. He stood on the passenger seat and pointed out approaching crab pots to Brant as they sped towards the point of the cape.

Natalie watched Ancora shrink behind them. She had to admit it was a beautiful day to be on the water. The wind drowned out the world and the sky was clear. Buoys passed by in a blur of color, but the cottages dotted along the shore took ages to pass. The vast expanse of water diminished the perception of distance. She leaned off the side of the boat and let the cool spray of the sea smack against her open palm.

Her hair whipped behind her shoulders as they sped past the shoreline. She closed her eyes and took in the heat of the sun. Despite it being a short outing, her skin would burn. Unlike Brant and Tawney, who both browned easier than a piece of toast, Natalie was so fair she worried one day she would become translucent.

She slid into the railing as Brant took a sharp turn around the point of the cape. Holding tight to the metal bar, she reached briefly beneath the waves. As they straightened out, Natalie squinted ahead. They approached a weathered shack sheltering aisles full of colorful produce. Several docks jutted out from the shore and led directly to the shop. A large sign swung from the end of the furthest dock that read LIGHTHOUSE MARKET.

Brant cut the engine and they drifted to the closest dock. Leo caught the first pole they came to and jumped onto the weathered wood. Natalie tossed him a rope off the bow and he pulled the *Learn'd Astronomer* along the dock until they were several pylons past the market sign. He tied a stern rope to another pillar, then Natalie and Brant joined him on the dock.

"Let's be quick," Natalie said, feeling exposed.

The heat was stifling. Natalie pulled her hair up into a ponytail to let the breeze flow across her neck. Sweat coated her calves, making her healing scabs sting.

She picked up a shopping basket at the end of the dock and entered the covered shop. Gravel crunched beneath her feet as she perused the aisles. Produce and cheap souvenirs were assembled in rustic bins on fold out tables. A large glass cooler by the cashier station was filled with bagged ice and dairy products, and another cooler close to their dock was packed with meat products. Local fishermen stood by hand-painted signs selling freshly harvested Chesapeake Bay blue crabs, oysters, and clams. Natalie maneuvered her way through other customers, seeking the limited shade provided by the shack.

Pretty packed for such a modest market.

Natalie retrieved the list Uncle Chris had given her and read it out to Leo and Brant.

"Eggs, milk, bread, salt water taffy, and then there are Tawney's additions of bacon, pizza, and soda."

"I'll find the bread, soda, and candy," Brant promptly departed into the crowd.

"I'll get the eggs and milk," Leo said, heading in the opposite direction of Brant.

"I guess that leaves me with the pizza and precious bacon," Natalie said to herself. She inspected the cooler next to her and opened the door, settling for the closest package of bacon. She dropped the meat into her basket and surveyed their pizza options. Natalie checked over her shoulder, briefly scanning the crowd. A tingling tickled her spine.

You're being paranoid, she told herself, focusing again on the pizza in front of her. She decided on a stuffed crust pepperoni and closed the fogged glass door. Someone stood waiting behind it, making Natalie jump.

Her silver hair flew wildly in all directions and her grey eyes inspected Natalie intently. A brown birthmark covered half of her forehead and right cheek, contrasting starkly with her pale skin. She wore the same navy blue jumpsuit she had worn when Natalie first saw her. Natalie clearly made out the emblem on the side of her sleeve.

Nautilus.

She cocked her head, admiring Natalie's face.

Natalie nearly dropped the basket as Brant added the bread into it. He casually put his arm around her waist and gave her a reassuring squeeze.

"Can we help you?" he asked the woman politely.

"I believe we've met," she croaked.

Sweat dripped down the back of Natalie's neck. She made eye contact with Leo across the market. He moved pointedly through the crowd towards her.

"Hmm, not likely," Brant pulled Natalie closer to him. He had a death grip on her waist. "My wife Angie and I are visiting from Maine. Have a good one!"

Brant guided Natalie away from the woman. Her body seemed to advance through molasses. Her legs were sluggish and clumsy, and she tripped on her own feet. Natalie caught sight of the grey-haired woman. She smiled after them.

"What a creep," Brant whispered.

"He's here," Natalie breathed. The market spun and she became simultaneously buoyant and anchored. She leaned against Brant to remain upright.

"He's going to get me. He's here." She scanned the crowd frantically for the large man.

He's here; he has to be.

"Who's here, Nat?" Brant eyed her with concern.

"She was in my house, Brant. They're here, they're here," Natalie wiped the sweat from her forehead.

"We need to go," Brant said sternly, practically dragging her towards the dock. "Where's Leo?"

"I only want to talk, sweetie."

Natalie yelped and spun on her heels. The old lady beamed up at her. A cylindrical metal rod dragged at her side as she trailed after Natalie.

Bolt, Natalie remembered Uncle Christopher's term.

Brant slid in front of Natalie, holding her still behind him.

The woman cocked her head and stared at them longingly. She spun the bolt almost lazily between her fingers.

"We have so much to discuss," she insisted.

"We own a vacuum, we've already found Jesus, and I'm politically indifferent," Brant explained in a rush. "Your time would be best spent elsewhere."

She pursed her lips and pressed on the shell insignia on her shoulder. A shopper from the crowd stared at them. Then another, and another. They swiftly moved through the market, never taking their attention off Natalie and Brant, until they blocked each exit. The other customers carried on about their shopping, apparently oblivious.

"Oh my God," Natalie whispered.

They're surrounding us.

"You're confused, child," the woman's wrinkles deepened with her frown. "I'm not here to sell you something; I'm here to save you from yourself. You've become murderers. All those innocent people in Norfolk, dead because of your apathy, hurt because of your negligence." The Nautilus elder reached out to them. "We can show you the truth."

"No," Natalie argued from behind Brant. "The bombing had nothing to do with us."

"Choosing not to act in the wake of tragedy, choosing to let

dead men lie, to let them rot," she clicked her tongue
disapprovingly on the roof of her mouth. "What would your
parents say?"

Natalie watched in shock as the cooler sheltering the pizzas
tumbled forward. Shoppers screamed and scrambled out of the
way. Glass shards scattered as the front of the cooler shattered.
The old woman turned to investigate the commotion, but never
saw the cooler hit the ground.

Leo burst from the crowd and tackled her onto the dock,
sending her bolt into the sea. He leapt up and pushed Brant
towards the boat.

"Go!"

Natalie was dragged behind them. The Nautilus followers
who blocked off the exits abandoned their posts to pursue
them. The woman still laid on the ground, just starting to rise.

A young man with a black ponytail sprinted for them from
across the market. He produced a bolt from across his back
and spun it rapidly at his side as he ran.

"We're not going to make it!" Natalie called to Leo and
Brant.

"Yes we are! Run!"

The gravel beneath her feet gave way to solid wood as she
sprinted across the dock. She glanced back again; the
ponytailed man followed a few paces behind them.

"We're not going to make it," Leo conceded.

Obviously!

"There!" Brant nodded to the *Learn'd Astronomer*. "Cross it!
Tack on the other side!"

"That's in the open!" Natalie countered.

"We don't have a choice," Leo pointed out as Nautilus
members guarded the ends of each dock. "They'll catch us
before we can even start the motor."

Natalie saw Brant dig into his pocket and take hold of his
spark as he jumped from the dock to the boat. The next jump
took him up and over the opposite side, out of sight. There was

a subtle flash, like lightning at high noon, barely noticeable against the glare of the sun.

Leo leapt onto the *Learn'd Astronomer* after Brant, and Natalie followed right behind him. As her feet met the textured white floor, someone took hold of her shirt and flung her towards the cabin. She bounced roughly off the driver's seat and slammed against the cabin door.

The man with the black ponytail sneered as he approached her. His navy jacket was out of place in the humid summer heat. The shining bolt spun swiftly at his side as Natalie fumbled with the lock on the cabin door.

Leo grabbed the man's jacket and pulled him back towards the stern. The bolt sliced through the air, sparking at its ends, missing Leo by inches.

The cabin lock clicked open and Natalie crawled inside. It was more cramped than she remembered. A bed large enough for two people occupied most of the tiny room, with a narrow sink in the corner and mirror on the back of the door. Unable to fully stand, Natalie crouched as she dug through cubbies along the wall and flipped up the bed cushions.

Come on!

Someone on the back of the boat grunted in pain.

You have guns stashed everywhere, Chris. There has to be something here!

"Nat!" Leo yelled from outside. "Get out of there!"

Natalie made to leave the cabin and tripped. She untangled her feet from something pointed and strapped and found her scuffed high-heeled sandals. Clutching one shoe, she emerged to find Leo pinned. The man pressed Leo's cheek into the rough floor and swung his bolt high in the air, aiming for Leo's head.

Natalie leapt on him. Holding the toe of her shoe, she drove its pointed heel into the man's arm. He cried out and Natalie backed away. The feeling of the shoe digging into his skin had made her want to hurl.

"Tanaka!" The old woman stood at the shore with her arms stretched out towards the ponytailed man. Other Nautilus followers raced past her as they closed in on the boat.

Natalie helped Leo to his feet. Blood trickled from a cut on his lower lip.

The man screamed in frustration. He swung the bolt aimlessly about the boat, its ends sparking with audible pops.

"Tanaka, stop!" the Nautilus woman yelled.

His Nautilus companions were so close Natalie heard their feet slamming against the planks on the dock. She dug for the spark in her pocket as the man they called Tanaka approached her.

"Nat, move!" Leo yelled, pulling her towards the edge of the boat.

Tanaka swung the bolt over his head, glaring at Natalie. Leo jumped to tackle him, but Tanaka pushed him away. Leo had barely hit the ground when he was scrambling back to his feet.

Tanaka brought the bolt straight down at Natalie. She held up the only defense she had: her high-heeled shoe. It snapped under the blow of the bolt and the metal rod grazed the inside of her right wrist. The pain consumed her. White-hot fire seared across her skin. It scorched down her fingertips and up her arm like lightning. A cloud seemed to black out the sun and the chaotic market fell silent. For an instant, Natalie was alone: just her and her pain. She screamed and clutched her wrist against her chest.

Broken. It was the lone coherent thought she could manage.

A gunshot rang out and Tanaka crouched instinctively for cover. Natalie clutched Leo's shirt as he scooped her off the ground. He cradled her in his arms and rolled off the back of the boat.

There was a moment of weightlessness. Natalie wished she could stay in it forever. The blinding white light flashed and a static tingling spread through her until she was grasping the old, splintered dock in Ancora. She was surprised to find the silence of the cavern comforting.

Leo pushed her up onto the dock, his chest heaving.

"Are you okay?" He reached out for her arm, but Natalie shook her head.

"Don't touch it," she begged. The initial blinding pain had passed, but her wrist burned as though sea nettles swam within her skin.

"I thought you guys were right behind me," Brant crouched over her.

"We were, but so was Nautilus. Come on, Nat. I won't hurt you."

Natalie reluctantly released her arm from her chest. She had never broken anything before, so she wasn't sure what it was supposed to feel like other than painful.

"Woah," Brant gasped.

"Get an ice pack," Leo instructed.

Natalie bit her lip as Brant ran out of the cavern.

"It's broken, isn't it?" she asked, feeling stupid.

"Not likely. Can you feel this?" Leo touched the tips of his fingers to hers.

She nodded.

"Good."

Brant skidded around the doorway with a malleable cold-compress pinched between his fingers and Enzi on his heels. A wet tongue slathered Natalie's forehead and she sat up, pushing Enzi away. He barked excitedly at them, darting from Natalie, to Leo, to Brant. Leo gently pressed the ice pack against her wrist and she wanted to melt into it.

"What did that?" Brant asked, his eyebrows lost beneath his hair.

"A bolt. Thankfully, someone shot at them," Natalie caught Leo pocketing a metal object off the dock. "You shot at them?" she gasped.

"I fired a warning shot into the water. It was enough."

"Who gave you a gun?" Brant crossed his arms.

"Christopher, before we left. He was worried."

"Then I'll be sure to tell him you knocked out a grandma. That'll calm him right down."

"I saved your sorry ass and you know it," Leo reached across Natalie and shoved Brant.

Brant picked up the shopping basket.

"Least we got the goods!"

"We stole?" Natalie asked, appalled at the thought.

"And vandalized," Leo added.

Tawney skipped through the doorway.

"Bacon! Good boy, Enzi!" she cried in delight. "Hey, where's the boat?"

Natalie waited while Tawney put the pieces together. She covered her mouth in shock.

"He's going to be so mad," she hurried to them and pulled Natalie to her feet.

Christopher filled the doorframe. His mouth was set in a deep frown, making him look older. Natalie bit her lip and hung her head in shame as his glare bore into her.

"What have you done?"

"Did you guys tack back here?" Tawney whispered.

"Hey, you're back!" Owen grinned, following Uncle Chris inside the cavern.

"Where's my bloody boat?" Christopher opened his arms wide at the empty boat slip.

Owen stopped short and cleared his throat.

"Did I miss something?"

"We didn't have a choice, Christopher," Brant explained.

"You always have a choice!"

"Well, I guess we could have chosen to get taken instead," Leo tossed him the boat keys. "The *Learn'd Astronomer* is fine, she's at the market. I doubt we'll be getting her back anytime soon, unless you fancy a shootout."

"Shootin'? Who was shootin'?" Christopher frowned at each of them. "Ya'll were shot at?"

"No, I fired a warning shot into the water," Leo explained.

"It was enough for us to get away."

"Nautilus found us," Natalie pulled the ice pack off her wrist and showed her injury to Uncle Chris.

"We don't know for sure," Leo interjected.

"We do," Christopher replied, examining her wound. "That's a bolt's mark. You're lucky you weren't killed; it must've been a partial blow. I told you not to let it touch you."

"This woman," Natalie blurted. "She was in my house the night of the Naval Station bombing; she had the nautilus shell on her uniform."

"How did they know to be there?" Owen asked from behind Uncle Chris.

"Hard to say," Christopher fiddled with the buoy keychain on his boat keys. "Possible they were scannin' the area and got lucky."

Natalie inferred by the tone in his voice Uncle Chris did not put much stock in luck.

"Awfully lucky," Leo snuck a glance at Natalie. She ignored him.

"So they've found us," Natalie examined the concrete walls of the cavern. Ancora didn't seem as safe as it had that morning.

"No, they didn't come here, but they figure y'all are close, for sure. Best be extra careful now. We'll relocate come tomorrow." A calloused thumb gently lifted her chin. Uncle Christopher's eyes were softer than they had been a moment before. "Let's get some ointment for that burn."

It's a burn? An electrical burn?

She was acutely aware of Leo touching her lower back.

"Nautilus granny called us murderers," Brant said. "Right after she pulled a bolt on us, and right before Leo knocked her lights out."

"Woah, nice!" Tawney gave Leo a high-five.

"Murderers? Why would she say that? They're the ones detonating bombs and setting serial fires," Owen complained.

"They want to make ya'll feel guilty. You can't let them. These are bad people tryin' to manipulate you into usin' your abilities to accomplish their own ends."

"What do they want to use us for?" Brant asked. "Maybe it's not so bad. Maybe it's not worth people getting bombed."

Christopher gave him a long stare.

"I dunno kid, but seein' as they're killin' people to get to you, I can't imagine they have anythin' good in mind. And on that note," he addressed them all. "Let's get you fed so you can resume your trainin'. We need to work faster than I thought."

Enzi rubbed up against the back of Natalie's legs as her friends walked back inside Ancora.

You're going to have to look eventually, she chided herself.

Natalie gingerly peeled back the ice pack from her right arm. She gasped. A brilliant red burn centered on her wrist with tendrils snaking towards her elbow and the palm of her hand. It was as though the energy from the bolt had dissipated through her skin on contact.

Don't let it touch you. Natalie raised an eyebrow at Enzi. *Noted.*

CHAPTER 18: NAUTILUS CHAMBERS

The screech of metal on stone broke the silence in Natalie's cell. She rose from her cot and sat on the floor beside the panel presenting her meal.

"Hello Chef," Natalie spoke to the wall. "What have you brought for me this eternal twilit eve?"

The panel swiveled around with a cup of water and a sandwich.

"Ah, delicious."

As always, the Chef remained silent. Natalie lifted the cup to her lips and drank. She spat the water out onto the dirt floor.

Ugh! It's salt water!

The panel began to revolve again and Natalie hastily scooped up her meal before it perished beyond the wall. To her surprise, the incoming portion of panel was not empty. A neatly folded pile of cloth occupied the small shelf that typically held her food. Natalie shoved the sandwich into her mouth and unfolded a navy form-fitting tracksuit with a silver embroidered nautilus shell on each arm. She nearly choked.

"You have got to be joking, Chef," Natalie muttered around the bread.

Natalie picked up the rest of her new uniform and a thick piece of paper slipped out from between the folds of clothing. It was a photograph.

Her fingers traced the familiar figures gathered around the long wooden table beneath the lantern-lit pavilion. Uncle Christopher sat at the head of the table, his beard still black and his belly less round. Natalie sat between her parents with her head resting on her wrist, undoubtedly engrossed in a book hidden in her lap. Her mother and father sat on either side of her. Her mother, frozen in time, twisted a curl of Natalie's ponytail between her fingers. Her father laughed at something as he held her mother's hand in front of Natalie's plate. His hair had not yet started to grey.

Leo and Tawney hung over the sides of their chairs, desperate to get a clear shot to fling food at Owen. Mr. and Mrs. Merrick passed Leo loaded forks of food for shooting, while Mrs. Davis fought to take Tawney's away from her. Owen lifted two empty dinner plates in defense, hiding behind his parents as they engaged in conversation with Tawney's father.

Brant sat next to his mother. Like Natalie, he was oblivious to the chaos going on around the table. His mother smiled warmly at him, her wig slightly askew, as Brant filled her plate. She knitted profusely, working away at a ball of rich red yarn, while Mr. Smith chatted happily with Natalie's father.

It was one of the few Formal Fridays that distinctly stood out in Natalie's mind.

This was the last time we were all together.

"Chef," Natalie called. She wasn't asking; she was sure now. *I know you're there.*

"Where did you get this?" She assessed the photograph again and thought of a more pressing question. "Chef, who took this?"

We're all in this picture...so who was watching us?

"Chef!"

"Shh!"

Natalie stared at the wall, hardly daring to breathe. The seconds passed into minutes, but no further sound came from beyond the panel.

Did I imagine it?

The screech of the panel turning sounded again and Natalie jumped. As it spun, a tan envelope came into view. It was bulging, barely large enough to contain its contents. Chicken scratch handwriting covered the outside.

HIDE ME

Remembering the video feed of her friends, Natalie figured she too was under surveillance. She carried the envelope beneath her Nautilus uniform and transferred it to her cot, slyly slipping it beneath the thin blanket.

Her mind raced.

What's inside the package? Maybe my spark?

Who is it from?

For what must have been the thousandth time, Natalie rubbed her wrist where the bolt had struck her. She hadn't seen her spark since she had been captured.

The envelope is too big for just the spark...

Natalie slipped the spandex of the Nautilus uniform between her fingers.

"To create and conserve peace and prosperity for all," Natalie quietly repeated Amir's description of Nautilus's purpose.

They're willing to abandon their values to accomplish their goals.

Natalie removed her tattered, dirt-encrusted clothing and slipped on the suit.

I'm not, but they don't have to know.

She wiggled her toes in the lightweight sneakers, thankful to have shoes again.

I have to get out.

She zipped up her jacket and the door to her cell slid to the right, sinking into the wall.

Please trust me.

Natalie strode into the glowing red passageway, the silver Nautilus shell glinting on her shoulder.

CHAPTER 19

B y the end of Tawney's self-defense class, Natalie was beat. The sun had set hours ago and the lamps in the gym cast a warm glow down from the ceiling. Natalie laid on one of the sparring mats with her head on Enzi's belly. She iced her wrist, engrossed in the logic puzzle. The metal box projected the glimmering orb before her and she followed the black swirling pathways with her finger, searching for a route to get the peg to the circle.

"Are you sure about this?" Tawney asked Leo a few mats over.

Leo pushed the sleeves of his hoodie up above his elbows. "Yeah."

"You don't sound sure," Tawney said hesitantly.

"Do it."

Tawney shrugged and turned her back to him.

Natalie observed her friends through the glow of the orb. Uncle Chris had instructed everyone to move on to target practice in the basement, but Leo managed to convince him this was more important. Owen and Brant were firing paintballs three floors beneath them, while Leo was determined to do the impossible: pin Tawney.

"Well?" Tawney asked impatiently. "Are we doing this or—"

Leo gripped Tawney's right shoulder. She spun and he pulled away, expecting her to grab him and flip him. Instead, Tawney dropped low and swept Leo's legs out from under him. He landed flat on his back with a heavy grunt.

Tawney helped him up.

Leo glanced at Natalie and she pretended to be absorbed in the intricate filigree of the orb.

"Again," Leo demanded.

Tawney grimaced.

"Get out of your head, Merrick," she told him firmly. "You already have all the tools, now use them. Envision my next move before I make it, like on the field."

Leo swiftly wrapped an arm around Tawney's neck. She calmly reached back and twisted his ear until he released her.

"Ow!"

"Do you need motivation? What matters most to you?"

Leo shook his head.

"If anything, I have too much motivation. I have to be able to do this."

Tawney squinted at him.

"Nat," she called.

"Uh, yes?" Natalie had not expected to be invited to their conversation.

"Get out."

"What?"

"Go be puzzled elsewhere," Tawney demanded.

Leo shrugged.

"Well...fine."

Slighted, Natalie took her logic puzzle and left. Enzi trotted out after her. Natalie stopped in the hallway and motioned for

Enzi to sit. His ears twitched as she leaned against the wall, listening.

"That's why we're doing this?" Tawney's voice sounded muffled through the drywall.

"I've nearly lost her twice already Tawney, at her house, at the market. You're right. I should be anticipating their moves, but I can't."

"Maybe it's because you're distracted," Tawney countered.

If Leo answered, Natalie couldn't hear it. She slumped against the wall. Enzi pushed his head against her to be pet.

He's fighting Tawney because he expects I'll need to be saved again. He thinks I'm weak.

Natalie thought back to what Uncle Chris had said in their first shooting lesson.

I want you to outsmart them.

She flipped the logic puzzle in the air and stood.

"Come on," she whispered to Enzi.

Natalie found her bed and worked on the patterned sphere until her vision began to blur. Within a few hours, she had traced hundreds of pathways, but none of the routes from the peg seemed to lead to the circular black hole. Afraid of losing herself in the maze, Natalie turned off the puzzle. She closed her eyes and a wrinkled face scarred with a brown birthmark smiled at her. Natalie stared up at the ceiling and sighed.

Sleep will not come easy.

She traced the mark on her right wrist made by the bolt. The skin had already lost most of its redness, but remained raised like a blister. Enzi sat up suddenly at the foot of her bed, staring out her bedroom door with ears perked to attention.

Natalie followed his gaze, holding her breath.

What is it, Enzi?

After a long minute, Enzi relaxed his head back onto Natalie's bed. She laid on her pillow and chided herself for being so jumpy. Ancora was still safe.

We tacked back within the cover of the cavern. No one will find us.

She repeated the mantra for what must have been the thousandth time that hour.

The tiniest of creeks sounded from the floor above. Enzi let out a low growl and launched off the bed, his ears flat against his head. His tail swooshed through the doorway and he took off towards the stairs. Natalie laid frozen in fear. She tried to listen, but she only heard her own heartbeat pounding in her ears.

Move. She commanded herself firmly. *Whatever it is, Enzi is facing it alone. Move, now.*

Silently, Natalie pushed the covers to the foot of her bed and sat up. She stood, lifting her weight off the bed carefully so it didn't squeak. She tiptoed to the door and cautiously peered around the corner.

A fast-moving body barreled into her, knocking her back against the wall. Leo caught her and kept her from falling.

"Did you see Enzi fly out of here like a bat out of Hell?" he whispered.

He was in black sweatpants, barefoot, and shirtless; his hoodie balled up under his arm. His body definitely reflected the lifelong soccer training. Natalie's cheeks flushed.

Maybe I did fall asleep, she wondered. *Let's see…*

"That was Enzi that blew past my room wasn't it?"

Natalie reached out and poked Leo's left bicep with her index finger.

"What are you—oh," Leo shook out the sweatshirt he was carrying and slipped it on over his head.

Huh. Not dreaming. Oh God, I just poked him.

"Sorry, I barged in."

No need to apologize.

"Nat, speak!" Leo shook her, sending a sharp pain through her left shoulder. She winced.

"Yeah, Enzi just got up and left. I was going to find him when you tried to tackle me to the ground. Anyway," Natalie rubbed her temples and stared at the floor to collect her thoughts. "I heard something upstairs and he took off. I'm sorry if he woke you."

"Woke me? Nat, Nautilus nearly had us this afternoon. I can't even lay down."

Selfish relief washed over her.

I'm not the only one struggling to cope.

"Come on," Leo pulled her into the hallway. "Let's go find him."

A tingling ran up her arm from the hand Leo had hold of, not unlike the sensation of tacking.

Blame this on stress and sleep deprivation. Get yourself together.

He led her quickly up the stairs before coming to an abrupt halt at the third floor landing. Natalie slammed into him.

"What—"

Leo shushed her and pointed past the library and gym. Natalie froze. Enzi sat with perfect posture captivated by the wall at the opposite end of the hallway.

"He growled at that wall twice yesterday," Natalie breathed into Leo's ear.

Together they made their way towards Enzi, staying as quiet as possible. About halfway to him, Enzi realized they were approaching. He glanced back at them, stood, and trotted right through the wall. His white fluffy tail swished out of sight.

"A rabbit hole within a rabbit hole," Natalie groaned.

"Be positive," Leo encouraged her. "Might be a cave of wonders." Leo gave her a loaded sideways glance. "This solidifies my argument though."

"If you're referring to your ludicrous ideas about Uncle Christopher—" Natalie didn't finish. Leo had boldly followed Enzi through the holographic projection of the solid wall and left her alone in the hallway.

She hesitated.

Leo's hooded head materialized through the wall. It was an unsettling sight.

"Come on!"

"Yeah, right," she steeled her nerves and followed Leo through the hologram.

One moment Natalie stood at what appeared to be the end of the hallway, the next she faced a closed door. It resembled any other door in the house: white, paneled, and outfitted with brass hardware. Nothing at all out of the ordinary.

Unless you include the holographic hide.

"No key," Natalie said with relief, noticing the deadbolt lock.

Leo turned the handle and the door swung silently inward.

"Not locked," Leo smirked as Enzi led the way inside.

"Sure, why bother locking the hidden door?" Natalie muttered.

The room beyond the hallway was uninviting. She fiddled with the sleeves of her sweatshirt in the doorway, fishing her brain for any sustainable excuse to not follow him. The darkness ahead of her was so thick Leo and Enzi had already vanished. The last time she had gone headstrong into the unknown it didn't go well. A kaleidoscope of color spilled over her; it bounced and danced off the whitewashed walls.

"See, I've found a magical lamp," Leo joked. He pulled Natalie in by the edge of her sleeve and shut the door behind them.

The room was significantly more cramped than Natalie had expected. Leo had turned on an ornate, stained glass lamp that stood in the far corner. It bathed everything in a blend of yellow, blue, red, and green. A wide bar-height table stood in the center of the room with crumpled papers and photographs scattered haphazardly on its surface. A clear fish-shaped dish rested on the corner of the table, half-full of colorful salt water taffy. The table and an oversized floral print recliner left barely enough room for the three of them to maneuver around.

A short, unfinished wooden door stood on the wall opposite the lamp. Natalie doubted it was tall enough to store a broom. She spotted two stainless steel bowls under the lamp: one small and one large. Enzi lifted his head out of the larger bowl and flicked his tongue over his nose.

"Pig," she teased him.

"Nat," Leo stared up at the wall, transfixed on one of three gigantic maps. One outlined North America, another depicted Western Europe, and the last showed the northern Atlantic Ocean.

The wood floor creaked under her feet as Natalie made her way around the recliner to join him. Leo pointed to the corner of Greenland where the outline of a spiral shell was inscribed in blue ink.

"A nautilus shell?"

She surveyed the maps closely. The deep creases in the old paper blurred many of the boundaries between countries. A familiar symbol inked in black caught her eye.

"Look there," she pointed to the northern corner of Scotland where the diamond and arrow shape glimmered. "The Coelacanth symbol. But what does the Coelacanth Project have to do with Scotland?"

"Or Florida?" Leo pointed to an identical symbol drawn onto the southern border of the United States.

Natalie shrugged, unable to tear her gaze from the symbol over Scotland. The ink was fresh.

Uncle Christopher marked this in recently. Maybe another Ancora?

Leo tapped sharply on the mouth of the Chesapeake Bay. She knew he intended to hit Norfolk, where a faded Coelacanth symbol had been freshly inked over with an ominous question mark, but the tip of his finger covered nearly half of the state.

"Guess he isn't sure if Norfolk is safe for Coelacanth after the bombing," Leo suggested.

Natalie traced over the mark herself. She left the tip of her finger covering the symbol, overcome by the expanse of map left exposed.

And these maps barely represent half of the world...I've spent my entire life beneath a finger's breadth.

A strange sense of excitement and gratitude rushed through

her. Natalie uncovered the eastern half of Virginia and ran her fingers across the Atlantic Ocean.

Our parents have given us the world.

Natalie traced across a third symbol drawn so faint she wasn't sure it was really there at all. The image was not foreign to her, yet she struggled to recall any one specific meaning behind it. At its core were three interlocking lenses arranged in a knot that circled on forever: never beginning, never ending. Filigreed fractals branched off each pointed ellipse adding intricacy, but the central shape resonated in her thoughts.

Triquetra? The term came to her from a dusty, forgotten shelf in her mind.

History has seen this symbol so many times it could be anything. Celtic, Christian, Wiccan, Japanese. Or has it been adapted again, into something new?

"So why do you suppose he's hiding all this stuff up here?" Leo derailed her train of thought. He shuffled through the mess of papers strewn across the table.

"He's not necessarily hiding it," Natalie said, not even believing her own argument. She forced herself away from the faded symbol and followed behind Leo, returning the disturbed documents back to their original, dust-outlined positions.

Of course, he's hiding it.

"Of course, he's hiding it!"

"Fine," Natalie conceded. "He's hiding it. However, he's done nothing but help us since we showed up uninvited on his doorstep. We have no reason to question him, Leo."

"According to him, everyone we know has been lying to us our whole lives, including my high school physics teacher, including him," Leo shook his head in disbelief. "Your blind faith amazes me."

"It isn't blind faith," Natalie retorted. "It's established faith. It's trust."

"So if Christopher had told you not to run into your house the other night, you would have actually listened?"

Natalie focused on a stack of photographs on the table beside them. Seaside cottage, seaside cottage, seaside castle, yacht, seaside cottage.

"You're right. I'm done."

"Come on, Nat, I was just—"

Enzi stood with his head cocked towards the door, tail wagging excitedly. Two high-pitched barks sounded from the hallway.

"Shh! Quiet, Angie!" Christopher hissed.

They're coming!

Panicked, Natalie scanned the room for a place to hide.

"In here!" Leo pulled open the short wooden door beside them.

"There's no way we'll fit," Natalie whispered.

"No time, get in," he shifted his weight from foot to foot anxiously: ready to move, ready to run.

Natalie ducked past him and through the doorway. Leo pressed into her, pulling the door shut behind them. She shuffled forward for space, feeling blindly for the back of the closet. Her foot fell through empty air and Natalie clung onto Leo to keep from stumbling. She steadied herself and placed her foot down firmly on a ledge. A few inches further, she found another drop and another ledge.

"Enzi?" Christopher stood just outside the door. "How'd you get in here, boy? Huntin' for treats, eh?"

"Stairs," Natalie breathed to Leo, pulling on his jacket to guide him.

She hugged the wall and descended as quickly as she dared. The wall curved in towards her, spiraling as they descended. Natalie hoped the architect had been consistent in setting the stairwell as she pushed herself to go faster. It was impossible to tell where the next stair fell, so she had to trust them to rise up and meet her feet as she went. Finally, when Natalie made to step down again, her foot fell hard on level ground. She paused, causing Leo to collide into her back.

"Sorry," she muttered, "stairs stopped."

Natalie felt along the wall to her left and reached out straight ahead as she moved forward. A few paces more and the hand out in front of her found another wall. It was rougher than the wall on her left, and had hinges on the side.

"I found a door," Natalie said as she gripped a handle. She turned it and pulled. The door swung toward her easily and the cool night air rushed in to greet them.

CHAPTER 20

Natalie flew through the open door. As fresh air flooded into her lungs, she realized she had been holding her breath. The shine of the full moon was blinding compared to the pitch-black stairwell. Leo pulled the door shut behind them and Natalie tried to get her bearings.

Ancora rose up high above her. She stood in its shadow, watching the wind blow the grasses on the surrounding sand dunes into rippling waves of silver. Brilliant shimmering stars shone overhead, exposing the tracks of ghost crabs scuttling across the sand. All she could hear were the ocean waves breaking against the other side of the house.

It was a beautiful summer night, but Natalie wanted nothing more than to get back inside. She pressed herself against the side of Ancora, hoping for its walls to open up and swallow her whole. She turned back to the door. Having to wait out Uncle Chris in the stairwell was better than being stranded outside like a sitting duck.

Natalie squinted in the twilight for the door, but it was gone. She frisked the layers of siding where she had passed through.

Nothing. No handle, no hinges, no seam.

"How can it be gone?" Natalie asked Leo, who did not seem to share her concern.

Leo shrugged.

"It must be designed to blend in."

He moved a few paces from her and leaned out to peer around the other side of Ancora.

"Come on," Leo motioned for her to follow. "Let's get back inside."

"What do you think I'm trying to do?" Natalie's feet slipped in the fine sand as she hurried to catch up to him.

"You're focusing on the problem instead of the solution."

"Shouldn't one acknowledge the problem before wandering around aimlessly," she retorted.

The sharp snap of a twig somewhere in the dunes made her stop short. Natalie sensed Leo come to a halt somewhere ahead of her. A thick, squat shrub covered most of the dune to their left. Its branches twitched in the breeze. Natalie's muscles tightened, preparing to run.

"Probably a squirrel," Leo whispered, focused on the bush.

"See many beach squirrels, do you?" Natalie hissed back.

Leo grinned at her.

"Someone's sassy."

"Better sassy than an—" she clamped her mouth shut. *Great.*

"Than what?" Leo asked eagerly.

Natalie shook her head and walked ahead of him.

"No way. They're Tawney's words, not mine."

Natalie's feet found solid concrete instead of sand. A footpath through the dunes led to a modest porch with a single rocking chair guarding the front door to Ancora. Leo climbed the few stairs to the landing and tried the handle.

"Tell me what Tawney said and I'll let you in."

"Nope."

"Worth a shot," Leo smiled. "It's locked anyway."

"As it should be. How are we going to get in?"

"Hide-A-Key?" Leo asked, checking under the doormat for a spare house key.

Natalie wrinkled her nose.

"I'm kidding. Let's wake Tawney up so she can tell me what she said," Leo left the porch and dug a pebble out of the sand.

"I doubt she'd say it again after everything that's happened the past few days."

"Why's that?"

"I guess life-threatening experiences have a way of...changing people."

"I disagree."

"How shocking," Natalie mused.

"I'm still me, but I expect I have a better handle on what's important in life and what isn't." Leo playfully tossed the rock to her and closed the distance between them. He was so close Natalie could smell the mint from his toothpaste as he spoke.

She wanted to ask what was important now that hadn't been before, but the words hid shyly in her throat.

"What's not important anymore?"

Coward, she berated herself.

"Choosing a college. Soccer."

"But soccer is everything to you."

Leo took the rock from her and booped the tip of her nose with it.

"You weren't listening." He walked swiftly away from her.

Natalie followed him around the corner of the house. He nodded at the first window on the second floor.

"That one, right?" Leo threw the rock up towards the window. It bounced off the glass with a sharp ping.

No response.

Leo dug another pebble out of the sand and threw it.

The curtains parted enough for Natalie to make out Tawney's wild curls. Natalie waved at her friend. Tawney threw open the curtains and pushed her window up and open.

"What are you guys doing out there?" she called to them. "You nearly gave me a heart attack!"

"Long story," Natalie said. "Can you let us in the front door? We're locked out."

"Wait, first, very important," Leo cleared his throat. "Natalie said you have a nickname for me."

Natalie gave him a hard shove.

"Quickly, please, Tawney. I don't like being out here."

"Sure! Is Brant with you?"

"We didn't mean to end up outside," Natalie explained, suspecting Tawney was disappointed she wasn't invited on their expedition. "It's just us."

"Then who's that?" Tawney pointed behind them.

The color drained from her face as Natalie spun on her heels. A lone figure stood on the peak of the dune behind them, silhouetted against the night sky.

"Door, Tawney," Leo said sternly. "Now."

Natalie did not look to see if Tawney did as he said. She let Leo move between her and the stranger. He guided her backwards, towards the porch. She clung to the back of his arm. Natalie checked behind them and wished she hadn't. Far past the porch, on the next dune, stood another figure.

We're being surrounded.

"Leo, there's another," she whispered to him, as though keeping her voice low would help hide them.

He nodded in response and from his pocket produced the same gun Christopher had sent with him to the market.

"You kept it?"

"Obviously," Leo answered. His head swiveled from one silhouette to the other. Neither had moved. "Figured I had better be more prepared if I'm going to keep getting into trouble with you."

Natalie's back pressed against the front door. Leo held her there.

"You're free to get into trouble with someone else

sometime," Natalie hissed from behind him.

"And I thought we were exclusive," Leo whispered back.

"I...I," Natalie was transfixed by the ominous figures.

"Hey, don't panic. Stay with me. Are you with me, Nat?"

"I'm with you," Natalie swallowed hard.

"Come on, Tawney," Leo adjusted his grip on the gun. It had been an eternity since she had been at her window.

As though on cue, the two figures began to steadily descend towards them. A whimper escaped her as Natalie buried her head into Leo's back. A cackling laugh floated to Natalie on the breeze and chills ran down her spine.

It's her!

Natalie pounded on the front door.

"Let us in!" she cried desperately.

"Stop or I'll shoot," Leo announced. His voice was steadier than his hands.

Natalie peeked around Leo's shoulder. The familiar silver-haired woman from the market stood at the foot of the porch stairs. She stared past Leo, straight at Natalie.

"Come with us, dearie," she cooed to them.

The figure accompanying her had also been at the market. Tanaka's thin lips pressed into a line above his pointed chin.

"What do you want us for?" Leo demanded.

She smiled endearingly at him. Tanaka removed the bolt from behind his back and spun it beside him. Cracks of white sparks flew off the ends.

"What is it you want us to do?" Leo clarified. "Maybe we can help."

"Oh, you will help," she nodded, climbing onto the first stair of the porch. She leaned on the railing for support.

"Not any closer," Leo gripped the pistol firmly out in front of him.

"You're not going to shoot me, dear."

The crack of gunfire cut through the night. Natalie jumped at the noise and the woman stumbled backwards from the porch, colliding into her companion. She screamed out and clutched at her right hand. Her blood shone silvery red in the moonlight. Natalie couldn't tell for certain, but she may have lost a few fingers. The sight made her cringe.

"Eleanor!" Tanaka eased the old woman into the sand.

"He may not but I will, for sure," Christopher emerged around the corner of the house, his gun still raised. "Come here, kids."

Natalie followed Leo to the porch railing and climbed over. She jumped off the side and landed in the soft sand.

"We were warned about you," the man with the ponytail spoke up, his voice low and smooth. He moved around Eleanor, who had collapsed whimpering into the sand. His almond-shaped eyes were as jet black as his hair and they glared at Christopher.

"Well, obviously they didn't do me justice." He nodded for Natalie and Leo to retreat further behind him. Natalie headed back towards where the disappearing door had been.

"Who sent you?"

Natalie wished she could block out Eleanor's screaming.

"We come for ourselves," Tanaka explained. "The Ward brought us together; he has shown us how to find peace."

Christopher's face twisted with rage.

"Who is your Ward?" he bellowed. "Gimme a name!"

A new figure appeared from behind the opposite end of Ancora. Natalie stopped short as Leo moved in front of her, gun held high. They were cornered: Nautilus ahead of them, Nautilus behind them.

"Uncle Chris," Leo called as the figure loomed towards them.

It was stout and wide. The closer he came the better Natalie saw him. Buzzed blond hair highlighted his square-shaped head and several lines of stitches crossed the side of his neck.

"It's him," Natalie whispered, fear taking over. "It's him." She dug her fingernails into Leo's shoulder, frantically

EXTANT

searching for a way out. She was a rabbit cornered between foxes, so ravaged by fear that her greatest threat became herself.

"There are more of us than there are of you," Tanaka said calmly. "Send them with us. Let them serve their full potential."

"They're going to get us," Natalie's chest ached.

"Let go, Nat," Leo wiggled beneath her while keeping his gun level on the heavy-set man.

He was so close Natalie saw each individual stitch in his neck. She bent her knees, getting ready. She knew she shouldn't, but she couldn't help it. She had to move. She was going to run for it.

"Leave now and we won't kill you," Christopher announced loudly.

"Get them, Tanaka!" Eleanor wailed in agony.

The man leapt at Christopher, his bolt electrifying the space between them. Christopher fired his gun without hesitation. Tanaka fell to the ground screaming, clutching his leg. Then suddenly Uncle Chris was at Natalie's side. He kicked a section of siding and a square of wall swung inward.

"In!" he yelled at them.

Natalie sprinted into the passageway. Leo followed close behind her and Christopher came last, sealing the door shut behind him. She heard the Nautilus thugs squabbling on the other side of the wall.

"You alright, Eleanor?"

Natalie knew his voice, it echoed endlessly in her nightmares.

A desperate wail answered him.

"Are you okay? Did you kill that man?" Natalie heard herself asking the questions. "Tanaka?"

"Dunno, just shot him," Christopher answered her in the dark stairwell. "They shouldn't have been able to find you here."

"Why did he say we were outnumbered?" Leo asked,

183

confused. "There were three of them and three of us, right?"

Christopher hissed between his teeth.

"Hell. Up the stairs, quickly now. We have to get to the boat cavern; the others are waitin'."

CHAPTER 21

"Gonna need you to shoot next time, kid," Christopher chastised Leo as they ascended the stairs.

Natalie found it was far easier going up the stairwell in complete darkness than down.

"I know," Leo snapped.

"You don't have to shoot to kill. And you," Christopher rounded on Natalie. "You need to carry a gun. A deal's a deal; this is your last warnin'."

"Why didn't Tawney let us in the front door?" she deflected.

Uncle Chris huffed heavily, already winded from the climb.

"There is no front door, not really. It's cosmetic, doesn't actually open at all. It's only a wall."

"Why have a door that isn't a door?" Leo asked, frustrated.

"Why have a door when you don't want people comin' in? Ancora needed a door to blend in, but anyone who should be gettin' in knows how. Which reminds me," he changed the subject. "How'd y'all get out?"

Natalie remained silent, taking deeper breaths to manage the never-ending spiral ascent.

"We found your secret lair."

Christopher snorted. Natalie reached the landing and leaned against the wall in relief.

"Ain't no secret lair," he chuckled, opening the door to said lair. A rainbow spilled into the cramped tunnel. "It's safe from prying eyes if anyone broke in, including Nautilus."

"And us."

Uncomfortable with where the conversation was headed, Natalie ducked into the office. It was even more of a cluttered mess than when she had seen it minutes prior. Papers littered the floor and the stained glass lamp laid strewn across the recliner. The cleanest part of the room were the walls; they had been stripped bare of their maps.

Frantic barking rose up from one of the lower levels of Ancora. She heard it for only a moment before he fell silent, but it was definitely him. She knew his bark anywhere.

"Nautilus is inside," she whispered. Her heart tried to drop to the floor. She wondered which she feared more: Enzi's barking or the heavy silence that followed it.

At least if he kept barking, I would know he's alright...

Christopher wrestled the recliner aside and popped up one of the floorboards, revealing a hidden compartment. He withdrew a handgun even smaller than the pistol Leo carried, which he shoved into Natalie's reluctant hands, and a clean, white envelope.

"I don't want this," she presented the gun to him, hating the feel of it against her skin.

"I don't care," Christopher told her. "A deal's a deal. We get to the boat cavern and we get out, you hear?" He dug a photograph out of the envelope and showed it to both of them. "This is where you go."

"How are you getting out?" Natalie asked, studying the picture. He had shown the same one during their first target practice.

"I'm goin' with you."

"You can tack, too?" Leo asked incredulously.

"No, kid, you're taking me with you," Christopher folded away the serene yellow cottage. He maneuvered his way across the room to the door.

"That works?" Natalie subtly passed her firearm to Leo while Christopher's back was turned.

He didn't answer her. Instead, Christopher cracked open the door and peeked through. Satisfied, he pulled it wide open. The hallway stretched out before her, empty and silent.

"Stay close," Christopher whispered. He leaned across the table and secured a handful of taffy from the fish-shaped dish. Stuffing the treasure into his pocket, he slipped out of the lair.

"You next," Leo nodded to her.

Natalie fell in behind Uncle Chris. The house was eerily quiet. The silence proved a comfort and a curse: if Nautilus was nearby, Natalie would hear them, but if Nautilus was nearby, they would also hear her. Christopher's shoes squeaked against the hardwood floor and Natalie was certain her heartbeat was echoing off the walls.

We won't reach the cavern unnoticed. We're louder than the Thanksgiving Day Parade.

Christopher reached the junction of the gym and the library and stopped. He flattened himself as best he could manage beside the open doorway to the gym. Without warning, he spun into the room. He kept his gun straight out in front of him, as though it had become an extension of himself.

Leo pulled his hood up over his head. Natalie watched him mock Christopher's movements in the library: a quick circle to survey the room, gun at attention.

Satisfied, Christopher resumed his position ahead of Natalie and they pressed on towards the staircase.

"Good thing the library was empty," Leo whispered to Natalie. "I have no idea what I'm doing."

"That's reassuring."

"Shh!"

Natalie tucked tight behind Uncle Christopher as they descended the stairs. Adrenaline amplified every sound. Her breath reverberated in her lungs. Her pulse drummed out of her ears, sporadic and thready. Every step took her deeper into the house and closer to Nautilus.

Halfway there, Natalie told herself as they reached the first landing. Realizing something was missing, she groaned. Natalie pulled on the back of Christopher's shirt.

"What?"

"My spark!" Natalie hissed. "It's in my room."

Leo hit the butt of his gun against his forehead.

"Are you sure?"

Her cheeks flushed with shame.

Stupid.

"It's on my bedside table. I was so concerned about where Enzi ran off to earlier I—"

"Alright, let's go," Christopher gestured at the hallway behind them.

"I'll get it," Leo offered. "She doesn't have a gun."

Christopher pinched the bridge of his nose.

"Bloody stubborn. Stay here."

Natalie peered from the shelter of the stairs as Christopher and Leo made their way through the hall, clearing bedrooms in their wake. She didn't feel safe in the stairwell. She didn't feel safe following them. The very ground she stood on had become unreliable. The illusion of Ancora's sheltering walls had been swept away.

Nowhere will be safe for us.

Leo dove into her bedroom. After an eternity, Christopher ran in after him.

Gunshots rang out from the first floor. Natalie yelped in alarm and covered her mouth to stifle the sound. Christopher and Leo were at her side in an instant. Christopher barreled past Natalie and flew down the stairs. Leo followed on his heels.

"Spark?" she asked.

Leo shook his head. Natalie bit her lip and focused on keeping her footing.

So stupid!

"We simply wish to initiate an open discussion," a velvet smooth voice floated up from the kitchen.

Natalie's heart sank. Between the wrecked office and Enzi's barking, it had been obvious Nautilus was inside. However, hearing them speak made it real. It dawned on her why Uncle Chris had shown her the photograph of the yellow cottage; it wasn't for a temporary escape.

We can't come back here. Ancora is dead.

The thought made her chest ache. Ancora had been an unexpected sanctuary. Her thoughts drifted up to the stack of books on the bedside table and the clothes in the dresser. She was leaving behind her last pieces of home.

Natalie wrestled her emotions into an iron chest in the recesses of her mind.

They're only things, she scolded herself. *I'll be lucky to get out of here with my life.*

Ahead of her, Christopher reached the first floor and strode towards the kitchen. Leo was more cautious. He lingered in the stairwell, blocking Natalie in behind him. She watched Christopher march straight for the boat cavern. He reached the archway to the living room and swiveled with his gun pointed towards the kitchen, beyond Natalie's line of sight. The drywall next to him ruptured as gunshots rang out. Christopher rolled behind one of the couches and out of view.

Natalie dug her fingers into Leo's arm. He tried to pull her forward, but she resisted. Every molecule of her body was telling her to stay put.

"We can't stay here, Nat," Leo told her, embodying the voice of reason. "Stay close to me."

She held her breath as they ran full out towards the living room. The kitchen briefly came into view as she slid behind the couch. A man in a sharp business suit stood behind the bar. His black hair was slick against the back of his head and a shining Nautilus shell was embroidered on the sleeve of his jacket. He stood with his arms casually behind his back.

Natalie crouched behind one of the couches. She pulled her knees up to her chest, making herself as small as possible.

"Y'all alright?" Christopher asked without looking at them. He stared around the other side of the couch towards the cavern.

"We're good," Leo responded.

Natalie doubted she was capable of verbalizing anything coherent. Christopher gave a thumbs up around the couch. Natalie leaned over to see who he was signaling to.

Brant and Owen hid in the hallway before the boat cavern, guns at the ready. Tawney bounced up and down behind them, waving frantically at Natalie with a black mop of fur tucked under her arm. She flashed a polished stone high above her head.

Natalie sagged against the couch in relief.

My spark.

"We have to pass this one to get to them," Christopher whispered, nodding towards the man in the kitchen.

"Come out and talk with me," the man coaxed. "My name is Amir Amani. You may find our goals are synonymous."

"Nah, I don't want to die," Brant called out.

Leo snorted next to her and Christopher flicked Brant a disapproving glare.

"Nautilus is violent purely in response to violence. Come peacefully and you will find peace. You see, my organization wants to build a better, joyous future for all, and you hold the key to inciting change."

"He's joking, right?" Leo whispered.

"Sorry, I left my keys at home," Brant replied. "And you burned it to the ground so, I guess you're S.O.L."

"Ah, this must be Mr. Smith I'm speaking to. I heard you

were quite the comedian."

Brant's jaw dropped open. For once, he had nothing to say.

"Truly, I am honored. I've heard much about you, Mr. Smith. I've heard about all of you and how incredibly special you are," Amir Amani's voice was softer than velvet. "You are a treasure to be shared with the world, not hidden away where your gifts are wasted."

Leo's gun came up sharply over Natalie's shoulder.

"Move and I shoot," he warned, his gun right next to her head.

She followed his aim. In the hallway stood the portly, stitched man from outside. His bolt dragged along the ground beside him.

"Who has joined us?" Amir asked from behind the bar, unable to visualize who was shuffling about in the hall.

"Rankin, Mr. Amani, sir."

Rankin. The name seared into Natalie's mind.

An ugly black and purple bruise encompassed Rankin's stitches and spanned the entire width of his neck. Natalie figured it must be painful because he struggled to turn his head. When he looked around, he had to pivot his entire body.

"That must be uncomfortable, Rankin," Leo nodded to the man's injuries. "Did you know Enzi is a professional guard dog? Oh, I guess you learned on your own."

A deep grumbling came from the direction of the cavern. Natalie crawled around Uncle Christopher to see Enzi prowling the hall. Owen held Tawney back by her shirt to keep her from going after the dog.

"No," Natalie said firmly. "Enzi, sit."

He protested with his hackles raised, teeth bared, and ears flattened back, but he did as she said. He sat out of sight of Amir in the kitchen; however, Rankin could see him clearly.

"Not that mutt," Rankin stumbled backwards.

"Watch it," Leo warned.

Rankin looked from the barrel of Leo's pistol to Enzi's

snarling jaws.

"Enzi, no. Stay," Natalie commanded. She lifted two fingers, reinforcing her verbal request with a visual one. Enzi's tail twitched in irritation, but he stayed.

A humming vibration resonated from the stairwell behind Rankin. Tanaka determinedly limped towards them. A frayed piece of blood-soaked cloth was tied tight around his left leg where Christopher had shot him. He fixated on Enzi, spinning his bolt faster than Natalie could follow.

Enzi stood and snarled, and two threatening barks escaped him. Natalie flinched as Rankin began spinning his own bolt. Sparks cracked loudly from the ends and that was all it took. Enzi charged towards the intruders. He ran out so fast, Amir had barely raised his gun before the kitchen bar was between them.

He aimed for the gap Enzi would have to clear before entering the hall where Rankin stood in front of Tanaka. The burly man slashed his sparking bolt wildly in front of him, his grimace contorted with fear.

Everyone was moving too fast. Natalie couldn't think.

"Enzi, no!"

Natalie leapt up from behind the couch, running straight for Enzi. She made to dive for him, but someone pulled her down, hard.

"No!" Natalie yelled.

She rolled over as Enzi leapt into the air. Amir Amani squinted at the white dog as he took aim. Rankin backed into the hallway, knocking over Tanaka.

He's going to die. Between Amir's bullet and the pair of bolts he ran for, Enzi was outgunned.

Natalie scrambled back to her feet and ran for him. She had hardly taken a step when Leo tackled Enzi mid-leap. They tumbled into the kitchen. Amir shuffled backward to avoid them. He aimed his gun at the intertwined mess of fur and sweatshirt. Enzi snapped blindly at Leo as he wrestled the dog to the ground. He held him tight with one arm around his head and the other pinning Enzi's hind legs to the floor.

Natalie's momentum took her another step. She kicked something cold and metallic. Leo's gun.

Shots echoed in the kitchen. Bullets sank themselves into the stainless steel refrigerator behind Amir. Brant stood exposed in the hall, his gun still raised.

Tanaka laid against the wall, clutching his leg. Rankin slowly rose to his feet. He turned his back to Natalie and Uncle Christopher as he swung his bolt high above Enzi and Leo.

Natalie snatched Leo's pistol off the floor and ran at Rankin. She jumped onto his back and slammed the butt of the gun into his stitches. Rankin screamed and dropped his weapon, clutching instead at the fresh blood spilling from between his stitches.

Christopher grabbed Natalie's arm, his gun pointed at Tanaka. The man's black ponytail swung as he pushed himself along the floor, back towards the staircase.

"Drop it," Uncle Chris growled to Amir.

Amir's gun clattered to the kitchen floor.

"We'll be goin' now," Christopher announced.

Leo rolled off Enzi, who shook himself indignantly. Enzi passed Rankin with a pointed snap of his jaws as he made his way to Natalie. Leo held his left arm tight against his side as he took his gun back from Natalie.

"That wasn't what I meant for you to do with it," he gasped. "But it was effective."

They crossed the kitchen to join Brant, Owen, and Tawney. Christopher backed up to them, keeping his gun high.

"Two groups," he instructed them.

"Where are we going?" Owen whispered, taking Angie from Tawney's arms.

"Nat and I know," Leo explained. Natalie thought back on the image of the yellow cottage, trying to recall all of the details.

"They can come with us?" Brant asked skeptically, waving his gun to the dogs and Uncle Christopher.

"Trust me," Christopher muttered, corralling them deeper into the hall.

Natalie felt Tawney grasp her hand and a small stone pressed between their palms. Brant slapped Leo on the back, who winced.

It's going to be a race, Natalie gritted her teeth. They would have to get to the cavern and reach the water before Nautilus regained their senses and their weapons and came after them.

"Now," Christopher said quietly.

Natalie spun and sprinted for the cavern. Brant was first through the door with Tawney close on his heels. Brant grabbed hold of Leo and Owen. With Angie balled tight into the crook of Owen's arm, they jumped off the dock and dissolved into a sea of white light.

Shots fired and Natalie's ears rang. She cleared the doorway and snagged a tight hold of Enzi's scruff. Her bare feet smacked on the wooden planks twice before Tawney caught Enzi's fur and jumped. Enzi eagerly leapt with her. Their momentum pulled Natalie off the dock towards the water, but she wasn't ready. She whipped her head around to see Christopher clearing the doorway.

"Uncle Chris!" Natalie stretched desperately back for him as Tawney and Enzi pulled her to the water.

Christopher threw himself towards the dock, reaching for Natalie's hand.

Then everything was lost in white.

CHAPTER 22

The flare faded as quickly as it had come. Slick, cold stone emerged beneath her. Enzi struggled to get a grip on the rock and she let go of his scruff. He climbed up onto a covered sandy beach and shook himself. He barked excitedly at Angie who darted from one corner of the beach to the other, sending sand spewing up the rocky walls.

The black rocks extended out into the water, creating a shallow pond along the few feet of beach. Water lapped quietly at the shore. A stone ceiling high above her curved around them, forming the walls of a black cave.

Something pulled on her hand, but she held tight to it.

"It's alright, kid. You got me."

Natalie didn't let go. She stared up at the ceiling and shook her head, trying to erase the past few minutes.

"Hey," Christopher patted her forearm. "You caught me; it's okay."

"What if I didn't?" Natalie whispered.

"Don't do that," Uncle Chris said sternly. "You got me.

You'll lose your mind thinkin' that way, worryin' about all the what if's. Things have a way of workin' themselves out in the end. You have to trust in that."

He pried her fingers from him and shuffled his way to the beach. Christopher plopped heavily on the sand and chuckled, popping a colorful taffy into his cheek.

"Nothin' like a little sparring to get your blood racin'," he mused.

"Sparring?" Brant said incredulously. "I'm pretty sure Satan just stood in our kitchen and that makes you giggle?"

He grinned.

"Guess he dresses nicer than I expected. And be sure, that ain't the Devil, only one of his demons."

"Where are we?" Owen inspected the slick algae on the rocks.

"California," Christopher replied casually, sorting through the contents of the white envelope he had saved from his office.

"Sweet!" Tawney beamed.

"Are you insane?" Owen startled Uncle Chris so badly he nearly dropped the envelope into the waves lapping at his feet.

"What's wrong with California?" Brant asked. "I've always wanted to surf."

"What's wrong?" Owen cleaned off his glasses, exasperated. "This state is one bad quake away from sinking into the sea! It's practically the most unpredictably dangerous place on the planet." He stared at the sand as though expecting the ground to open up at any moment.

"Nah, mate, that's Australia," Brant jumped onto one of the larger black rocks with his knees bent and arms out wide. "California is the land of sun, sand, and surf."

"Eager to get in, eh?" Christopher called to Leo. He had crossed the stretch of sand and leaned his forehead against the door that led out of the cave.

"Yeah."

Natalie didn't like his tone. It was flat and lifeless. She shuffled through the fine sand and joined Leo by the wall.

"What's wrong?" Brant asked from his rocky perch.

Natalie turned Leo to face her.

He slumped against the door, pale and trembling. Blood soaked the front of his sweatshirt and dripped freely beneath his left arm, which he cradled tight against his stomach.

He's been shot.

She clung to Leo's shoulder as much to keep him upright as she did to steady herself.

"Oh God," Tawney and Uncle Chris hurried to Leo's side.

"Sorry," Leo muttered. His eyelashes fluttered as he fought to stay conscious.

Christopher scooped Leo up in his arms and nodded towards the door.

"Inside, to the left," he instructed.

Owen pulled the door open and the two dogs bolted in beneath Christopher's feet, making him stumble.

"Bloody mutts," he grumbled, shuffling in behind them. "One of you boys fetch me a bar stool."

The cottage was larger than it had appeared in the photograph. Dark tile floors flowed through a modest kitchen and living room. White couches formed a half-circle against narrow panes of textured glass that filled a curved bay window. Flowing white curtains hung from the ceiling and a thick rug covered the center of the room with a short, circular table atop it. Drops of blood shone crimson on the cream rug as Christopher carried Leo across the room.

Natalie kept pace with Christopher to stay by Leo's side. Her fingers brushed his forehead as she pushed his hair back. His skin was slick with sweat, yet cold to the touch.

He's going into shock.

"Towels," Christopher requested. "Bathroom, door on the right."

Owen sprinted ahead and returned a moment later with an

armful of deep plum towels.

"There," Christopher ordered, pointing to the closest couch.

Owen laid the towels on the couch as Brant dragged a high barstool from the kitchen and placed it next to Leo.

"There are first-aid kits under the sink in the kitchen," Christopher said to Tawney. "Bring the big one."

Tawney did as requested and returned with a large tackle box cradled in her arms. Christopher laid Leo on the couch. Leo sucked in a sharp breath between his teeth as Chris manipulated his arm.

"Is it only your arm?" Christopher asked him.

Leo didn't answer. Christopher snapped his fingers in front of Leo's nose and asked again.

"Hey! Were you hit anywhere else?"

Leo shook his head.

"When were you hit?"

Leo feebly shook his head again.

"Stay awake, kid. You need sugar, eat this," Christopher unwrapped one of his precious candies and put it in Leo's mouth.

"Pineapple," he whispered.

Natalie opened the tackle box, which had been deemed a first-aid kit by the almighty power of a Sharpie. She passed Uncle Chris a pair of bandage scissors with trembling fingers. Christopher's mouth was set in a thin line as he cut Leo's hoodie sleeve from wrist to shoulder.

He's worried. This is bad.

"You've ruined it," Leo moaned as he tried to pull his arm away.

"Stop moving," Christopher scolded him. "Answer me. When were you hit?"

"Wasn't," Leo responded.

Natalie supplied Christopher with a steady stream of gauze and saline as he wiped the blood off Leo's arm.

"Ah," Christopher relaxed his furrowed brow.

"What?" Brant hovered close to his friend's side.

"He wasn't shot. Fetch him some water, ibuprofen, and amoxicillin from the kitchen. Meds are in one of the drawers."

"I've got it," Owen hurried away.

Intrigued, Natalie leaned closer as Christopher wiped away fresh pooling blood. For a second, she saw five deep punctures in Leo's forearm. The largest one overflowed quickly with blood again.

Natalie's stomach clenched with guilt.

Oh no, oh no.

She smeared some numbing cream on gauze squares and pressed it over the wound. Leo winced and tried to push her away.

"I know it burns; it'll pass. I'm sorry," Natalie replaced the gauze as blood soaked threw them onto her fingertips. "I'm so sorry."

Leo gave up trying to stop her and rubbed his thumb over her knuckles.

"It's okay, Nat," he whispered.

"Relax," Christopher took the gauze from her. "I've got him. Go get some water."

Natalie rushed to the sink. She shook as she washed Leo's blood off her fingers. Owen dug feverishly through the cluttered drawer of medications next to her.

"I don't understand," Brant bounced slightly on the balls of his feet as Leo struggled to remain conscious. "If he wasn't shot then what happened?"

Pleased with his investigation of their new home, Enzi padded in and put his muzzle on Leo's lap for pets. Leo rubbed him behind his ear for a moment before sinking into the couch, no longer able to open his eyes. His breathing was shallow and fast.

He's lost a lot of blood.

"Enzi bit him," Natalie confessed, using the counter to keep upright.

Christopher donned blue nitrile gloves and poured a green soapy liquid over Leo's wounds.

"Bad dog!" Brant yelled at Enzi, lunging at him. Enzi flinched and skittered to Natalie, his tail between his legs.

"It's okay, Enzi," Natalie coddled him. "It's okay." She pulled Enzi tight against her.

"Bad human!" Tawney threw a pillow at Brant from one of the other couches.

"He attacked Leo! Look at him! He could die!" Brant threw the pillow back to her.

"He didn't mean to; he didn't realize!" Natalie defended him.

"Oy!" Christopher interrupted. "He's gonna be bloody fine if y'all shut it and let me suture!"

Natalie sat on the floor with Enzi as Christopher deftly worked a pair of hemostats and a pack of suture from the first-aid kit. Brant crossed his arms and slumped onto the edge of the couch.

Owen arrived sheepishly from the kitchen with a bottle of water and a handful of pills.

"You know," Owen started hesitantly. "Antibiotic resistance is rising...we shouldn't have him take amoxicillin unless he really needs it."

"Do you know how much bacteria is in a dog's mouth? Trust me," Uncle Chris gestured to Leo with bloodied gloves. "He needs 'em."

Owen put the pills in Leo's mouth and lifted the water up to his lips, encouraging him to drink.

"Ouch," Leo whispered as Uncle Chris stabbed him with the needle end of the suture.

"Gonna be about ten minutes of ouch, kid," Christopher smiled. "No tattoos for you, eh?"

Leo shook his head and laid back into the cushions.

"Why does he look like shit if he's going to be fine?" Brant asked.

"He lost a lot of blood," Christopher answered, focused on his work. "But bodies are incredible little machines. They can make more blood, so long as we stop the loss."

"Ancora?" Tawney interrupted.

Natalie followed her gaze to the wall opposite the bay window. Large, antiqued letters decorated the space above the kitchen table.

ANCORA

"But I thought Ancora was the beach house back home?" Owen asked, voicing Natalie's own confusion.

Christopher grinned.

"See how quickly it became home? That's exactly it. Ancora is more a state of mind than any one place. There," Christopher tied off the last stitch. "How you feelin'?" He asked Leo as he applied antibiotic ointment and a large bandage over the five stitched punctures.

"Worried," Leo said, clenching his jaw as he sat up a little more.

"I told you, you're gonna be fine. Rest, hydrate, medicate: the cure to all ailments."

"Not about this," Leo said as Christopher laid an ice pack across the blue bandage wrap. "How did Nautilus find us?"

"I dunno, kid," Uncle Chris furrowed his brow. "It's concernin'."

"Another question," Owen leaned in. "I understand you were stocking Ancora, well Ancora I, before we got there, but who is stocking this place? The kitchen is packed."

"I have some friends loyal to the cause."

"I thought the Coelacanth Project was a secret?" Tawney squinted at him.

"It is."

"So were these loyalists in on it? How can you trust them?" Brant crossed his arms. "Seems as though anyone who has anything to do with us either wants to protect us, use us, or kill us."

"Continue assumin' that until this war is done," Christopher warned.

"War?" Natalie asked, alarmed.

"Figure of speech," Uncle Chris waved the comment away. *In what language?*

Christopher rose with his tackle box, marking the end of their conversation.

"Our stretch of beach is fairly desolate. I'm takin' Angie for a stroll by the water before the sun sets if anyone wants to go. Except you," he kicked Leo's foot.

"Outside?" Tawney pressed her nose against the window. "You really mean it?"

"Under the hot California sun," Christopher confirmed. "We're pretty far from home now, should be safe enough."

"Yes please!"

"We should stay here with Leo," Brant said pointedly.

"Yeah, alright." Tawney slumped her shoulders in disappointment.

"He should be up on his feet by mornin'," Uncle Chris shrugged. "We'll go then, yeah?"

Tawney beamed at him. "Yes!"

"Do you mind taking Enzi?" Natalie asked. "He loves the beach."

"Sure thing," Christopher fluffed Enzi's fur as he ran past him.

"Oh, and Uncle Chris," Natalie said hesitantly, "don't let him eat the sand."

He blinked at her.

"Eat the sand?" he repeated slowly.

"Yeah," Natalie rubbed her arm, embarrassed. "I know it's weird; he's obsessed."

"Bloody dumb dog," Christopher scratched the back of his head. "Sure, I'll watch him."

"And Uncle Chris—"

"If you tell me he drinks seawater, I'm leavin' him here."

"No, no, just," Natalie paused. The idea of Christopher leaving them alone made her feel vulnerable. "Hurry back," she finished.

"For sure."

He left through the kitchen with Enzi and Angie trotting beside him. It was a few long minutes before anyone spoke. Finally, it was Leo who broke the silence.

"We can't wait another day to look for our parents, Nat."

We'll be waiting for you.

Natalie bit her lip. The timing couldn't be worse.

"You're not fit to go anywhere," Owen objected. "Especially not hunting around for our parents."

"I'll rest up and I'll be fine. I want to hear the truth from their mouths, not Christopher's."

"On that," Brant's mouth was set and his tone unusually serious. "He seems to expect everything. Ancora I was stocked and operational before we came to him and then this Ancora was prepared, across the entire country, before we even knew we were coming here. It's awfully convenient."

"He had an office," Leo added. "In Ancora I, behind a hologram on the third floor. Full of maps and photographs. Nautilus has all of it now. But today was not their first time in that room."

Owen knocked on the coffee table.

"Last night, when Enzi was losing his mind while we trained, was Nautilus in the office then?"

Natalie observed Christopher and the two dogs outside the window. He threw a ball far down the beach and Enzi took off, covering Angie in sand. Christopher doubled over in amusement.

"Awfully convenient," Brant repeated, spinning his knit cap on the tip of his finger.

"What are you saying?" Tawney peeled away from the window to question them.

"It's possible Nautilus has been with us this entire time,"

Brant said.

"Hiding in the house?"

"No, Tawney. Brant is suggesting Uncle Chris works for Nautilus, which is ridiculous," Natalie scoffed.

"He's the one who told us to question everything," Leo managed to barely open one eye.

"Not his fidelity! He already told us it's his job to protect us and prepare safe houses for us."

"He also told us the Coelacanth Project was dissolved after our parents decided they didn't want us to train," Brant defended Leo's argument. "If the project was dissolved, why are these training houses still stocked?"

"The project may have been terminated, but our ability to tack wasn't. So long as we live, we risk being exploited. He didn't keep up Ancora for a paycheck," Natalie's face burned red she was so worked up. "He did it for us."

"Well, for our 'gift,'" Leo picked apart her words.

"He saved your life!"

"After, potentially, putting it in danger. I'm not saying I'm sure. I'm admitting it's possible. I'm not sure of anything."

"You don't always need proof to appreciate something is true," Natalie pushed back.

"Actually, Natalie is quite right," Owen spoke up from the corner, cleaning his glasses on his shirt. "Nearly every great scientific truth was once considered impossible."

Natalie was distracted from Owen's speech by a flash of refracted sunlight outside the bay window. Angie and Enzi raced along the beach towards the cottage and Christopher stood where the waves kissed the sand, facing the sea.

"...a heliocentric galaxy, electricity, flight, wireless communication, nuclear fusion, the list goes on. That's the history of humanity: we circumvent the impossible with belief before action."

"And then we corrupt it." Natalie played with the stone in her pocket.

"The point was," Leo waved their digression aside. "We need to find our parents. They will set everything straight."

"You said this secret office had maps?" Tawney absentmindedly flicked a curl of hair. "Did you see anything that might point to our parents?"

"Possibly," Leo glanced at Natalie before continuing. "There was a place marked with the Coelacanth symbol and a newly inked question mark next to it."

"Where?" Owen sat with his elbows on his knees.

"Directly over Norfolk," Natalie confessed.

Brant flopped onto the couch opposite Leo.

"Were there marks for Nautilus, too?"

"Yeah," Leo took a sip of water. "A few scattered places in Western Europe and the U.S."

"There's no reason to hide this from us unless he's with Nautilus," Brant accused.

Movement outside the window again caught Natalie's eye. Christopher was heading back towards the house. Enzi lifted the tennis ball in his mouth high above Angie's head as they walked. She jumped and pawed at him doggedly, eager to take it from him.

"I'm not discussing this anymore," Natalie crossed the room to the stairwell. "I suggest you all stop as well."

A door opposite of the rocky lagoon they had arrived in swung inwards. It dazzled the room for a moment with its vivid yellow siding as Christopher passed through.

Natalie climbed the stairs swiftly with Enzi at her heels. She rose as high as the house would take her, as far away from everyone as possible. She passed the first landing and kept climbing until she came to a door at the end of the stairs. Natalie passed through without a second thought and squinted in the sunlight.

Terrified she might be seen, Natalie dropped to her knees. Enzi paced the railing of the rooftop patio as the sea breeze puffed up his fur. It was warmer than it had been on the east coast, but without the stifling humidity. Natalie crouched against the yellow siding.

The sun dipped its rays into the waves. Natalie had grown up where the sun rose from the ocean each morning. Watching it sink beneath the sea made her realize how far from home she was.

Home is gone, Natalie reminded herself. *Home is gone. Mom is gone. Dad is gone. Ancora is gone. Christopher was nearly gone, and Leo was nearly gone, too.*

Natalie broke into violent sobs. It was too much.

Uncle Chris can't be with Nautilus. He's our only chance.

CHAPTER 23: NAUTILUS CHAMBERS

Natalie emerged into the circular white room. Again, it had been transformed. Ceiling high silver columns formed a ring around the center of the room. The metallic structures reflected the fluorescent lighting, making the space appear to glow from within. Inside the circle, a set of black stairs rose to meet a high platform. Amir Amani stood atop the staircase watching Natalie approach; his dark suit stuck out dramatically in the sea of white light. Behind him stretched a row of empty seats, framing the large television Natalie had seen on their first meeting in the white room.

Natalie stopped just beyond the glowing red passageway.
We're not alone.

Eleanor, Tanaka, and Rankin climbed the stairs leading up to Amir's stage. Eleanor's right arm was suspended in a sling against her chest, while Tanaka supported himself on a pair of crutches. Each gave Amir a slight nod as they passed him and claimed one of the chairs on the platform.

"Nat!"

Tawney jumped up and down across the room from Natalie, waving frantically. Brant, Owen, and Leo stood spaced out around the ring of columns, each in Nautilus uniforms matching her own.

"Tawney," Natalie smiled in relief and ran towards her.

"No, no! Stop!" Leo stood several feet ahead of Natalie with his arms stretched out.

Confused, she slowed to a halt. Her friends were spaced evenly between the metal columns, each with an ominous red passageway far behind them. Along the walls, Natalie noticed identical columns rose up between each of their passageways.

Leo approached her on her left, stopping where the column in the ring and the column on the wall aligned. He raised his hand and pushed it into what should have been empty air. His palm flattened as though pressed against glass.

"It's a force field," Owen grumbled from somewhere behind her. "It's kind of impossible really."

Natalie ran her fingers along the invisible wall dividing her and Leo. She aligned her hand with his. Where their skin should have touched there was pure pressure, pushing her away. A knot twisted painfully in her abdomen and she gritted her teeth against it.

I was wrong. This is worse than the cell.

"You will find each other again," Amir's voice floated to her from his pedestal. "By coming together through Nautilus, you will be more than anything you could have been before. Come into this inner circle and join Nautilus. Vow to work with us to create peace and you will find peace within yourselves."

Natalie let her hand fall away from Leo's. She carefully composed her expression before confronting Amir. He spoke loudly, so his voice filled the room, but he focused on her. She felt exposed beneath her placid bluff.

"How would tacking secure the omnipresent peace you preach?" Owen asked from his slice of the room. His red hair was the lone burst of color in the surrounding shades of white and grey.

"I realize you are not accustomed to ignorance, Mr. Johnson. This must frustrate you terribly. I do promise you, upon vowing allegiance to Nautilus, you'll learn the greatest truth is also the world's greatest secret."

"Your ambiguity is tantalizing."

"Wow," Tawney leaned casually against the force field separating her from Brant. "You managed to irritate Owen. That's a first."

"Your argument lacks substance," Leo squarely faced Amir. "Why would we listen to someone who talks about peace and blows up cities?"

"What is any act of violence but simply a means to an end when attempts for a peaceful resolution have fallen on deaf ears?"

"Maybe what you want isn't possible," Brant said quietly. He sat on the floor hugging his knees. He appeared paler than he had before.

"It is," Amir insisted. "You can save the victims of a merciless world from a meaningless, premature death."

"No death is meaningless," Leo argued.

Amir sighed.

"What did anyone learn from the Norfolk bombing? Safety is an illusion? Terror surrounds us? Humanity avoids the damning fact that fate lacks empathy and we lack control. But you," Amir Amani gestured around at each of them. "You can change everything. You can tip the balance because you have control. You can create peace."

"The Coelacanth Project was created to help humanity navigate the possibility of nuclear war. We're meant to lead real-time peacekeeping negotiations between nations. You've misconstrued us to be something we're not," Owen's analysis neared on sympathetic.

Natalie glanced at Leo, but he was fixated on Amir.

Are you with me?

"What if we decide not to help you?" Brant stared vacantly off into space. "More people get blown up?"

He's going to break soon. Natalie absentmindedly ran her fingers along the raised white scar decorating her right wrist and palm.

I have to do something.

Amir cocked his head at Brant, reminding Natalie of Enzi when he's thinking.

"Why would you not want to help us, Mr. Smith?"

"Why would we? Humans are not capable of peace."

"I do believe, upon reflection, you will come to the same realization as all of us here within Nautilus have. To not acquire peace in our time, when we have the capability to do so, is nothing less than criminal. Those who allow suffering to continue are as guilty as those who initiate suffering." Amir spoke with intense passion and commitment. He was unfairly compelling.

Natalie fought against the doubt creeping through the halls of her mind like a toxic fog.

I'm doing the right thing, she told herself. *His words are lies. Nautilus brings war not peace.*

"If, for whatever reason, you do not want to follow Nautilus's path, we will be forced to persuade you in other ways," Amir gestured to the television screen as it flickered to life.

Natalie sank to her knees. The image panned slowly over each of their parents. Some were bruised, some bled, and some had dirt-caked and tear-streaked cheeks. The photographs were headshots against a stark white background. They could have been taken anywhere at any time. Black dots spotted Natalie's vision. Her friends' voices drifted across her in muffled waves.

It's over. Nautilus has them. Nautilus has us. The Coelacanth Project is dead.

Her mother's image filled the screen. Her cheek was split and swollen, and dried blood covered the length of her jaw. Natalie recoiled at the thought of someone laying a hand on her mom. She couldn't bear the idea of her being in pain, of her suffering because of Natalie's mistakes.

"You see, there are more than strangers desperate for your allegiance," Amir spoke soothingly. It made Natalie's blood boil. "People are suffering," he spoke directly to her.

We should have never left Ancora. It's my fault they have her.

Her mother's hair was tousled and unkempt, but her brown eyes shone intensely. She stared defiantly into the camera. Natalie stared back. She didn't see the mother who read her to sleep, who helped her with her homework, or who took her to adopt a puppy from the shelter.

She saw a woman dedicated to protecting her family. She saw a researcher, a scientist. She saw courage.

Question everything.

There was something missing. Whether the photographs were taken minutes before, days before, or completely faked, it didn't matter. Natalie's mother stared at her from Amir's stage without a hint of doubt in her eyes.

She wouldn't want me to tack for Nautilus, Natalie knew. *Even if they do have her.*

Natalie pushed herself up from her knees.

She would want me to fight.

Natalie was vaguely aware of Tawney cursing and throwing her shoes at Amir's platform. Part of her registered Brant slumped where he sat, laying his red-capped head on his knees as his shoulders shook.

Control your fear.

"Release them immediately," Owen yelled at Amir. "You won't accomplish anything by blackmailing us."

Leo stood with his arms crossed, squinting at the photo reel.

None of them noticed Natalie drifting towards the platform. Her feet were more confident of their destination than her mind.

Forgive me. Trust me.

It wasn't until she crossed into Amir's central circle that a crushing silence fell over the room. She stopped at the base of the stairs leading to his platform.

"Nat," Tawney's voice cracked. "What are you doing?"

Natalie didn't look at her. She didn't look at anyone but Amir.

"Sweet child. Will you serve Nautilus on its quest for peace?" Amir Amani smiled graciously down at her.

"No, Nat," Owen's plea was so quiet Natalie suspected he hadn't actually meant for her to hear.

Natalie ascended the first stair.

Trust me.

"I will."

"No!"

The betrayal in Tawney's scream shook Natalie to her core. She scanned the platform, distracting herself as she continued up the stairs. To her surprise, Eleanor beamed at her. Her right hand was bandaged, with her ring and middle finger completely missing. Uncle Christopher had shot those fingers clean off outside of Ancora I. Leo had tackled the old woman to the ground at Lighthouse Market. Yet here she sat, with tears of joy trickling down her wrinkled face, staring at Natalie as though she were a wayward grandchild coming home at last.

Natalie stood before Amir. He studied her.

Don't think. Don't think a thing.

"I will stand with Nautilus because I want to achieve peace in our time. My life has been wrecked by violence. My parents are missing and my home was destroyed. I've been lied to my entire life about what I can do. Now that I know, I want to play my part."

Play my part.

Amir remained silent. His face was a mask: poised and impervious.

He won't believe it until I do. Trust me, Amir Amani. I am broken, I am lost, I am tired. Bring me home.

Natalie felt tears brimming her eyes and she let them fall. She allowed herself to feel the pain she had been stifling since the night of the bombing. He needed to see it.

"You were right before, Mr. Amani," her voice cracked. "I am afraid, but not of what I expected. I realized all of my fears are linked to the mistakes of my family and can be calmed by Nautilus. So I offer my allegiance, my deference, and my cooperation. I'm only scared of what will happen if the Ward fails to achieve peace." Natalie lowered her head, unable to stand Amir's penetrating gaze. She wasn't sure how long she could manipulate her emotions. The silence stretched on and Natalie bit the inside of her cheek.

If he doesn't believe me, our parents are dead. We're dead.

Slender fingers lifted her chin. The corners of Amir's mouth twitched into the smallest smile.

"We are saved. Come child and rejoice, for you are home," Amir embraced her. Behind him, Eleanor choked out a sob and clasped her hands together.

"Are you the Ward?" Natalie whispered to him, desperate to focus on anything except his arms around her.

"No, child," Amir held her at arm's length. "We represent just a small facet of Nautilus's chambers. The Ward guides us towards our gilded future while we, in exchange, protect him. He is at Nautilus's center."

"Have you met him? May I meet him?"

Amir's smile tightened and Natalie feared she had overstepped.

"I want to express my gratitude; he has given me hope."

"Perhaps," Amir answered curtly, then smoothed his tone. "Perhaps you will, once you've served Nautilus to your greatest potential."

If I serve my family to my greatest potential, Nautilus and its Ward will fall.

"Now, more importantly," Amir raised his voice to be heard by the entire room. "Will your friends follow you?"

"I will," a voice echoed quietly beside Natalie.

Brant stood next to her on the stage. His cheeks were sunken and pale, but his bloodshot blue eyes were hopeful as he gazed over at her. Tawney unleashed a string of obscenities up towards the stage.

"It seems not everyone shares your insight to our mission. What a shame," Amir clicked his tongue in disappointment.

"Please," Natalie proceeded cautiously. "I ask for my friends to have an opportunity to reflect on how supporting Nautilus's fight for peace may ultimately help us find peace for ourselves by providing an outlet for our gifts."

She had practiced the line in her head a hundred times. For the first time since ascending the stage, Natalie's gaze fell on her friends beneath her. Tawney furiously turned her back to her, slamming her fists against the invisible barricade. Silent tears spilt down Owen's face while Leo squinted up at her, thinking.

Understand what I'm saying, she begged. *The only way out is through.*

"I ask that you give them the same gift you gave me: time."

"Of course, of course!" Amir clapped in delight and the television screen faded to black behind him. "Achieving inner peace with your decision is the first step on your journey to world peace with Nautilus. Please," he gestured to the glowing passageways behind each of them. "I will call upon you again, soon, disciples of the Ward."

Trust me, Amir Amani. Trust us, Natalie thought desperately, hoping her friends realized the benefit of playing along sooner rather than later.

Natalie descended the stairs and forced herself to walk calmly towards her tunnel. Leo rushed along the force field between them, calling her name, desperate to catch her attention. He held his healing forearm against his chest as he repeatedly smacked his other palm flat against the invisible wall.

Just before she reached the passageway, Natalie met his concerned gaze. She blinked once, slowly.

The bat of her eyelashes stopped him in his tracks. She strode into the red tunnel and left her friends behind in the white room.

Getting close to Nautilus is the key out of this labyrinth. But first, Natalie broke into a run as the tile turned to dirt beneath her shoes. *I have mail to open.*

CHAPTER 24

"Nat?"

Natalie calmed her breathing to something that resembled normal. The sun had been drowned by the sea, leaving the moon and twinkling stars to illuminate the roof of Ancora II. She threw her head back, trying to convince gravity to pull her tears back.

"Natalie? You out here?" The door swung open and stopped inches from her. Enzi put his front paws up on Christopher to greet him. Angie shuffled around the door and promptly settled herself in Natalie's lap.

"Hard to hide with this pup around, huh?" Uncle Chris mused. He sat next to Natalie and Angie abandoned one lap for another.

Natalie sniffled.

"Hey now, what's this?" Christopher wiped a fresh tear from her cheek. His calloused touch was the most comforting thing she had had in days and her sobs overcame her all over again.

"Uh," Uncle Chris patted her awkwardly on the back.

"There, there."

Natalie threw her arms around his chest. He was warm and solid and smelled faintly of cigarette smoke. She pulled away, drying her tears on her sleeve.

"Are you smoking again?" Natalie asked him sternly.

"I, uh, well, no you don't," he wagged his finger at her. "Don't deflect. I'm not up here cryin' on the roof."

"I can't get a handle on this, Uncle Chris. How is everyone else functioning? They even seem to be having fun sometimes. I've spent every moment since the bombings in Norfolk terrified. Terrified our parents are hurt, or captured, or Nautilus will find us. And now Enzi's maimed Leo," Natalie rubbed her forehead. "Everything is a mess."

Christopher passed her an orange and white piece of taffy. She removed the wax paper wrapping and pinched the candy between her teeth. The salty orange and vanilla flavor and unique hard but chewy texture reminded her of every summer she had ever shared with him. Boat rides, family dinners, bonfire s'mores at midnight: the nostalgia was comforting, but also a sad reminder of how much had changed.

"He'll have scars, but he'll be alright. And fear is essential. It keeps you alive. It keeps your priorities in order. However, you mustn't let it command you. Your purpose must be stronger than your fear. And remember," Uncle Chris scratched Angie's belly as she rolled over in his lap. "Fear comes from within. It can be channeled like the energy you use for tackin'."

Natalie watched Enzi sniff along the rooftop patio.

"My fear won't listen to me."

"The universe will listen to you if you're brave enough to speak to it," Christopher leaned against the side of the cottage and gazed up at the sky. "All those stars, they're surrounded by an abyss of darkness, but they burn anyway. Their light crosses the universe forever, long after the star itself has gone dim, just to be seen by you: an insignificant human on an insignificant planet. Imagine the courage that takes."

He had drifted far away, lost in another world. Natalie saw

more of Christopher than ever before. The insight underlined how little she knew about his life. She tried to stop herself from speaking, but the question spilled past her lips.

"What did you do before you came to the Coelacanth Project?"

Christopher tore his attention from the sky above and chuckled.

"Research."

"That really clears things up."

Christopher winked at her.

"Some secrets get better with time," he quickly changed the subject off himself. "Don't assume your friends are immune to fear. They struggle with you."

"What do you mean?"

"Brant has barely eaten anythin' in two days and Owen has been obsessin' with the physics of tackin' to distract himself from everythin' else. Literally studyin' himself to sleep. Meanwhile, Leo can't sleep at all. I'm gonna give the boy sleepin' pills with his dose of antibiotics tonight to give him some relief." Christopher jabbed her weakly in her good arm. "Then you sit up here, obsessin' about things you can't change. And Tawney," he paused for a breath. "Tawney doesn't know how to deal with anythin' she can't punch away. Y'all have been sufferin' alone when you ought to be leanin' on each other."

Natalie pulled her knees to her chest and rested her chin on one of them. If what he said was true, she had been incredibly selfish.

Maybe I've been blinded to their suffering by my own.

"You know what this whole week reminds me of?" he asked, interrupting her thoughts.

"No, Uncle Chris. I can't recall anything even remotely similar to the past couple of days," Natalie laughed a little at the absurdity of it. It was good to laugh; it pushed the fog from her mind.

"Teachin' you to ride a bike. You remember?"

Natalie remembered it well. Kids at school had noticed she was eight years old with training wheels on her bicycle. They teased her relentlessly and finally she refused to ride the bike at all. She loved its purple color and shining silver tassels on the handlebars, but it wasn't worth being picked on.

Uncle Christopher observed she was suddenly reluctant to ride and bribed the truth from her with an ice cream sundae. He started lessons that afternoon. It took days, but finally, one day, she did it. He was holding onto the back of her seat and he told her he was going to let go. She begged him not to.

"Okay," he said. "I won't let go."

The pavement blurred beneath her. She pushed hard on the pedals and the wind blew her hair behind her shoulders. She had never gone so fast before.

"I'm flying!" Natalie giggled.

She glanced back to Uncle Chris, but he was an entire block away, clapping and cheering her on.

"Yeah, I do remember," Natalie said finally. "You lied to me."

"But you flew."

"Honestly, it's one of my favorite memories of you."

He peered sideways at her.

"Is that so?"

"Yes," she replied, embarrassed. "Is that so strange?"

"Considerin' you fell and scraped your bloody knee, yeah it's a little strange. I'm pretty sure you have a scar."

"I do, on my right kneecap," Natalie pulled up her pant leg to prove it to herself. "That's from that day?"

"You fell on the curb. Your mom yelled and yelled at me," he laughed. "You were sobbin' and tellin' her you were flyin' before you fell."

"That's all I remember," Natalie shrugged, her left shoulder twinged in protest. "I don't remember the fall at all."

"That spark is your brand new bike," Uncle Christopher told her.

Natalie took out the five-sided stone and let it sit in her palm.

"We will have to take those trainin' wheels off soon."

She traced the scar on her knee with her fingertip. It shone white in the starlight, like the mark left by the bolt on her wrist. She sat quiet for a long while, occasionally catching sight of a meteor streaking brilliantly bright across the sky.

"Looks like tacking," Natalie commented after a particularly radiant one.

Christopher huffed once next to her.

"It really does."

"Uncle Chris," Natalie started, remembering a comment made in Ancora I. "What's a ward?"

"A ward is someone protected, usually a minor."

"I understand the definition. I meant in relation to Nautilus. What ward are they talking about?"

"Ah, you mean the Ward." He squinted up at the stars, as though searching for the right words. "At Nautilus's center is one person. They orchestrate operations behind the glitterin' veil of promised peace and prosperity. Very few people are privy to their true goal or identity and Nautilus's pawns are brainwashed to blindly follow and protect the Ward at all costs."

"Do you know who the Ward is?"

"Nah, kid, I wish I did. It's one of two unknowns that keep me up at night."

"What's the other?"

Christopher rubbed his neck and sighed.

"How this ends."

A warm blanket of silence enveloped them: comfortable and familiar. Natalie didn't press for any more information on the Ward; she knew he had said all he would on the matter.

"You need to quit smoking, Uncle Chris," she scolded after a while.

"You're right. I'll pop up to the store and buy a fresh pack

of quittin' patches. Oh wait, I'm America's Most Wanted.
Maybe next year," he chuckled. "Speakin' of drugs, Leo's due
for his next dose. Which reminds me, Leo was thoughtful
enough to save these for you when lookin' for your spark."
From the inside of his windbreaker, he revealed three
bloodstained books and the sleek metal casing of the logic
puzzle.

Natalie forced back fresh tears. She put Dr. Seuss, Michael
Crichton, and Plato in her lap and clicked on the holographic
projection of the orb.

"I thought they were lost," she admitted.

"The important things in life have a way of findin' their way
back to you, usually by way of a friend."

Natalie spun the glowing orb. It rotated around the white
peg pointed towards the sky.

"Any tips on this impossible task you've given me?"

"For sure," he smiled. "Question everything. Wake up."

Natalie wrinkled her nose at him.

"Don't you know who's credited with the invention of the
logic puzzle?" Christopher teased her.

"I'm sure it was ages ago. The Greeks maybe?"

"Charles Lutwidge Dodgson."

Natalie shook her head.

"It doesn't ring a bell."

"Ah, then maybe his pen name? Lewis Carroll."

Natalie's mouth fell open. She relaxed against the siding of
the cottage behind her and furrowed her eyebrows at the
shimmering hologram.

The author of Alice's Adventures in Wonderland!

"Wake up, Alice," she muttered.

Curiouser and curiouser.

"Well, Leo will be needin' these." He shook a yellow pill vial
from his jacket.

"I should take them," Natalie clicked off the hologram. "I'm
not sure he'll take anything from you right now."

"Hmm? Why's that?"

Natalie hesitated. Leo would not approve of her telling Christopher his theory. Then there was the 0.01% chance Leo was actually right. Natalie pushed that thought from her mind.

It's Uncle Christopher.

"He and Brant are fairly convinced you're working with Nautilus."

To Natalie's surprise, he smiled.

"Good."

"Good?"

"Means they're listenin'. If you're goin' to succeed in protectin' yourselves and those sparks, y'all need to treat everyone as a potential threat."

"I don't believe you're with Nautilus," Natalie said defensively. "But Leo argues I'm too trusting."

"Trust is often pursued by pain, yet life would be hollow without either. Go on, it's your dog that bit him. You better make sure he heals from it."

"That's a little harsh," Natalie opened the door and started down the stairs. Enzi's white tail led the way.

"The truth is harsh, kid, just you wait."

Natalie stopped in the stairwell, certain she was not supposed to hear his last comment. She hugged her stained books against her stomach as the chilling clutch of fear crept up her spine.

Channel your fear.

Enzi whined impatiently several stairs below her and she hurried to catch up to him.

Just you wait.

CHAPTER 25

Natalie reached the first floor and the silence gave her pause. The recessed ceiling bulbs had dimmed and Leo sat on the couch alone with his arm propped up high on the barstool. The glow of the television across the room lit his grim expression. She took a seat next to him and Enzi forced himself on the couch between them. He laid his head on Leo's lap.

"Where is everyone?"

"Bed," Leo replied, fixated by the program on T.V. "Listen to this," he turned up the volume.

"The Hampton Roads area, from Virginia Beach to Williamsburg, is being evacuated west of Richmond due to a bomb threat issued this evening," a female voice echoed over footage of traffic crawling out of coastal Virginia. "According to the F.B.I., the terrorists behind the threat have issued a statement demanding undisclosed individuals who possess information on how to access and disarm the bomb come forward within twenty-four hours, or the bomb will detonate.

Authorities have not yet discerned exactly where the bomb is located. The President was relocated early this morning to a private bunker—"

Natalie clicked off the television. Gradually, she adjusted to the dim glimmer reflected off the starlit sea.

"They're talking to us, Nat."

"Nonsense. We have no idea where a bomb is or how bombs work. Take this," Natalie passed him the three medications from Christopher's pill vial. Leo put them all into his mouth and chased the pills with an entire glass of lemonade.

"We have some idea," he insisted. "Our parents' office is in Norfolk, close to that first bombing. That's where they want us to go."

"Which is exactly why we shouldn't."

"If we don't go, people could die."

"If we go and get captured, it's over. Nautilus would have us and the power of tacking at their command," Natalie countered.

"Not at their command."

"Maybe you're strong enough to resist torture, but I doubt I am."

"What if our parents are in that office?"

Natalie opened her mouth to reply, only to shut it again. *We'll be waiting.*

"It's unlikely," Natalie said, though she believed the opposite.

"The spark symbol on Norfolk was the closest Coelacanth marking to our houses on that map in Christopher's office. And it happens to be in the same city as our parents' office?" Leo argued. "Our parents are there, Nat, and you know it."

"We've been in that office building a hundred times before and we have never seen anything related to the Coelacanth Project."

"But we've learned what to look for," Leo insisted. "You know what your problem is?" He leaned towards her. Enzi whined as he was squished between them.

"No, Leo, what's my problem?" Natalie scowled at him.

"You overanalyze everything," he said bluntly. "You spend all of your time assessing the information around you, instead of taking a second to simply exist. Then your brain gets so exhausted processing life that when you need it to make a decision, you panic. Like when you ignored every horror film ever made and went into your house the night of the bombing." His words were unkind, but his tone teetered on the cusp of wonder. The sentences stumbled out of his mouth in a rush, as though he had been holding them back for ages.

Natalie flushed, entirely unsure if she was being criticized or receiving an oddly delivered compliment. Leo leaned in closer. His breath was warm and sweet on her lips. She watched him study her face, his hazel eyes tracing the curve of her cheek.

"Right now, you're thinking too much." Leo moved so his lips barely brushed against hers as he spoke, softer than a feather against her skin.

"You don't want me to think?" Natalie whispered. Delicate and adrift, her mind had morphed into a cloud. Her thoughts were frozen fractals suspended on a breeze of serotonin and adrenaline.

"That's not what I said. You're brilliant. Just don't let your brain stop you from going after what you want. Use it."

She leaned into him. He tasted like lemonade.

"Natalie," he breathed.

Lightning struck through her clouded mind, clearing it like wildfire. She couldn't remember when he had last said her full name, and he had certainly never said it like that.

He pulled away enough to squint suspiciously at her.

"Did you give me sleeping pills?"

Natalie didn't answer.

"Thank you," Leo pressed his forehead against hers. "But you should know, I'm a lightweight, so I may not wake for days."

He pulled away and Natalie caught herself drifting after him. She took in fresh air to clear her mind. Leo sank into the cushions. Natalie retrieved a blanket from another couch and draped it over him and Enzi.

"Is Enzi okay? I tackled him hard."

"He's fine," Natalie shifted awkwardly towards the stairs. "Thank you for what you did. I'm so sorry about your arm."

"He didn't mean it," Leo clumsily petted Enzi's head. "And I knew that reckless, protective instinct of yours was taking over. It was the only way to save you both."

Natalie stood with him until his breathing became even and slow. Certain he had fallen asleep, she took the first stair.

"Where did you want to go?"

Natalie shook her head, not following.

"What do you mean?"

"When we were tacking we couldn't go to your first choice, so you took us to the site of the bombing instead. Where did you want to go?" he was barely able to muster more than a whisper.

"It's stupid, just a bookstore," she whispered. "Go to sleep."

"What bookstore?" he pressed.

Natalie moved behind him and leaned her elbows on the back of the couch.

"Well," she started, "there's this bookstore in Paris. It overlooks the Seine, with a gorgeous view of Notre-Dame Cathedral. It's practically a labyrinth, with hidden passages and alcoves, all overflowing with books. There is a coffee shop, and reading cubbies, and even a bookstore cat, Mythos. I've always wanted to go; it's silly."

"I wanted to go to Barcelona to kick a soccer ball around. That's silly."

"Then why were we dancing?" Natalie asked.

"Supposed to be an adventure," Leo shrugged then winced. "Dancing was scarier. So we danced."

Natalie wasn't sure what to make of that.

"Goodnight, Leo."

"We're going to find them," he said, drifting off to sleep. "I promise."

"Don't promise."

"I promise. Tomorrow morning, we're going."

Enzi eyed her climbing up the stairs with his ears perked in two perfect triangles atop his head. She motioned for him to stay and he lowered his head onto Leo's lap. Natalie proceeded upstairs without him.

In the hallway on the second floor, three doors were ajar. One leaked the glow of a dim yellow lamp. Natalie pushed the door fully open with a soft knock.

"Tawney?"

"Careful!"

Natalie floundered clumsily over strips of thin leather strewn across the carpet and took a seat next to her friend on the floor. Tawney lifted a drill with a thin bit attached and pointed it at her hand.

"Tawney!" Natalie yanked the drill away from her. "What are you thinking?"

Baffled, Tawney picked up one of the leather strips from the floor. She dangled it in the air.

"Making bracelets."

In the middle of the piece of leather was one of their sparks. A hole had been drilled through each end of the stone, the strip of leather passed through, and then the two ends looped together so they could be adjusted.

"Oh," Natalie returned the drill and focused on where the leather passed through the holes in the sparks. The center of the stone wasn't grey as on the outside, but a golden yellow.

"What did you think I was doing?"

Natalie remembered Christopher's warning that Tawney struggled to process her emotions.

Tawney making bracelets is definitely weird, but not concerning.

"Since when do you do arts and crafts?"

"Since you nearly lost your spark when Nautilus invaded Ancora I," Tawney paused and inspected the hole she had made in the spark between her fingers. "It was actually Owen's idea. This way they are always on your wrist, touching your skin. If we're in a pinch, you jump and go. It's genius."

"Tell him," Natalie elbowed her.

"Oh, I did. He couldn't form sentences for nearly an hour. Walking encyclopedia? Yes. Socially competent? Not so much."

"Maybe it depends on his company."

Oblivious to Natalie's insinuations, Tawney pointed to her.

"Gimme," she said.

Natalie produced her own rock from her pocket and reluctantly surrendered it.

"This isn't going to break it...right?" Natalie watched apprehensively as Tawney pressed the drill bit against the smooth edge of the stone.

"Christopher said it's fine."

A minute later Tawney slipped the new bracelet onto Natalie's left wrist, turning the spark so the diamond and arrow point insignia faced outward. Its length spanned nearly the entire width of her wrist, with the leather straps from either end tied in a knot.

"I love that they made the symbol a fish, to mimic the real Coelacanth."

Natalie furrowed her eyebrows at her.

"What do you mean?"

Tawney lifted Natalie's arm between them. It was the first time she had ever studied the stone horizontally. Tawney tapped the diamond and the arrow point symbol and Natalie saw it: the archaic outline of a fish.

"I can't believe I didn't notice," Natalie studied the stone more closely.

"Brains can be stubborn."

Natalie leaned against Tawney's bed.

"I keep seeing the old woman. Eleanor. She is in every

shadow. She's in my dreams."

"We're better than that old hag, Nat," Tawney stowed her drill and pulled her knees up to her chest. "Every time I try to sleep, I imagine my parents getting tortured. I'm so angry with them and scared for them at the same time. How can I be mad and sad and scared?" She rested her chin on her knees.

Natalie had never seen her friend so pained and defeated. It made her heart ache. She realized why Leo had made his promises; to him she must appear just as broken.

"We're going to find them."

"We have no idea where they are."

"Yes, we do. We're going to check their offices tomorrow morning. And if they aren't there, we'll keep looking. We're going to find them. I promise."

Tawney dropped her knees to the ground and sat cross-legged.

"Tomorrow morning? That's a whole day sooner than what was decided in the library."

The image of the evacuation taking place on the other side of the country filled her mind. Thousands of cars fighting to escape the threat of destruction across eight lanes of stagnant traffic.

"We can't wait, not with the threat of another bombing over our heads."

"If we're going to do that, you need some help," Tawney said with a grimace. "Your tactical skills are...frankly, they're terrible, Nat. Why won't you use the gun? You weren't too bad with the paintball targets."

Natalie shook her head.

"I don't want to."

"You're being stubborn."

"Yes," Natalie agreed. "But I don't want to fight that way. You don't have control of a bullet once you fire it. It's literally out of your hands. Your target could move or someone could get in the way; you could aim to injure and accidentally kill them. I have enough unknowns in my life as it is. But I want to fight, Tawney. I can't be helpless again," Natalie added, remembering how easily Rankin had manhandled her up the stairs of her home. "I don't want others to fight for me."

Like Enzi and Leo, constantly in harm's way because I'm overanalyzing.

"Then you had better solve that puzzle Chris gave you. Maybe he's going to make you a wise sage beyond the need for weapons of lesser men," Tawney snorted.

Natalie laughed.

"No, I don't expect it's about fighting. If I can outsmart the puzzle, maybe I can outsmart Nautilus." She took out the metal box and activated it by pressing in on its sides. The glowing orb materialized before her. She manipulated the ball with her touch, tracing endless black pathways across its surface.

Tawney poked the pin projected out of the sphere and it bobbed in place, like a buoy on the water.

"Maybe you're overthinking it."

Natalie glared at her and Tawney raised her arms in surrender.

"Was only a suggestion. It's your toy."

She stared at the hologram. Natalie wanted to crawl in through one of its many crevices and hide forever, protected by an intricate maze no one could solve.

Natalie sensed exhaustion taking control. She blinked repeatedly to keep focused and sank further and further into the side of Tawney's bed. After fighting it for several minutes, she finally waved goodnight to Tawney and made her way down the hall to one of the open bedroom doors. The first one she came to had a big, white dog sprawled across the bed.

I guess this one is ours.

It was smaller than her bedroom in Ancora I, and lacked the personal touches from home. There were no painted letters above her bed and the drawers in the oak dresser overflowed with clothes her size, but they were not actually hers. She placed her stack of comfort Leo had rescued on her bedside table and inspected them more closely.

Jurassic Park, thankfully, did not have a speck of blood on it. Plato had taken a decent hit, but the cover of *Oh, the Places You'll Go!* was saturated.

I'm going to miss that library.

Natalie thought back to towering bookshelves and was grateful to have a piece of it with her.

Thanks to Leo.

Her thoughts darted about her mind like aimless ants desperate for their burrow. She kept replaying Leo's words, kept feeling his lips on hers, watching his eyes map her face.

Frozen by my fear and my rationale, Natalie huffed. *How do I think myself out of overthinking?*

The hours passed painfully slow. She fiddled with the spark on her wrist and struggled to keep her eyes open. She traced the pathways of the orb, but the lines blurred together and grew until they encompassed the entire globe. The white peg hovered in purgatory along the edge of the black sphere.

"Ready?"

The voice jolted her awake.

Leo stood in the doorway, barely visible in the shadows with his black jeans and sweatshirt. Tawney, Brant, and Owen trickled into view behind him.

Natalie jumped out of bed, all drowsiness gone.

"Let's go find our parents."

CHAPTER 26

Natalie followed behind Leo and Brant as they made their way down the stairs. Foggy morning sunlight filtered in through the sheer white curtains, drenching the cottage in molten gold. Tawney pulled her to a stop as they reached the living room.

"Listen."

A low grumbling echoed through the house.

"Snoring," Tawney snickered.

"It's possible we slipped him a dose of his own medicine," Leo high-fived Brant. His left arm, still bandaged, was slung against his chest with a navy scarf.

"You drugged him?" Natalie asked.

"Enough to make sure he sleeps through the day," Brant assured her.

A weight Natalie had not realized she was carrying lifted from her. She hated to speculate how betrayed Christopher would feel if he knew they were sneaking out to do exactly what he warned against. Now he may never find out.

He imagines he's keeping us safe, but nowhere is safe.
They weren't safe inside Ancora; they weren't safe outside
Ancora.
*We'll be in danger whether or not we try to find our parents. Being
together is better for everyone.*
Natalie followed her friends through the arched door to the
rock-enclosed grotto. Enzi dashed through the opening after
her.
"No, Enzi," she led him back to the living room and
scratched his head. "Stay. I'll be back soon."
He watched her close the door with his ears pointed. He
stuck his nose against the crack between the floor and the door
and dug at the tile.
"Let's go," Tawney pulled on the back of Natalie's shirt.
Natalie knew it was too risky to take Enzi with them. He
would draw attention and be easily recognized, but it still hurt
to leave him behind. She fell in line with her friends who stood
on the edge of the water lapping quietly against the sand.
"Let's go," Natalie agreed. She marched forward into the
ocean and blinding light swallowed her up. A second later, the
brilliance and tingling was replaced by pitch-black nothingness.
White flashes popped up around her, vanishing as quickly as
they occurred. She reached out blindly and her fingers brushed
against an aluminum wall on her right.
"A door should be up ahead," Owen whispered.
He shuffled past her. A moment later, a door swung open
and the space was bathed in warm sunlight. Boats rocked gently
in the water, tied up and abandoned under the protection of the
boat motel. Natalie followed Owen and her friends outside. She
kicked a rock into the corner of the doorway to keep it open
for them.
Fully covered and directly across the street from their
parents' office, Mitch's Boat Motel was incredibly convenient.
She remembered riding up to the marina on Christopher's boat
and meeting their parents for lunch on several occasions. The
more she thought about it, the more Natalie became convinced

the location of Mitch's Boat Motel was no coincidence.

Perfect coverage for tacking right next to their office? Definitely planned.

"Woah," Brant whispered, scanning the street.

It was deserted. Traffic signals flashed, but no cars lingered beneath them. No one bustled along the sidewalks on their way to work. A street normally filled with the scent of coffee and doughnuts and talk of business had fallen eerily silent. The mandatory evacuation snuffed out a productive, bustling city. Natalie had never seen the streets so devoid of life.

"This is creepy," Tawney shivered despite the heat.

Natalie couldn't agree more. She felt exposed on the pathway.

"Come on," Leo encouraged them. "Let's get inside."

"The sooner the better," Owen shielded his glasses from the glare of the mid-morning sun.

Natalie crossed the street, still looking both ways despite the utter lack of cars. They congregated on the landing of the familiar, unmarked, whitewashed office building. One story tall, it was the shortest structure on the block. The inconspicuous black door waited for them.

"Be ready," Leo advised.

Natalie watched him closely, concerned he may fall out at any moment. He adjusted his scarf sling and held his pistol at his side. Despite the unusual paleness of his cheeks, his mind seemed clear and sharp.

With a nod, Brant swung the door open and Leo rushed in first. Tawney and Owen followed close behind, while Brant slunk in after Natalie. Leo and Tawney made quick work of the one level office building. They moved through the open space with their guns high in front of them and, in a matter of seconds, cleared the office.

"Clear."

"Clear," Tawney echoed. "Well, this place is trashed."

Instead of individual offices or cubicles, their parents had shared one large space. Desks lined the walls and clean white paint reflected the natural light let in through wide windows. Déjà vu tickled the back of Natalie's mind as she made her way through the once neat and organized room. The family photographs that had hung on the walls littered the floor, their glass shattered and their backings ripped out. The many desks had been gutted and overturned with the contents of their drawers spilled out onto the floor. Natalie could hardly move without stepping on a piece of paper or photograph or broken glass. Her heart leapt into her throat.

It's exactly what Nautilus did at home.

"Nautilus has definitely been here," Leo said, moving gingerly through the debris.

"What are we looking for exactly?" Tawney asked. "I don't see any sign of our parents."

"Something we didn't look for the last time we were here," Natalie explained.

"You know: holograms, false walls, loose floorboards, a lifetime of lies and deceit. Think like Uncle Chris," Brant smirked.

"I'll keep guard. I say if we don't find anything in ten minutes, we call it for today," Leo suggested.

"This is odd," Owen flipped through a stack of paper.

He passed a piece to Natalie. Two columns of large decimals ran the length of the page. There was no title or header or anything to give meaning to the list of numbers, but the format was familiar.

"They're coordinates," Owen muttered, twisting a piece of his lengthening red stubble in thought.

"I wonder if Nautilus found what they wanted," Tawney kicked aside some broken glass.

"Let's hope not," Natalie returned the strange list of longitude and latitude locations to Owen.

"Check this out!" Brant called from around the corner of the room.

Glass crunched beneath Natalie's shoes as she made her way

across the field of debris to Brant. A gigantic blue nautilus shell scarred the back wall of the room. Over it, a black symbol had been marked: a diamond with an upward arrow point invading from beneath. The exact same symbol as the one on their stone.

A rising fish.

A short message was plastered beneath it.

MORTEM ANTE CLADEM

"Coelacanth has been here since Nautilus raided the place," Owen gawked up at the wall in front of them.

"Leo, check this out," Brant called across the room.

Natalie heard Leo shuffling through papers and other litter on the floor to join them.

"What's it say?" Leo's eyebrows furrowed.

"Mortem ante cladem," Natalie read the message below the symbol aloud. "It's Latin. It means 'death before defeat.'" Its implications hit Natalie hard. Their parents would not settle for being captured or used as bait.

"They're going to die to protect us," Owen blanched.

"No, we're going to find them," Leo rotated his gun, distracted. "Let's see what else we can find and get out of here."

"They've got more guts than I thought possible," Tawney whispered. She touched the outline of the Coelacanth symbol and leapt back as though it had burned her.

"You okay?" Owen made to move closer, but she held up her hand. He stopped.

"It's still wet," she revealed, her palm drenched in black paint.

For a moment no one moved.

Natalie pushed forward and touched the writing for herself. She rubbed the slick paint between her fingers.

"They're close." She fought the excitement threatening to overrun her. Her fingers trembled as she felt along the walls, prying for any loose drywall or trick baseboards.

"Question everything," she muttered. "Think like Uncle Chris."

Tawney did laps around the room, slipping on strewn papers as she felt for holographic walls. Brant and Owen kicked aside debris and jumped on the floor, searching for secret doors.

"We need to go," Leo announced, peeking through the curtains.

"Leo!" Tawney whined in protest. "They're here!"

"So is Nautilus." He took hold of her shoulder and led her towards the door. "Come on, they're running from the end of the street. We have to go."

"But the bomb," Natalie's fingers worked fast, tracing the baseboard along the wall of the painting. "It's set to detonate tonight."

"Probably a bluff," Leo said. "We'll come back tomorrow."

"You're lying."

"They've taken care of themselves this far; our parents will be fine," Leo argued.

Natalie knew he was saying whatever was necessary to get her to leave.

"We're the reason they're in danger!"

"Because of what they made us, Nat. Now let's go," Brant picked her up from beneath her arms.

"No, Brant," Leo hissed from across the room, but Brant ignored him.

He threw Natalie across his shoulder and she saw red. She beat her fists against his back and struggled to kick him. He was carrying her away. Away from her parents, away from the truth. She drew in a deep breath and cleared her mind.

Don't panic. Be patient...be patient.

Natalie snatched a dislodged curtain rod off its perch on the wall as they passed it. She whacked Brant hard across his calves, making him jump. He didn't let go. She swung the rod of metal around and ran the end into his side.

"Ugh!" he cried out and collapsed, sending Natalie

tumbling.

She braced herself for the impact against the wall beside them, but it never came. Natalie dropped and rolled when she finally hit the clean, carpeted floor. She popped to her feet, curtain rod in tow, and gaped back at the seemingly solid wall before her.

Natalie leaned through the hologram back into the ransacked office. Leo, Owen, Brant, and Tawney gaped at her.

"Get in here!"

Owen pulled Brant to his feet and they crammed in behind Natalie. The space was barely large enough to fit them all. Natalie squeezed herself between the back of the tiny room and Brant, who was still cradling his side. Owen hung half out of the hologram to keep an eye on the navy Nautilus suits growing larger in the window.

Leo gave Natalie a disapproving glare as he tucked in with them.

"We should have gone when we had the chance."

"They're here somewhere, I'm sure of it," Natalie defended herself.

Leo gestured to their tiny space with his gun.

"Are they?"

"You can be such an arrogant ass sometimes, you know that?" Tawney whispered to him.

"That's my nickname?"

"You told him?" Tawney frowned at her.

Natalie leaned against an ornate tapestry hung on the wall beside her.

"No, Tawney, but you just did."

"Shh!" Owen hissed, retreating fully inside the holographic cubby with them. Sweat beaded on his forehead as he held up his gun.

Natalie heard the office door click open and heavy boots crash through the mess scattered on the floor beyond their hiding space. She hardly dared to breathe.

Nautilus was inside the office with them.

And I've brought a curtain rod to a gunfight.

CHAPTER 27

"This is creepy," a man complained beyond the holographic wall. "The city's deserted, sir. There's no one here."

"That's why I had to come do this myself," a smooth voice answered. "A motion detector was activated; therefore, the city is not as deserted as you claim."

I know you.

"But sir," the first man's voice was closer than before. "Even if someone is here, the bomb will take care of them."

"And what if one of the Coelacanth kids is here? Do you possess the strength to tell the Ward you lost his path to peace? You should be denied the gracious gift our mission will bring."

"No, please, Mr. Amani, sir."

Natalie met Leo's gaze when he glanced back to her. He raised his eyebrows.

"Ah," Amir Amani spoke from beyond their hiding place. "'Mortem ante cladem.' 'Tis a shame. Coelacanth may have benefited with us if their stubbornness would yield to logic."

Natalie concentrated on the hologram. If Amir leaned against the wall to the right of the painted message, he would be in the hide with them.

"They've moved on. Check the surrounding buildings and get me the security footage in the marina."

Natalie exchanged panicked looks with her friends. The boat motel was the only option to tack back to Ancora under cover.

"Yes sir," the subordinate answered. "Ugh!"

A loud rustling and a thud sounded from beyond the holographic wall.

"Oh, get up!"

Owen and Leo pushed back away from the hologram, both fixated on the floor. A single piece of paper laid in purgatory: half inside their holographic hide and half inside the room with Nautilus. No sound came from beyond the hologram. Natalie didn't move; she didn't breathe.

Owen attempted to adjust the paper, but Leo stopped him. *Maybe they won't see it. It's one piece of paper on a floor littered with hundreds. They won't see it.*

Someone tugged on her sleeve. Tawney faced opposite the incriminating paper, captivated by the tapestry behind them. Engrossed in the hologram, Natalie ignored her.

Tawney pulled harder and pointed at the corner of the ornate wall hanging. Natalie observed the bottom corner of the tapestry sway out away from the wall, then back in, as though drifting on a breeze. With some difficulty in the crowded square room, she peeked behind the swaying edge of fabric. A black tunnel barely half Natalie's height lay behind the tapestry.

Natalie pulled the fabric out towards her and shoved Tawney into it. Silently, Natalie got everyone's attention and they followed suit. Owen was practically doubled over, shuffling forward blindly.

Leo filed in last. Before he ducked into the tunnel, he pointed back at the holographic wall. The piece of paper slipped a hair to the side and then vanished back into the ruined office.

Abandoning all attempts of silence, Leo pushed Natalie ahead of him. Unable to maneuver it in the narrow space, she dropped her trusty curtain rod and sprinted into the tunnel. A few paces in, the ceiling rose and she was able to stand. A dim light shone from far ahead of her, blocked out by the silhouettes of her friends as they hurried towards it. She drew in as much of the damp tunnel air as her lungs would hold and pushed herself to run faster.

Nautilus is right behind us. Channel your fear.

The uneven stone floor became smooth and worn beneath her shoes. Leo ran up alongside her.

"So far, we're heading towards the water," he said. "Too convenient to be a coincidence."

Natalie nodded.

"Our parents must have gone this way, too."

The light at the end of the tunnel twinkled. Natalie caught a glimpse of movement in the darkness on her left. She doubled back so fast her feet nearly slipped out from beneath her. Off the main tunnel, the stone wall gave in to another passageway.

I could have sworn...

Natalie stared into the shadows, her mind working.

"Nat!" Leo hissed. He ran back to her. "What are you doing? Move!"

"I saw something," Natalie leaned into the passage. A cool breeze met her skin.

"Nat, Nautilus is on our heels," Leo pulled her. "Let's move."

Their friends had dispersed along the path ahead of them. Natalie bit her lip.

This might be my only chance.

Leo swiveled from her to the tunnel in front of them and shook his head. She knew what he was thinking; she could see it.

He's remembering the night in my house. Me barging in, stupid and unprepared. He remembers me being carried up the stairs and him being kicked away.

Natalie realized she was shaking. Every sane cell of her body was screaming for her to forget the passage and keep running after the others. Yet she stared into the tunnel beside them.

"Nat," Leo tried to pull her towards the exit. "Stay with me."

Natalie slipped out of his grasp. She had made up her mind. "Don't wait for me."

Natalie darted into the tunnel. The passageway was pitch-black and sloped downward under her feet. Unable to see her hand stretched out in front of her, she stayed low and moved fast. She checked over her shoulder repeatedly, expecting the blazing glare of Nautilus flashlights to be closing in on her.

Suddenly, the hand out ahead of her smacked against something solid. Natalie managed to slow in time to save herself from running clear into it. The wall was smooth and cold to the touch. Her fingers traced the edges, searching, until she closed them around a handle.

It turned.

Natalie pulled the door towards her and blue light poured into the tunnel. She entered a wide room with a low ceiling that made her feel unusually claustrophobic. Blue projection screens spanned the walls with a repeating message in white that read 'input error'. A dozen desks, most of which were occupied by massive computer monitors, formed a circle around a clear model of the Earth.

Natalie stumbled on a bundle of wires that snaked along the floor as she drifted towards the rotating globe. Mimicking the Earth's rotation, the glass sphere spun at an angle, supported by a wide pedestal. It was captivating. Illuminated white lines dictated the boundaries of frosted continents and countries. Familiar symbols decorated the map. Blue Nautilus shells were etched on various countries while Coelacanth's spark symbol glowed on others, sometimes even occupying the same space.

Like right...here.

Natalie tapped the globe directly over coastal Virginia. The model stopped its rotation and went black. The projections around the room flickered and the blue glow was replaced with reports from Hampton Roads. Natalie moved around the room from screen to screen, amazed at their scope. They covered everything: the weather forecast, news reports, the founding of Jamestown, the annual Neptune Festival, tidal projections, satellite images. Every screen had something new each time she turned.

A nighttime satellite image towered above her. Norfolk blazed with fissures of light branching away from it like veins from the heart. It was evidence of life. A beacon of hope against the abyssal void of darkness stretching away into the Atlantic. Uncle Christopher's words echoed in her mind.

Satellites. Blips of energy, sparks of light. They're searching for us. He didn't mention our parents might be doing the same.

"Natalie!" Leo fussed from across the room.

She started in surprise, but remained focused on the glass sphere. In its center, only visible through the clear, unfrosted glass that covered the seas, was the same symbol she had seen marked onto one of Christopher's maps: the triquetra.

"Our parents aren't just in hiding," Natalie explained, tapping again on the globe. "They're researching; they're looking for something. They must be trying to find us."

Leo strode across the room and pulled her to him. His cheeks were flushed and his eyebrows drawn together in frustration.

"You have to stop doing that."

"I told you not to wait," Natalie argued. "I couldn't let myself leave when there was a chance—"

"I don't care about the reason, Natalie. I don't. I'm with you. No matter how determined you are to get us killed, I'm with you. Get out of your head and let me help." He let go of her arm and leaned against the nearest desk, adjusting his sling. His gaze drifted around the room.

All Natalie could do was stare at him. Her mind was buzzing, but instead of an overwhelming rush of thoughts, there was white noise. The return of the blue glow from the projection screens highlighted the profile of his face.

"You're with me," Natalie repeated.

Leo squinted at something behind her.

"Nat, down!" Leo yelled.

Natalie dropped to the floor as Leo let out shots towards the wall behind her. She flipped onto her back and caught sight of a heavy-set figure crouched beneath a desk.

"Don't shoot me, Leo!" she cried.

Natalie scrambled to her feet as Leo's gun clattered to the floor, his mouth open in shock. The woman's blonde hair shone silver in the globe's radiance as she ran for another passageway.

Natalie sprinted after her.

"Mrs. Davis!"

The plump woman shuffled around a desk and came face-to-face with Leo.

"Mrs. Davis," Natalie repeated.

Tawney's mother let out a defeated sigh. The closer Natalie got to her, the less Mrs. Davis resembled herself. Her expression was worn, as though she had aged several years in the past few days. Her hair was knotted atop her head and her lips lacked their usual dazzling red hue.

"Is my mom here, too?" Natalie blurted. "And dad? What are you all working on? Are you looking for us?"

"You shouldn't be here," Mrs. Davis hissed. "Does Christopher realize you left Ancora?"

Natalie huffed in frustration.

I didn't come all the way here for a lecture!

"Please, Mrs. Davis, where are my parents? The globe," Natalie pointed to the spinning glass Earth, "aren't you all trying to find us? We're here. We're all together again."

"No Natalie, we knew exactly where you were," her gaze darted repeatedly to the tunnel Natalie and Leo had entered through. "By the time we got home, our houses were in flames and you all were well on your way to Christopher's. It was the original plan for you to go to him; you would be safest in Ancora. You could learn the truth about yourselves while we searched for...for something bigger. Oh, look at you."

Mrs. Davis held Natalie at arm's length, but she batted her away.

"What do you mean you're searching for something bigger? We need you! Come home! Everything is gone, my house, my life. Where are my mom and dad?"

"Keep it down, child!" she hissed. "You've already brought Nautilus to our doorstep; don't make it worse."

"Make it worse?" Natalie yelled.

Leo attempted to comfort her, but she shoved him off.

"You all did this to us! We didn't ask for this!"

Tawney's mother covered Natalie's mouth, silencing her.

"I'm sorry this ordeal got messy, but Nautilus cannot find this room. We have to find the key before they do. Christopher lied to us, but it was for you. You can trust him."

She removed her hand and Natalie was so dumbfounded by the influx of meaningless information she had nothing to say.

"You must leave," Mrs. Davis gave Natalie a kiss on the forehead. "Give that to my fierce girl, now." She hugged Leo briefly and fled into a passageway opposite the one they had entered through.

Natalie made to follow her, but Leo touched her shoulder. He didn't pull her back or tell her to stop. She stopped on her own. He laced his fingers between hers.

"Our friends are waiting for us," she said quietly.

"Yeah, they're probably freaking out, Nat. Let's go."

"We'll find them again," Natalie stared at the empty space Tawney's mother had left behind.

"We will," he agreed, "when Nautilus isn't making camp in the room next door. Come on."

Natalie followed Leo silently back through the low passageway to the main tunnel. When they reached it, Natalie broke into a run, heading for a dim circle of daylight far ahead. Her muscles ached, but she welcomed it. It made her certain the room was real, the globe was real, and Mrs. Davis was real. Their parents were alive and safe.

I'll find you again.

The light grew brighter and she pushed harder. She feared if she slowed, she might change her mind and chase her parents instead.

Tawney and Owen waved from the opening, hurrying her forward. Natalie burst through without slowing, Leo right behind her. The tunnel opened into Mitch's Boat Motel, the same marina they had tacked into. Sunlight reflected through the open guillotine doors far beyond the last docked boat. Brant, Tawney, and Owen fell in line alongside her as Natalie's footsteps slammed on the planked wood of the dock.

Natalie jumped into a spacious boat and launched herself over the other side with the yellow cottage of Ancora II pictured clear in her mind. A blinding white brilliance rushed up to meet her, but before she reached it something closed around the back of her shirt. Strong arms yanked her back and slammed her flat on her back in the boat.

Natalie gasped for air. She tried to scream, but her lungs refused to inflate.

Turn back! Turn back!

She struggled to get upright and crawled back towards the dock. An invisible spear of ice twisted itself into her chest as she heaved herself up on the side of the boat.

Two men in navy blue jumpsuits had Tawney trapped between them on the dock. She easily evaded the blundering attempts of one to catch her. The other lifted a round object to his mouth and, in an instant, Tawney collapsed to the ground.

Shots fired through the aluminum walls of the marina. The man who stood above Tawney stumbled backwards, clutching his arm. Owen ran at him screaming, gun still raised, prepared to fire again.

A brunette woman with a silver nautilus shell on the sleeve

of her shirt spun out from behind one of the docked boats and slammed something into Owen's thigh. He fell to the ground, motionless.

They have us.

Natalie groaned as she pushed herself to her feet, fighting off the pain of having the wind knocked out of her. She lifted up her arms in surrender.

Brant laid still, half inside the tunnel entrance. Leo was a boat over, squirming beneath a Nautilus man who had him pinned.

"Please," Natalie managed, her lungs burning. "Take me. Let them go. It's my fault. Take me instead."

"Nat, get out of here!" Leo yelled at her.

"Let them go and I'll do whatever you want. Don't hurt them."

Someone grabbed a fistful of Natalie's hair and yanked her head back. She squealed in pain and clawed desperately at the arm holding her. They didn't budge. She was vaguely aware of something heavy splashing into the water near her.

A grunt sounded from behind her and she was released. Natalie sank forward in relief, clutching her stinging scalp. A stocky bald man grumbled as he lumbered away from Natalie to confront Leo.

Leo's previous assailant flailed in the water beside the other boat, struggling to get his bearings. Leo pointed his gun at the Nautilus man standing between them. His sling lost, he cradled his injured arm cautiously against his chest.

"I don't want to shoot you," Leo told him.

"Don't I know it," the man snickered.

Natalie was acutely aware of how outnumbered they were. At least twelve other Nautilus agents filled the room and Natalie did not recognize any of them. Brant, Owen, and Tawney lay motionless on the ground, too far away for her to tell if they were still breathing.

We can't fight them all, not the two of us.

"I don't want to shoot you," he repeated. "That doesn't mean I won't."

The man snorted in amusement and lunged for Leo. Leo shot him in the foot and the man fell to the ground, slamming his fists against the cushioned seats.

Natalie pulled the metal bolt off his back and rotated it clumsily at her side. The Nautilus man Leo threw overboard scrambled onto the stern behind her. She spun the bolt through the air and touched the shiny end to the man's arm. He screamed once and slumped against the boat, silent and still.

Leo gasped. Natalie watched as he pulled a tiny dart out from his shoulder. His eyes rolled back into his head and he collapsed onto the floor of the boat.

A sharp pinch stung the side of Natalie's neck and her vision began to blur. An older woman with wild silver hair and a tan birthmark covering most of her face ran towards her. Her right arm was bandaged and slung.

Eleanor.

"Oh, my dear," her voice came to Natalie through a thick fog.

Eleanor's frail touch eased Natalie to the ground. Her vision blurred and a ringing echoed in her ears. All at once, the world fell away and she floated in fog.

"We'll help you find peace."

CHAPTER 28: NAUTILUS CHAMBERS

It's my fault we were captured, Natalie berated herself as she hurried through the red tunnel, away from the white room and its invisible barriers.

It's my fault we were drugged and kept in the dark for days. It's my fault Nautilus has our parents. It's my fault they're suffering. My fault, my fault, my fault. But if I can convince Amir Amani to trust us, maybe we can get out of this pit.

Eager to open Chef's gift, Natalie climbed into her cot before the door to her cell had closed. After watching her friends' surveillance feed, she did her best to portray exhaustion. She stretched dramatically, yawned, and pulled the scratchy blanket above her head.

Chef's envelope laid waiting right where Natalie left it. She ripped open the seal and poured the contents out onto the bed beside her. Five smaller, twine-bound envelopes and folded cardstock tumbled out, followed by five grey stones with thin leather straps attached to the ends.

My spark!

Natalie pulled one of the bracelets onto her wrist. Like an anchor, it was heavier than it appeared. She smiled; it was as though a piece of herself had been returned to her. Natalie zipped the other four sparks into her jacket pocket and investigated the rest of the pile. The white envelopes were all marked with a letter: T, L, O, B, and N.

One for each of us.

She opened the one decorated with a neatly inked 'N' and removed several Polaroid photographs. With only a few stray moonbeams passing through the thin blanket, Natalie had to squint to make out the pictures.

The first was a little girl with wispy brown pigtails and a toothless smile smeared with strawberry ice cream. She sat in a stroller, clutching a ruffle-socked foot with sticky pink fingers. Natalie turned the photograph over and a short description was written on the back.

First Ice Cream Cone.

The next photograph was of her pointing to a purple bicycle with sparkling tassels and a big red bow on the handlebars. She was smiling wide despite missing both of her front teeth.

First Bicycle.

Another photographed the books atop Natalie's headboard, the ones she reached for first at bedtime.

Natalie's Favorite Reads.

Natalie ran her fingers delicately along the edge of the next Polaroid. Her mother and father stood beaming outside of their home. Nearly twenty years younger, her father's hair was still golden blond and the corners of her mother's eyes didn't crinkle as much when she smiled. Natalie sat perched on her father's hip with her head resting on his shoulder, waving her tiny fingers apprehensively at the camera.

I can't be more than two years old, Natalie realized. She stared at the photograph, wanting nothing more than to be in their arms again.

Curious, Natalie peeked into the other envelopes. Tawney scowled at the camera, wearing a sparkling pink ballerina tutu around her waist. Owen proudly sported charred eyebrows and scarlet cheeks with his homemade volcano at his first science fair. Brant and Leo wore pirate hats and waved plastic swords from their tree house.

Natalie put the memories aside and picked up the folded cardstock. Out of it slipped a square brown tag with a short message scribbled on it.

FOLLOW ME: LRRLRLLLRU

Unsure what the cryptic message was supposed to mean, Natalie put the note aside and unfolded the heavyweight paper. A filigree letterhead embossed the top quarter of the page with the familiar Coelacanth symbol etched in its center. Natalie traced the outline with her thumb as she read the document carefully.

The Coelacanth Project
October 6, 2005

It is with great enthusiasm and reverence that I formally welcome you to the Coelacanth Project. Although the world will never know of your sacrifice, I hope you find peace in the essence of our mission. The Coelacanth Project is a private program dedicated to the prevention of nuclear war and other catastrophic events through the service of five biochemically unique individuals.

These individuals, who will ultimately become global sentinels for peace, are equipped with additional cellular receptors. These exclusive receptors enable their bodies to interact with the special metal aurichalcum in a solid, concentrated form and in a dissolved ionic state in seawater. This interaction permits a conduction of charge that elevates the atoms that comprise their bodies to a higher state of excitement. The subsequent release of this energy allows them to transport the electricity and themselves from one place to another via a connection of seawater and driven intent.

As you well know, this power has vast potential for peacekeeping efforts in an era of growing global tension. However, we must also consider its capability for exploitation. I implore you to unite with your fellow Coelacanth associates and conserve the obscurity of our mission.

Your charges will be as follows:

Brant – Mr. Frederick Hutchinson and Ms. Nora Delacruz, henceforth known as Mr. Robert Smith and Mrs. Jennifer Smith.

Leonidas – Dr. Philip Kurr and Ms. Suzanne Sharpe, henceforth known as Mr. Michael Merrick and Mrs. Elizabeth Merrick.

Natalie A. – Mr. Benjamin Shepard and Dr. Madison Finch, henceforth known as Mr. John Morrigan and Mrs. Mary Morrigan.

Owen – Dr. Caleb Randolph and Ms. Avery Kinney, henceforth known as Mr. Thomas Johnson and Mrs. Margaret Johnson.

Tawney – Mr. Wyatt Barnett and Ms. Natasha Morin, henceforth known as Mr. Samuel Davis and Mrs. Patricia Davis.

Let us embark on this grand adventure together and secure a peaceful future for humanity.

I am forever indebted to your service and your sacrifice.

Christopher E. Reyes

Executive Director
Coelacanth Project

Natalie couldn't breathe. She threw off the blanket and read the document again in the full radiance of the moon.

No. That's not possible.

She dug out the last Polaroid she had seen of her and her parents outside their home. She flipped the photograph over and read the inscription signed on the back.

Welcome Home Natalie.

She crumpled the photograph in her fist and threw it at the door to her cell.

No, no, no!

Natalie dragged her thin bedding off the cot and tossed it across the room. The envelopes scattered along the floor. She tried to form a coherent thought.

Question everything.

She didn't want to believe it. She shook her head, working through the details.

It cannot be real. Adopted? No. My parents are my parents.

The more she thought, the more she panicked. It made too much sense.

No parent would allow a group of radical scientists to touch their child.

The clock high on the wall above her ticked away the seconds. Tick-tock, tick-tock.

But I wasn't theirs.

Black spots clouded her vision. She doubled over next to the cot, gasping for air. No matter how much she inhaled, it wasn't enough. She was suffocating.

I'm not theirs.

Cold sweat beaded on her neck. She hit the wall with her fist.

Mutate her, change her, sacrifice her.

Natalie let out a guttural scream that threatened to rip apart her throat.

Lies. All lies. My entire life.

Adopted. I'm ADOPTED. My parents aren't my parents; I don't even know their real names. I don't know my name.

"Chef?" Natalie yelled.

No answer. Her head was spinning.

My entire life has been a lie. I don't know those people. Who are they?
"Chef!"
Who am I? Where am I from?

The room swayed beneath her feet as she picked up the damning documents and envelopes from the floor.

If they aren't my parents, who is? Question everything. Do I even have parents? Maybe we were made in test tubes.

"Chef, are you there?" Natalie leaned her head against the wall above the panel. The room was spinning around her, forming a nauseating blur of grey. "Is this true?"

Silence.

Natalie was sick of silence.

"Is this true?" Natalie yelled, her voice cracking.

She pounded on the wall with her fists, screaming for Chef. "IS IT TRUE? ANSWER ME!"

"Go," a voice commanded beyond the wall.

Natalie choked back her tears. Surely, she imagined the response. No one had ever answered her before. Nothing lived beyond the wall.

"Follow me," the voice whispered.

Natalie had been so distraught she failed to notice the door to her cell had opened. The pitch-black of the unknown awaited her.

She shoved the document and envelopes into her jacket and hastily wiped her cheeks.

FOLLOW ME: LRRLRLLLRU.

It has to be the way out.

"Thank you, Chef," she breathed before rushing into the darkness.

CHAPTER 29:
NAUTILUS
CHAMBERS

A *dopted.*
Natalie moved quickly through the black passageways.

I don't even know my last name. Just an 'A.' Anonymous? Anyone? Alone? No one would genetically manipulate children with a home, children who were loved. No parent would do that.

She struggled to force all thoughts of the strangers who raised her out of her mind.

Focus.

LRRLRLLLRU.

She repeated the directions over and over, drowning out any other thought. She traced along the wall beside her and finally found open air.

Left.

She took the adjacent tunnel, pushing herself to go faster.

How could they?

Her thoughts drifted uncontrollably back to the Coelacanth document. Her right hand bumped across the uneven cracks in the stone wall until it slipped into nothing.

Right.

Natalie rounded the corner and collided with something solid and warm. There was a tangle of legs and arms as she kicked furiously to get away. Images of the burly and bruised Rankin overwhelmed her.

No, no, no!

To her surprise, her attacker retreated as quickly as she did.

"Ow!" he squealed as one of her random kicks found its mark.

"Owen?" Natalie questioned hesitantly.

"Nat?" Owen sounded as relieved as she felt. "That hurt!"

"Sorry," Natalie crouched next to her friend. "You got directions out?"

"Yeah, a few minutes ago. Then the door to my cell opened and the red beacons never came on so I made a run for it."

"That means we all probably got them," Natalie's pulse quickened.

We might actually get out of here.

"Did you get anything else?" Natalie tried to sound casual.

"No, why? Did you?"

"No," Natalie answered hastily, her cheeks burning. "Actually, yes." Remembering the sparks in her jacket, she removed one and passed it to Owen.

"Here's hoping we're close to the water."

Natalie pulled Owen to his feet. He kept hold of her jacket as she hurried through the passageway. Again, her fingers left cold stone for open air.

Right.

She pushed herself into a run for a few paces at a time, but her mind refused to trust her blind movements.

Left.

She caught a faint whisper ahead of them and stopped. Owen collided into her and his glasses clattered to the floor. He muttered in irritation as he crawled around by her feet. The whispering stopped, but Natalie was certain she had heard it.

She ran through the options quickly in her head. Either it was Nautilus or it was one of her friends. Fifty-fifty shot. Considering they were running around in the gloom, trusting some sketchy instructions, possibly from Nautilus itself…

"So are we going to get out of here or twiddle our thumbs until they realize we're gone?"

Natalie grinned.

"Ladies first."

"Ha, you're funny, Nat. Or do you prefer 'Seashell Princess' now?" Tawney spat bitterly.

Natalie's smile fell.

"I was doing that to—"

"Later," Leo's voice sounded from the other side of the passage.

Leo.

Natalie didn't let herself entertain the consequences. She strode through the unlit tunnel, eliminating the distance between them. Her hands found his chest and then he was everywhere, surrounding her. He wrapped an arm around her waist as he tilted her face up to meet his. His lips touched hers gently at first, until Natalie pulled on his shirt, and then he kissed her harder, ravenous.

Leo broke away and rested his forehead on hers. His fingers traced the curve of her cheek, leaving fire in their wake. An iron weight settled in her stomach: heavy and toxic. Their kiss had done more than unite them. It burdened her with hope.

"That's four of us," Owen sounded off in the darkness somewhere next to them. "Where's Brant?"

"Seashell Princess Junior? He's probably being made an

honorary Nautilus Sister as we speak," Tawney snapped.

"I'm right here," Brant announced from somewhere in the darkness. "I didn't see any other choice."

"There's always a choice."

"You with me?" Natalie whispered to Leo.

"I'm with you."

A blaring alarm echoed throughout the tunnels, silencing her friends' argument.

Time's up.

"Let's go," Natalie yelled over the alarm. She barreled down the passageway, tripping and bumping into her friends in the shadows.

Right.

She was in a full out run. Someone stumbled beside her and she pulled them up, hardly missing a step.

Left.

Red beacons pulsated from the ground beneath their feet, bathing the tunnels crimson before drowning them in absolute darkness. It was more off-putting than running through the black passages.

Left.

Every time the lanterns came on Natalie was sure Nautilus would be there, waiting for her to run right into their grasp.

Left.

The alarm shut off but Natalie did not slow. Her footsteps boomed in the residual silence. Her fingers found open air.

Right.

Natalie ran until she came to the end of the passageway. There were no more turns; it was a dead end.

"U," Leo was illuminated by the red glow. He gingerly rubbed his left arm. "Under? Up?"

He stomped on the dirt floor while Owen and Tawney explored the walls. Brant watched the passageway they had come through. As the next red glow came from the floor, Natalie investigated the ceiling. Even at its brightest, she couldn't visualize the top of the tunnel.

"Lift me," she said to Leo.

"I'm smaller," Tawney volunteered herself.

"Sorry, Tawney, we need height," Leo said, following Natalie's gaze towards the ceiling.

Leo gripped Natalie's waist and, in one swift motion, her feet left the ground. She reached up the wall beyond the red light. Her fingertips grazed over cold stone and dirt. She dug into every crevice for something, anything. Slick metal passed under her fingers and she latched onto it. A rung about the width of her shoulders was hidden against the wall. Natalie grabbed on tight and pulled. It barely moved an inch.

"We're out of time," Brant announced from the corner.

Natalie yanked on the rough bar, gaining another inch.

"We have to go," Brant said, retreating into the passage.

"Let go," Natalie called to Leo.

"What?"

"Let me go!"

Leo released her hips and her entire weight hung from the bar. It creaked for a heart-wrenching second before it finally gave way. Natalie was falling, the ground rushing up to meet her.

"I've got you," Leo slowed her descent and they tumbled into the dirt.

A silver ladder hung from the obscured ceiling. Natalie scrambled to her feet and started to climb. Owen's words hung ominously in her mind.

Here's hoping we're near the water. If we aren't beside the ocean, we won't stand a chance.

Her head slammed against the ceiling. Natalie recoiled and rubbed her throbbing skull. Reaching above her, she found a circular handle.

It's a hatch, she realized, attempting to turn the lever. It didn't budge.

"What's the hold up, Nat?" Leo was directly beneath her.

Anxiety leaked into his voice.

"Switch," Natalie instructed. She leaned entirely to the left side of the ladder and allowed Leo to squeeze past her.

The lever screeched in protest, but Leo won out. He pushed the hatch door outwards and silvery moonbeams poured in. Leo vanished beyond the door and Natalie climbed out behind him.

A frigid breeze whipped her hair as she emerged into the night. She hugged herself tightly, her back to the wind. The sheer number of stars shining above Natalie captivated her. Lacking the pollution of street and city lights, they illuminated the night. An unmarked, low-lying building stood a few hundred feet to their left in the middle of a frostbitten wasteland. Knee-high peaks of snow and ice stretched as far as Natalie could see. Green and purple ribbons swirled beneath the stars far above her. Despite its chill, the breeze carried a welcomed sound.

"Waves," Natalie chattered in relief.

As Owen emerged from the hatch, Leo rounded on Natalie. He barely seemed to register the cold. His left arm stayed tucked tight against his abdomen, still sore from his encounter with Enzi's teeth.

"You were brilliant," he told her. "Your performance in the white room, the slow blink. Perfect."

"You remembered," Natalie shivered as she passed him a spark from her pocket. "Ten minutes ago, the fastest way out was for Nautilus to trust us. There wasn't a chance in hell of fighting our way out, so," Natalie shrugged. "Think your way out."

"Brilliant," he squeezed her hand tight in his. Warmth flowed from him. She welcomed his touch and the heat it brought.

Brant clambered out of the hatch and Leo pulled away.

"Thank you," Natalie finally replied to Leo's compliment while passing Brant his spark.

"You're welcome?" Brant put the stone bracelet on his

wrist.

"What are y'all waitin' for?" A round mound hustled towards them from the eternal twilight haze. He was bundled in so many jackets and scarves, Natalie only recognized him by the sound of his voice.

She ran to meet Uncle Chris. She threw her arms around his wide waist and buried her face in one of the plush scarves.

"Is it true?" Natalie breathed into the fabric.

"Not now," Christopher patted her on the back. "We've got to move, kid." He gently pushed her away and held a photograph out to all of them. "Focus. Commit it to memory. This is where we're goin'."

Natalie studied the building, the curves of its walls, its beacon.

Ancora III.

Uncle Chris folded away the photo and started stripping off his layers of coats, passing one to each of them. Natalie donned hers instantly, grateful for the additional barrier against the chill. Christopher proceeded to produce a handful of pistols from beneath his many layers. Natalie grimaced as he forced her to take one.

"I knew you would get us out," Owen took the gun from Christopher.

"Wasn't me," he admitted.

Natalie pinched the weapon between her thumb and forefinger. The steel was freezing cold against her bare skin. A warm touch nudged her arm and took the gun from her. Brant gave her a swift wink as he pocketed the weapon. She nodded in thanks.

Christopher waved a pistol about as he assessed their modest group.

"Oy! Where's—"

An ear-piercing scream echoed from beneath their feet. A flash of red and navy blurred past Natalie as Owen made for the hatch.

Tawney!

She ran after Owen and peered into the depths of the tunnel. Two Nautilus followers fought to pull Tawney off the ladder. She clung to the rungs with her body intertwined in the metal.

Christopher roughly pushed Owen out of the way and aimed his pistol into the hatch. Owen hit the frozen ground hard, but was up in a second. He shoved Brant square in the chest.

"Why didn't you send her up first?"

"They were closing in on us," Brant argued.

"So you left her behind?" Leo shook his head, disappointed. "Don't be a coward."

Brant flinched.

"I did exactly what Nat did," Brant pointed at her. "You aren't calling her a coward."

"Nat was being clever. You were only trying to save yourself."

Natalie barely heard them arguing. Tawney peeked up at the barrel of the gun and screamed again.

"Duck," Christopher told her.

Natalie stared in horror as he fired off two quick rounds.

One of Tawney's assailants fell away from her and did not get up. The other reached under Tawney and propelled her upwards. Christopher caught her arm and pulled her out of the tunnel. Tawney laid on the ground where he left her.

"Damn you, Christopher," she gasped.

Natalie helped her friend to her feet and embraced her.

"I didn't mean what I said," Tawney whispered to her.

Natalie passed Tawney her spark as Uncle Chris gave her a fluffy pink jacket.

"It's alright," Natalie assured her.

A tall Nautilus woman with dark skin and glossy purple lipstick emerged from the hatch. She had one of the long Nautilus bolts strung across her back. Brant made to punch her, but Christopher caught his arm.

"Watch it, kid. Good help is hard to find."

"Cutting it a little close, Reyes," the newcomer chided, shutting the hatch behind her.

Christopher snorted.

"I made it, didn't I?"

"Chef?" Natalie blurted.

The woman winked at her and pulled Natalie into a tight embrace. Natalie clung to her. Chef was real; she had been in the winding tunnels with her and not just a figure in Natalie's imagination. The envelope poked Natalie beneath her jacket. Its secrets burned into her skin.

"It was time you knew," Chef whispered to her.

"Is it true?" Natalie breathed into Chef's shoulder.

"Safety first, then we'll talk," Chef guided Natalie out to arm's length.

"We need to move," Christopher gave Tawney his own pistol and produced another from his pocket for himself.

"Any snacks in there?" Brant asked, half-joking, half-hopeful.

"Short trek across the tundra," the woman nodded towards their right. "Let's hustle." Chef removed the shaft from her back and gave it to Natalie. "I heard you kicked some Nautilus ass with a bolt a few days ago. I also heard you won't use a gun."

"You ditched the pistol already?"

Natalie shrugged in apology to Christopher before hesitantly taking the bolt from Chef. The rod was thin enough for her to close her fist around it, but it was heavier than it appeared. Silver bands capped either end of the textured black metal.

"This is a Nautilus weapon," Natalie said.

"So was I, once." Chef strapped the bolt across Natalie's back. "You have to rotate it to generate a charge. I'll teach you how to use it in Ancora."

Something slammed hard against the inside of the hatch.

"That won't hold them long," Chef nodded towards Christopher. "Your move, Reyes."

"Let's disappear."

CHAPTER 30

Christopher gestured across the field of snow and ice. Despite the wide-open space, the dim light made it difficult to see very far.

"Don't stop when you reach the cliff. Just go. We'll meet in Ancora."

Natalie ran across the tundra. Her breath flowed behind her in icy clouds and the frozen ground crunched beneath her shoes. Brant and Owen ran ahead of her, and Tawney sprinted to catch up with them. She beamed as she passed Natalie.

"It's so good to move!"

Natalie followed her past the first few uneven mounds of ice. Barely a hundred paces away from the hatch Natalie was forced to slow to a winding shuffle. The ground was slippery and littered with craters impossible to see in the starlight. She nearly fell flat out more than once. Her heart fluttered in her chest, willing her to move faster, but it was impossible.

"Argh!" Christopher flailed as he sank ankle deep into a hole in the snow. "Bloody hollows," he scoffed.

"Are we—"

A vicious snarling far behind them, followed by a short-lived scream, cut off Natalie's question. She looked back to the hatch, but it had been swallowed up by the blue twilight haze.

"They're already out of the tunnels," Chef announced, pulling a pistol from her belt. "Get to the cliff. I'll cover you."

Christopher pushed Natalie and Leo forward.

"Go!"

She ran the best she could. The icy wind stabbed into her lungs. Natalie followed on Tawney's heels, but she was able to leap over mounds and divots that Natalie had to slow for.

A white blur passed on her right and came to keep pace with her. Pink tongue flapping in the wind, Enzi leapt across a small trench in the ice. Beside him Angie sprinted, ears flat against her head.

"You brought the dogs?" Natalie yelled to Uncle Chris.

"Couldn't exactly...get a...pet sitter," he huffed back to her, struggling to keep up.

Natalie sprinted across a particularly flat expanse of ice and nearly toppled right over the cliff. Brant pulled her back by the fabric of her jacket.

"Did you forget?" he gasped, catching his breath. "You tack, not fly."

"Thanks for reminding me," her chest heaved.

The ground dropped straight down beneath them, littered with large, jutting rocks. Far below them, white-capped waves crashed against the cliff. Angie darted in and out between their legs while Enzi stood, hackles raised, facing the hazy horizon.

"We're dead," Brant announced.

"Let's just jump," Tawney said, making to do just that.

Owen pulled her roughly back.

"We're really far south, Tawney," his teeth chattered. "Incredibly far south."

"Yeah, so? Christopher and Chef-lady said to jump."

Shouts echoed from beyond the small clearing of ice they

could see clearly. Brant, Owen, Leo, and Tawney lifted their weapons towards the dense twilight fog. Natalie pulled the bolt off her back and held it awkwardly in front of her.

Chef emerged into their patch of ice first. She backed towards them with her gun high, covering Christopher who jogged to join them.

"Jump!" Chef yelled to them.

"We could die!" Owen argued.

"Better the chance than the guarantee," Uncle Chris countered.

Natalie exchanged hesitant glances with her friends. The water was a long way down.

A man in a sable suit emerged from the obscure winter field, his arms up in surrender. His polished black shoes and silver cufflinks reflected the starlight.

"Children," Amir Amani greeted them, shaking his head. "Why do you run from us? We offer you the world. And you," he frowned at Chef, "turning weapons on your family. It is against our teachings. What will our Ward say?"

Chef pointed her gun steadily at Amir. Her gaze shifted from him to the depths of the twilight. The occasional navy blur and crunch of ice gave them away: Nautilus hid in the shadows.

"You should know children, before you go any further, that your actions affect more than your own fate."

It was odd. The wind blew frigid cold, but Natalie noticed sweat glistening on Amir's brow.

"I want you to come to us as Nautilus welcomes you: with open hearts and minds. But I cannot lose—" Amir stopped himself. His voice had cracked, along with his perfectly composed veneer.

For a moment, Natalie glimpsed the Amir Amani beneath the velvet voice and ironed suit.

He speaks for Nautilus, but this is personal.

"Nautilus does not react kindly to those who dishonor their

promises," Amir was himself again. His delicate voice camouflaged the threats beneath his words. "The dishonest and disloyal are not conducive for peace."

"No promises were made to you," Leo said bluntly.

"By adorning those uniforms, you made a symbolic promise to join our cause. Ms. Morrigan and Mr. Smith both built on that symbolism with voiced words of commitment. However," Amir gestured someone forward out of the cover of the darkness. "We do appreciate how difficult this must be for you to choose between the misguided teachings of your blasphemous uncle and the rightful path of peace. It can be hard to deviate from the guidance of your parents, no matter how wrongful their path may be. So, let us make it simple!"

A man stumbled forward to join Amir. His clothing had been torn in several places and his shirt, possibly white at one point in time, had been stained red and brown. His wrists were bound and a mixture of dirt and blood caked his face. Regardless, Natalie knew him instantly.

Chef's aim faltered for a moment. She shared an anxious glance with Christopher.

"Dad?" Brant stepped forward, but Tawney stopped him.

"Your parents so bravely tried to stop us from taking you in the marina. Yet they fail to realize their efforts simply extinguish your true potential. Join us now and there will be peace for you and your family."

"Nautilus won't touch them," Owen muttered. "It makes more sense to keep them as motivation for us."

Natalie had a gut feeling and made a split decision to run with it.

"What will the Ward do to you if we fail to concede?"

Amir maintained his smile, but it was rigid and forced. Brant's father tore his gaze away from his son and focused on Amir, apparently interested in his answer.

"The Ward is the physical embodiment of all Nautilus aims to achieve. Forgiveness is a cornerstone of peace. You should concern yourself more with the safety of your loved ones. Run and they will die," Amir announced. "They exist merely to ensure your cooperation."

Amir pulled a gun from his jacket and pressed the barrel to Mr. Smith's forehead. Mr. Smith did not struggle or protest; he simply stared up at the starry sky.

"No! No, don't hurt him," Brant's gun fell to the snow as he fought feebly to escape Tawney's grasp.

"Good lad. Now convince your comrades."

"No, Brant, we can't go with them. We'll never escape again," Leo held his friend back.

"I can't do this again!" Brant screamed at him. "You don't know! I can't, I can't do it." Tears sparkled on his cheeks.

"Nautilus has all of your parents," Amir chimed in. "Brant would not be alone in his loss if you choose to make your induction more difficult than necessary."

Natalie clung to the document hidden beneath her jacket. *Mom and Dad…*

But they're not Mom and Dad, not really.

They lied. They lied my entire life.

"Go ahead," Natalie said firmly to Amir. "Kill them and you kill any chance of us working for Nautilus. You kill any chance to free yourself from whatever the Ward has on you. Now, we will give you one chance, Mr. Amani. Release them."

"What are you doing?" Brant cried.

"He could actually kill them," Tawney whispered, her gun slack at her side.

Are we still going to risk our lives to save parents who aren't our parents? Natalie shook the question from her mind.

Amir stared at Natalie, the corner of his mouth twitching.

"He won't," Natalie said to assure her friends as much as herself. "He won't kill them."

Get desperate, Amir. Make a mistake.

"You possess nothing to bargain with Ms. Morrigan," Amir smirked, but his voice had fallen. "We have your parents and unlike them, unlike yourself, Nautilus keeps its promises. We will eliminate those who impede our efforts to achieve peace. I promise you that."

He swiftly pointed his gun to Chef and fired without hesitation. She dropped in a heap before them and did not move.

Natalie screamed and covered her mouth.

Before she could do anything else, Christopher shoved her hard towards the cliff. Natalie stumbled and fell backwards into her friends. Owen and Tawney screamed as they toppled over the edge towards the water below.

Amir Amani let go of Brant's father, who fell to his knees, and marched towards them. Brant made to run towards his dad, but Leo pulled him towards the cliff. Amir fired his weapon again and Uncle Chris cried out, clutching his leg. He tried to move towards them and stumbled, unable to stand.

Natalie seized one of Christopher's arms and began dragging him towards the cliff. Leo took the other and together they pulled faster. Enzi took the hood of his coat between his jaws and dug his paws into the frozen snow.

"Brant!" Leo cried out.

Brant glanced from his father to Uncle Christopher, distraught.

"We can't help him if we stay here, Brant," Natalie tried to make him see reason. "We can't help any of them inside those walls. We have to go."

Brant gazed towards his father again.

"We'll free them." It wasn't until Natalie said it that she realized she meant it.

They gave up their lives for us.

Mr. Smith gave the subtlest of nods.

They would do it again.

Brant spun and hurried back to them. He clutched the same arm Natalie held and pulled. Amir fired his gun again and a patch of ice erupted a few feet from Christopher's chest.

"Do this, girl, and I will destroy everything you hold dear. I will make you suffer as I have suffered. I will do whatever it takes to secure your allegiance to Nautilus." Amir advanced, his gun fixed on Christopher.

Natalie let go of Christopher's arm and pulled the bolt off her back. She swung the metal rod above her head and slammed the edge against Amir's wrist, knocking his gun to the ground. Without stopping, she spun the shaft around and propelled the entire weight of her body as she hit the back of his knees and sent Amir sprawling.

Natalie stood over him, the bolt a sparkless threat in his face.

"You don't know how to use that, girl," he snarled at her, his mask of kindness shattered.

"You will stop hunting my family. You will not touch them. You will not touch us. You will not control us. Ever."

The ice across the clearing crackled as new and familiar Nautilus members slowly made their way across the ice sheet. Their bolts sparked brightly through the darkness, illuminating many raised guns amongst them. Tanaka sneered as he deftly rotated his bolt on either side of his body. Rankin edged closer behind Eleanor. The old woman frowned and dragged a bolt alongside her in the snow.

"We're leaving," Natalie focused again on Amir. "Free our parents before you're forced to."

"You have no power against me."

"I gave you an out," Natalie hissed. "You were too cowardly to take it."

Natalie shoved off him and resumed her place at Christopher's side.

The Nautilus followers with handguns opened fire and bullets cascaded around Natalie. The frozen ground exploded around her feet as Amir screamed for his people to stop.

"If the children die, the Ward will have your life for it!" Amir crawled for his own gun. He made to take aim at Christopher again, but it was too late.

Natalie had reached the edge of the cliff. She didn't check

behind her; she preferred not to visualize the scattered rocks and possible death waiting far below. She scooped Angie off the ground and stuck her into Uncle Christopher's coat. The ice gave way beneath her right heel.

"Nautilus will find you," Amir screamed. His neatly gelled hair stuck out at odd angles. "I will find you. I swear it. When the Ward is done, you will die for this! I will squeeze the life from you myself."

Natalie gave a final tug on Christopher. The last thing she saw was Chef's body lying lifeless on the ice before gravity swept her away. Enzi jumped off the cliff beside her. Natalie screamed until she was out of breath. The wind whipped her hair and she toppled wildly, unable to right herself. She tried to draw in fresh air but the wind stole it away. She forced herself to visualize the photograph Christopher had shown her. The water, the curved building, the beacon.

Focus.

Gunshots seemed to erupt from all around her. It didn't make sense.

Focus.

Someone near her yelled.

Leo? Focus!

Natalie hit the water hard. The air was forced from her lungs. She slipped beneath the waves and the frigid water consumed her. The cold was everywhere. She should not have touched the water. She should not have perceived the cold.

Panicked, Natalie felt her wrist for her spark. Her fingers were numb and clumsy, but it was there.

Something is wrong.

CHAPTER 31

Natalie spun blindly in the water, unable to tell which way was up. Any movement might take her closer to air or closer to drowning. Gravity was gone and the world inverted.

I'm going to drown.

Natalie forced herself to stop moving. She allowed the water to orient her on its own. After an eternity, she consistently drifted in one direction. Desperately resisting the signals her lungs were sending her brain to breathe, Natalie trusted the drift.

Please lead to air.

She swam, but the cold was paralyzing.

I'm not going to make it.

Her head broke the surface and the wind stole what little heat she had left. Natalie drew in a deep, piercing breath. Enzi paddled on her immediate right, fighting the onslaught of waves threatening to push them both against large rocks they had miraculously missed.

Natalie rose with the swells, searching for her friends at every peak and using the troughs to swim for a meager spit of shore. Enzi whined and kept at her side. Her teeth chattered uncontrollably, making it even harder to see clearly. A black blob materialized and paddled along next to Enzi. As the two dogs neared the shore, Enzi scruffed Angie in his mouth and carried her to the base of the cliff. Between her and the dogs, Natalie spotted a large mass bobbing with the waves.

Finally.

She made for the figure and Enzi dove back in.

"N-n-n-," she tried to tell him 'no' but it was useless. He was already paddling towards her. She reached the floating body and took hold of a puffy winter coat.

Uncle Chris.

Unable to grip anything with her frozen fingers, Natalie linked her arm with his and kicked steadily for shore. Enzi took part of his coat in his mouth and swam hard. The waves worked with them, pushing them towards the base of the cliff. A groan sounded from the floating pile of fluff.

Alive, was the sole coherent thought Natalie could manage.

Her legs rebounded off something in the water when she kicked. Rocks scraped against the front of her jacket.

Land.

She crawled forward. Angie sat ahead of her, trembling. Her long black fur hung soaking wet around her paws. Natalie collapsed onto her back, nearly convulsing she was shivering so hard. Uncle Christopher was unusually still next to her. Brilliant ribbons of green and purple flickered across the sky.

Northern lights, Natalie noted. Her toes felt oddly warm, the first sign of her body starting to shut down. Natalie observed the auroras dancing above her, feeling the numbness spread to her ankles. Her mind would make-believe she was comfortable before death took her. It was a great kindness evolved by nature, a final parting gift. Shadows crept into her peripheral vision.

Northern lights? No...southern lights...

Damn.

Enzi's big blue eyes stared at her. Natalie forced herself onto her hands and knees and dragged Christopher back towards the water. Enzi cocked his head at her and backed away to sit with Angie.

The water lifted Natalie off the shore. She pushed Christopher ahead of her, kicking hard, pushing all thoughts out of her mind.

Kick, kick, kick, kick, kick.

When Enzi became small behind her she tried to call for him, but nothing came out. She tried to whistle, but her chattering teeth would not allow her to make any form out of her lips. Desperate, she lifted one of her arms and slapped it flat out against the top of the water, making a loud smack. Needles stabbed into her skin, but it did the trick.

Enzi scooped Angie into his mouth again and trudged back into the water.

To trudge, Natalie giggled, nearly delirious. Her mind slipped back to the colorful street in Spain. The dancing, the warmth...it felt like a dream. A paw fell roughly across her face and Natalie realized in horror she had lost consciousness.

Recognizing her time was limited, Natalie took a deep breath and sank beneath the waves. She pulled Christopher behind her, swimming as hard as she could. Her free hand fumbled blindly behind her until she bumped something soft and furry. Natalie looped her arm around Enzi's neck and kicked.

And kicked.

And kicked.

Pressure built in her ears. Her limbs were so numb she couldn't tell if her feet were moving. Natalie felt a rush of water as she was suddenly forced downward. Her arms and legs drifted uselessly behind her. A tingling tickled her.

Dead.

It grew stronger. A white light shone from beyond her eyelids.

EXTANT

Focus...focus.

A new force commanded her. It was stronger than the buoyancy of the water. She was no longer floating, she was weightless. The glowing light flashed and dissipated as swiftly as gravity returned. Natalie slammed into the sand and a warm breeze greeted her. She gasped for air and laid flat out on the beach. Her body trembled to warm itself despite the summer air surrounding her.

Natalie crawled to Uncle Chris and shook him. Beneath the fluffy jackets, he laid still, his eyes closed. She shook him harder. Still no response. Natalie kneed the layers of coats hard.

The mound of jackets rose with a heavy sigh.

Alive.

Enzi circled her, Angie still scruffed in his mouth. He dropped the miniature dog into her lap. She was shaking, but not getting up. Natalie petted Enzi's head and clutched Angie close to her.

Find help.

Her thoughts were quickly becoming clearer. A tingling much different from tacking spread through her. Feeling was returning to her fingers and toes.

This is going to hurt, she knew.

Natalie scanned the beach. The rising sun cast a golden glow on the water and the hotels lining the coast. Two women emerged from the Barclay Towers Hotel on her left. Each had their hair tied back and sneakers laced up for an early morning run on the boardwalk. Natalie tried to wave to them, but collapsed back into the sand.

"Help," she croaked.

Christopher coughed violently next to her. Natalie attempted to roll him onto his side, but he was too bulky. She settled for tilting his head as he expelled mouthfuls of ocean water. Blood stained the sand burgundy around his leg.

"Are you alright?"

Having seen her frantic waving or heard Christopher vomiting, the two women approached. The younger of the two stayed far back, her nose wrinkled suspiciously, while the older one knelt next to Natalie.

Mother, Natalie figured. A pang of sadness hit her chest.

Enzi slathered the new arrival to their group with kisses. The woman gently shouldered him away and touched Christopher's puffy winter coat with suspicion. Natalie didn't blame her. The entire scene was bizarre.

"Ph-phone?" Natalie asked.

The jogger produced a smartphone from her pocket and tried to pass it to Natalie. She fumbled with the device. Her fingers trembled so badly, Natalie gave the phone back.

"9-1-1," Natalie requested. "F-for my uncle."

The woman dialed and spoke to the operator. A seed of guilt planted itself in Natalie's mind. She was so kind. Shallow lines on her cheeks revealed the remnants of a frequent smile and a simple necklace with a dolphin charm swung around her neck.

"Yes, ma'am. My name is Kaela Verene; we are outside the Barclay Towers. Ah, he's middle-aged, barely conscious, cold to the touch, and—"

"Shot," Natalie interrupted, pointing to Christopher's leg.

"Has a recent gunshot wound," Mrs. Verene repeated into the phone. Her eyebrows drew together in concern. "There's also a little dog, she isn't moving," the woman shook her head to something the operator said over the line. "Yes, I understand the dog is not priority—yes, alright we can apply pressure to the wound."

Mrs. Verene removed her pink running jacket and pressed it firmly onto Uncle Christopher's leg. He groaned in protest.

She'll care for him. She had literally given him the clothes off her back.

Forgive me, Mrs. Verene.

"Sent-t-tara of Virginia B-beach?" Natalie confirmed with Mrs. Verene. Her uncontrollable shivering made her stutter.

She nodded, listening to the operator on the line.

Natalie rested her hand on Uncle Christopher's shoulder.

"R-rest, hydrate, m-m-medicate," she repeated the instructions he had given Leo after his bite wound. "I'll come b-back," Natalie promised him. She repeated the promise to Mrs. Verene.

I can't be here when the EMT's arrive. Too many questions. I couldn't even give his real name; he's still a wanted man.

"What do you mean?" Mrs. Verene asked. "You're in shock, sweetie. You should sit. Nora, can you sit with her?"

Nora, who appeared to be around Natalie's age, shook her auburn ponytail and did not budge.

"Take care of him," Natalie begged. She cradled Angie in her arms as she backed towards the crashing ocean waves. "I'll be back."

"Miss, we'll take care of you," Mrs. Verene pressed the phone to her ear with her shoulder. "Besides, you've nowhere to go right now."

"What's that?" Natalie faked concern and pointed towards the hotel.

Both Kaela Verene and her daughter Nora turned to look. While they faced away from her, Natalie took hold of Enzi's collar and stepped backwards into the shallow wave rolling up the sand.

I'll come back.

The curving walls, the beacon, the waves.

A white flash enveloped her and a weightlessness lifted her up. The pain of her body regaining feeling overpowered the usual tingling. An instant later, Natalie pulled herself onto a newly planked pier and a cylindrical, striped tower rose high above her.

CHAPTER 32

"What kept you?" Tawney crossed the short pier to meet Natalie beneath a covered boat slip.

Natalie swayed in the weak breeze. She struggled to stay standing.

"Woah there," Brant slipped his arm around Natalie's waist. Her feet lifted off the ground and she sank into his hold.

Enzi shook sand and salt water from his fur and pranced ahead of her. He led the way out of the boat slip and towards the towering lighthouse. Black and white stripes spiraled up its sides and a yellow beacon spun at its peak, warning approaching ships of its shallow surroundings.

Natalie rested her head on Brant's shoulder as he carried her up the pier and into Ancora III. The gentle rocking as he walked was comforting. It reminded her of summer boat rides with Christopher...she hoped there would be dolphins...that was always her favorite part...

Someone shook her.

"Hey! Stay awake!" Tawney snapped her fingers in front of

Natalie's nose.

"Yeah," Natalie croaked, wondering when she moved from Brant's arms to a chair. "I'm fine."

"Is she alive?" Tawney asked, peering at the lump of wet fur in Natalie's lap.

Natalie rubbed Angie's side. The dog laid still and drew slow, shallow breaths.

"Get her warm."

Tawney scooped Angie into a blanket and moved to a nearby fireplace. She worked on the dog, buffing her fur dry. Enzi settled himself in front of the flickering flames.

"Where are we?" Natalie asked. She examined the room to distract herself from the feeling her toes were on fire.

The room was not large. She sat at the end of a rough wooden table in a kitchenette. Grey tiles manufactured to resemble wooden planks covered the floor. A single overhead lamp dimly illuminated the rounded walls and futon couch across the room from where Natalie sat. A few square windows filtered in the rays of the rising sun. An iron spiral staircase rose upwards from the center of the room and faded into the ceiling.

Owen descended the stairs with a bag of ice pressed against his left eye.

"We aren't quite sure. I expect somewhere in the southern half of the North Atlantic based on sun positioning."

"What took you so long?" Tawney asked, focused on her work.

"Christopher was shot; he needed a hospital. I found someone to help him," Natalie rested her head against the back of the chair and squeezed her eyes shut to block out the pain of the numbness receding. "I didn't think to dive."

Tawney huffed.

"Me neither. Thought he was drowning me!"

Natalie squinted through her eyelashes as Owen pulled the ice pack away from his face. An ugly black bruise bloomed around his left eye.

"Ice melt is fresh and floats on top of the salt water. It's less dense. That's why I didn't want to jump in the first place. We can't tack in fresh water."

"Details," Tawney rotated Angie and started drying her other side.

"Life-threatening details."

"So," Brant interrupted. "Leo stayed with Christopher then?"

Natalie's eyes flew open. Brant was busy drying Enzi with a towel.

"What?"

Dumbfounded faces stared back at her. Angie whimpered.

"Leo isn't here?" Natalie asked. Her head spun. "You're certain?"

"We thought he was with you," Tawney whispered, all color drained from her face.

Natalie stood. Her thawing feet burned as though she walked on hot coals.

"Nat," Brant blocked her path. "Nat, let's be rational."

"Enzi, stay," Natalie ordered as she lumbered back through the arched doorway and out under the morning sky.

"You can't go back!" Tawney yelled from the doorway.

"Do you suggest I leave him?"

"Please, consider what we're saying," Owen said gently, placing his glasses back on his nose.

"Nat," Brant called for her.

Nearly at the empty, covered boat slip, she ignored him. She made to march straight off the pier's edge, but Brant seized her arm. He spun her around to meet him.

"You're not leaving," he insisted. "You'll die."

"Let go."

"You could drown, or be shot, or freeze to death. It's suicide," Brant pleaded with her.

"Thanks for that delightful image. Let go."

Brant pulled hard on Natalie's arm in an attempt to get her back to the lighthouse.

Frustrated at losing precious time, Natalie swung the bolt off her back and slammed it flat against the back of Brant's knees. He faltered and let go of her bicep.

Natalie stepped off the pier. The now familiar brilliance consumed her and she took a deep breath. She envisioned the base of the cliff, the frigid white-capped waves crashing against the black rocks, the tiny sheltered shore, Leo and Uncle Chris and Brant and the dogs all leaping desperately from the cliff, all falling with her…

I have to get back there.

Images of Leo slipping beneath the waves clouded her thoughts. She imagined him wounded and unable to swim. She imagined him not understanding why he couldn't tack, not swimming beneath the layer of fresh water.

I have to get back there.

A moment later, the light dissipated and black, freezing cold water engulfed her. The shock stole the air from her lungs. Somehow, it seemed colder than before. She reached high above her for open air.

Breaking the surface, her fingertips met a frosty gust of wind. Natalie braced herself. Her head emerged from the sea and the cold was crushing. She gasped and struggled to take another breath. Her body had already begun to tremble. She maybe had minutes to search for Leo.

Large waves moved her up and down from crest to trough, giving her fleeting glimpses at her surroundings. Moonbeams threw harsh shadows and the green and purple auroras shifted across the sky. She had risen among a cluster of large protruding rocks with the cliff nearly twenty yards ahead of her.

Above the noise of the surf, Natalie heard gunshots. She kicked to one of the larger boulders and struggled to grip its slick surface without being able to feel her fingertips. Unable to get a good hold, Natalie resorted to pressing her entire body against the rock.

What are they shooting at now? Natalie wondered. *Maybe they can see Leo?*

She chewed her lip anxiously. If they saw Leo, they would catch her trying to get to him.

A few more gunshots sounded, followed by a scream and a splash somewhere between her hiding place and the cliff. Natalie peeked around the rock and saw a floating mass near the cliff, along with a smaller one, and something gleaming white in the moonlight.

That...can't be.

Natalie moved out from behind the rock to see more clearly. There was no doubt. Enzi was paddling quickly towards the larger of the two masses, which had to be—

Christopher! And that...that's me!

Natalie swam back behind the boulder and put her head against the stone while her heart tried to beat clear out of her chest. She couldn't tell if she trembled from shock or the cold.

That's me! This already happened!

Natalie stared at the spark around her left wrist.

This isn't possible.

Something Amir told her tickled the back of her brain.

Time is the most powerful weapon of all.

I traveled back in time.

She clung to the stone for dear life. It was sturdy and real and she didn't want to let go.

Maybe I'm unconscious. I'm dreaming.

A frigid wave swept her up and she fought to keep hold of her stone anchor. The freezing water stole her breath as it briefly submerged her face beneath it.

Not unconscious.

I traveled back in time.

This is why Nautilus wants us, how they plan to achieve peace. Tacking alone could never achieve that. It makes so much sense, yet no sense at all. Natalie gasped for air as the pieces started to fit together. *That's why our parents were angry.*

She remembered what Tawney's mother had said in their hideout.

'Christopher lied to us, but it was for you.'

He lied.

It was never about tacking, not really. We aren't meant to prevent war or conflict. We are meant to erase it.

Natalie peered around the rock again and saw the other Natalie was busy maneuvering the unresponsive Uncle Chris towards shore.

I traveled back in time. She repeated it over and over in her mind, trying to make reality easier to swallow.

But how?

I didn't do anything differently.

Natalie convulsed so hard her head hit the boulder. She had forgotten the cold, but her body hadn't. She kicked out from her hiding place and began searching the cove for any sign of Leo. A faint glimmer shone from deep beneath the waves.

Brant. Natalie figured he must have reached the layer of salt water and tacked to the lighthouse.

This is actually perfect, Natalie realized. *It will be much easier to find Leo.*

Confident the darkness and surf provided enough concealment from past-Natalie, she swam around the cove in search of Leo. Natalie resisted the urge to call out for him. If Nautilus heard her, she would expose everyone.

What happens if past-me sees present-me?

Natalie pushed the thought away. It didn't matter. She had a thousand questions and none of them mattered.

I have to find him.

At the peak of each wave, she desperately scanned the water and at each trough, she kicked further into the center of the cove. She checked on the Natalie with Uncle Christopher. They had reached the shore. In a minute or two, past-Natalie would realize she must return to the water.

Despite her efforts, there was no sign of Leo. She couldn't

make out anything in the surrounding waves breaking the pattern of the surf. Her body began to convulse again. She had seconds left at best.

"Leo," Natalie whispered between chattering teeth. Desperate, she scanned the collection of rocks and the shore. She skimmed the top of the cliff, wondering if perhaps he had never jumped at all.

No, he was next to me.

Past-Natalie had returned to the water with Christopher in tow. Natalie watched as her past self sank beneath the waves and swam for the salt water below them.

"Leo!" Natalie no longer cared if Nautilus heard her. She was out of time. Her voice was swept away by the wind. She spun where she floated, her toes tingling painfully.

Nothing. There was no sign of him.

Natalie surveyed the murky water around her. No glow had risen from where past-Natalie had submerged.

Too long, Natalie thought. She remembered the pressure she had felt beneath the waves, forcing her deeper.

I'll come back, Natalie promised. *I'm with you.*

Natalie kicked to where her past self had descended and dove. Her legs flopped behind her, heavier than lead weights. She had no idea if they were kicking as she told them to. She swam straight for the sea floor with both arms stretched ahead of her, feeling, searching.

Something collided hard with her and she spun towards it, reaching blindly through the water. Natalie closed her arms around whatever she could get a hold of and pulled. A sharp tingling of electricity spread from her fingertips. She let go of her cargo and thought of the lighthouse.

Its curved walls, the black and white stripes, its warning beacon, the devastated faces of my friends...

Natalie clutched the drenched document still hidden beneath her jacket.

Liar.

Her mind drifted back to her talk with Uncle Chris on the roof of Ancora II.

Was everything a lie?

Her thoughts were sluggish. She remembered the warmth of the California air, the dogs running down the beach after a ball… Gravity rushed up beneath her and Natalie pushed herself to her knees. She coughed water onto the warm sand between her hands.

Sand?

Callused hands helped her to her feet. Christopher squinted against the sun sinking beneath the waves behind her.

"You shouldn't be here!"

Natalie had to hold his forearms to stay vertical. They thawed her frozen fingers.

"Where am I?" Natalie asked, on the verge of hysterics.

How is Christopher standing? Where is the lighthouse?

Beyond Christopher, a modest cottage with vivid yellow siding and a rooftop porch basked in the glow of the setting sun.

Ancora II…

"Go back," he instructed her. His voice was firm and insistent, yet he beamed at her.

"Uncle Chris I-I," Natalie stopped and started again. "Chris, something's wrong with me."

"Oh, kid," Christopher cupped the sides of her face. "You're perfect. Not a hair out of place."

"No, I think," she swallowed hard, reluctant to say it aloud. "Go back."

"I traveled back in time," she blurted.

"I know, kid. I know."

"I traveled back in time," Natalie whispered again, staring at her hands as though they were to blame. She absorbed his words slowly. "You know?"

"Nat, listen to me. Go back. You're the most dangerous thing on the planet. We don't know what happens when you fiddle with the timeline, so don't. The Coelacanth Project is meant for extinction-level situations only, you hear? Don't meddle. No matter what. Don't let Nautilus use you."

"They had us locked away," she choked back tears. "There wasn't any sun for days, and now—"

He shook her.

"Go back," he commanded. "Lead them home."

Christopher pushed Natalie backwards into the sea and she disappeared in a flash of light.

CHAPTER 33

The weightless white flash deposited Natalie beside the wooden planks of the pier. She clung to a pylon as gravity strove to pull her earthward. Someone lifted her up onto the sundrenched wood and she collapsed on her side. Shivers violently rocked her as a tightness clutched her chest.

"Nat!"

I couldn't find him. I failed.

A heavy blanket enveloped her and someone sat her upright. She bit her lip, vainly striving to hold back the tears already spilling over her cheeks. They were oddly warm against her icy skin.

"No Leo?" Owen knelt next to her.

"He-here?"

The smallest shake of Owen's head sent Natalie over the edge. She sobbed. Her entire body convulsed, overwhelmed by the physical and emotional torture.

"L-lost," Natalie cried into the blanket. "P-p-parents capttured, C-C-Chris shot. Wh-what," she drew in a sharp breath that stabbed her lungs. "What have I done?" Natalie tore the spark off her wrist with fumbling fingers and threw it as hard as she could.

It didn't go far. Tawney picked it up off the pier and pocketed the stone.

"Let's get you dry," Brant attempted to carry her, but Natalie shook her head.

She forced herself to her feet and, leaning against Brant for support, she shuffled her way inside the lighthouse. Tawney ran ahead of them. By the time Natalie reached the couch, a clean change of clothes, a towel, and a blanket waited for her.

"Do you want help?" Tawney offered. A lively Angie wagged her tail in the shelter of Tawney's arms.

Natalie refused and they left her. She removed the bolt from her back and propped it carefully against the wall. Trembling, Natalie unfolded the heavy cardstock from her jacket and hid it beneath the couch to dry. Too exhausted to find a better hiding place, she hoped no one would find it. She wasn't ready to share the contents with the others.

She pulled out the group photograph Chef had given her of their last complete Formal Friday and laid it beside the Coelacanth document. Natalie set out the individual envelopes of Polaroids in front of the fireplace. Each created a puddle of water on the floor beneath it. She suspected they were ruined, but set them up to dry all the same.

It took her a painfully long time to get out of her soaking wet Nautilus uniform. The dampness made it cling to her skin while her numb, uncooperative fingers struggled to grip the fabric. Freed from her navy jumpsuit, she used the towel to dry off as much as possible before donning the loose fabric pants and thin, long-sleeved shirt.

Natalie laid on the couch and pulled the fleece blanket tight around her. Guilt churned her gut at the thought of the Coelacanth document hidden beneath her.

They deserve the truth.

But she was too exhausted to give it to them. Enzi crawled into a ball at her feet and as she lost consciousness, part of her hoped to never wake.

Natalie woke alone, when the sun was still high in the sky. Every muscle throbbed as she rose from the couch, but her mind felt lucid again. She checked under the futon to find her secret had remained untouched. A sigh of relief escaped her. She slipped the paper and photograph into her shirt and headed up the spiral staircase to hide it somewhere more secure.

The first landing was as open as the ground floor, but instead of a couch and a kitchen, there was a four-poster bed and a wardrobe. An open window welcomed in a summer breeze that billowed out the floor-length white curtains. Tawney was crossing the room in a handstand, deftly shifting her weight from one arm to the other. Natalie tried to continue unnoticed up the stairs, but Tawney caught her.

"Nat!" she exclaimed, collapsing in a joyful heap on the floor. "You're awake!"

"Yeah," Natalie crossed her arms against her stomach, hoping Tawney missed the square impression against her shirt.

I should tell her, but it doesn't feel right.

"Where am I staying?" Natalie asked.

"Follow me!" Tawney slipped between the stairs above Natalie and bounded from one stair to the other. "One up here is supposed to be yours."

They passed two floors identical to Tawney's, each smaller in diameter than the last. When they stopped at the fifth floor, the staircase continued upwards.

"There are two more bedrooms up there," Tawney explained, following Natalie's gaze. "Then there's the light! It's pretty cool. Want to climb higher?"

"Maybe in a bit," Natalie peered out the window. The surrounding sea sparkled in the sunlight.

"Where's Enzi?"

"On the beach with Brant and Owen, and Angie, too. There isn't another house around for miles."

"We need to be extra careful here," Natalie warned. "They shouldn't stray far from the lighthouse."

If Leo is okay, he knows to come here. If we leave, he would have no idea where to find us.

"I'll remind them," she turned to leave, but Natalie caught her.

Natalie held Tawney at arm's length and looked her over. A scab covered the majority of her chin and thin scratches scoured both cheeks. One of her palms was bandaged and she still carried a pistol around her waist. Her round brown eyes squinted suspiciously.

Give that to my fierce girl.

Natalie pushed Tawney's brown curls away from her face and kissed her forehead. Tawney threw her arms around Natalie's shoulders and squeezed. Natalie's body ached in response, but she didn't move away.

"We'll find him, Nat," Tawney whispered.

"I know," Natalie lied. "I'll be down in a minute."

As soon as Tawney had disappeared down the stairs, Natalie pulled the envelope from her shirt and opened the wardrobe. A rack full of flowing soft shirts met flush with a high column of drawers. Natalie opened the bottom drawer and tucked the Coelacanth letter and all of its heavy implications away. She supported herself against the wardrobe, mentally dodging all of the thoughts her mind wanted to obsess over. The adoption, time travel, Uncle Christopher; she didn't want anything to do with any of it.

Natalie caught sight of four old friends balanced on a modest bedside table. Plato, Crichton, a bloodied Dr. Seuss, and the logic puzzle were neatly stacked, awaiting her arrival. Propped against the stack of books was a crumpled white envelope. Natalie opened it and fanned through dozens of photographs.

Seaside cottage, seaside castle, seaside cave, seaside cottage, seaside lighthouse, the photographs went on and on: more Ancora's than they could use in a lifetime.

To her amazement, Natalie smiled. Christopher was still looking out for her, helping her find home in the chaos. She gingerly hid the envelope of safe houses and *Oh, the Places You'll Go!* alongside the Coelacanth document in the bottom drawer of the dresser. Forever stained with Leo's blood, the book was too painful to look at. He had saved her life and when it came time to repay the favor, she had failed him.

Natalie took the logic puzzle and the group photograph of a Formal Friday long past, and drifted back down the stairs. An idea was forming in the back of her mind, something inspired by Uncle Chris and Chef. She swallowed a heavy lump in her throat.

Chef died to get us out of Nautilus and I don't even know her real name.

Natalie reached the ground floor and noticed the few surviving Polaroids had been placed above the mantle of the fireplace. She scanned through them again as Tawney, Brant, and Owen filed in from outside.

Brant and Owen, both slick with sweat, sat heavily on kitchen chairs, while Tawney led Angie and Enzi to a treat jar. Natalie repeatedly glanced at the empty seat that remained between Brant and Owen. She thought at any moment Leo would materialize in that chair, as though nothing happened.

"I wanted to apologize," Natalie set the logic puzzle on the table and clicked its sides to activate the hologram. Once again, the glittering orb materialized before her. "It's my fault we were captured. Which led to everything else…"

"Nat—"

"Tawney, please," Natalie tucked a piece of hair behind her ear. "Nautilus has our parents. They're Nautilus's greatest advantage against us and they know it. Uncle Chris will surely be in the hospital for a while and after he's out, he's done. I don't want him involved anymore. It's too dangerous and this is our fight. And, of course, I couldn't find Leo," Natalie drew in an unsteady breath and laid the group photograph in the center of the table. "This photograph and those Polaroids were all given to me by Chef."

"Why did she give them all to you?" Tawney asked.

"I suppose it was easier for her to slip everything to one person rather than risk her safety four times over. She gave us a reminder that our parents love us."

"Of course they do. Why wouldn't they?" Brant asked.

Natalie's cheeks burned.

We're adopted.

It was on the tip of her tongue, but Natalie couldn't do it. She stared into the logic puzzle, distracted by particles of dust in the air refracting the fragile beams of the hologram.

Question everything.

What if it isn't true? I'd be upsetting them for nothing.

A lie. She knew it was true. It made perfect sense.

It doesn't change anything.

Another lie. It changed everything.

They should hear it from our parents.

Her conscious quieted. That would suffice, at least for the moment.

All the more reason to save them from Nautilus.

"Nat?" Owen interrupted her thoughts.

"Sorry," she shook her head to clear it. "There's something else." Natalie picked up the bolt and twirled it absentmindedly between her fingers. "When I tacked back to find Leo...I, well, I went farther than I anticipated."

Tawney, Brant, and Owen stared at her.

"Do you mean," Owen adjusted his glasses. The corners of his mouth twitched hesitantly into a tiny smile. "Are you saying you...well, you know?"

Natalie nodded.

Owen stared up at her, wide-eyed.

"Could you tell what kind? There are three major theories —"

"Hey, what's going on?" Brant cut him off. "Theories about what?"

"I traveled back in time," Natalie whispered.

Brant and Tawney investigated the floor, as though captivated by the faux wooden tiles.

"Natalie, you've been through a lot," Tawney started.

"Yeah, we all have, and there's a lot more going on here than we've been told. Tacking is just the surface. Think about it. If we can travel through time, suddenly Nautilus's drive to find us and their sermons on creating peace make a lot more sense."

"I'm not sure," Tawney bit her lip.

"How did you do it?" Brant fiddled with the spark on his wrist. "Travel through time?"

"Absolutely no idea," Natalie admitted. "I didn't do anything differently. I just so desperately wanted to get back there to him."

"What was it like?" Owen asked in awe.

"Well, it was like tacking. Exactly like tacking. I had no idea what had happened until I saw us fall from the cliff. I thought I had lost my mind."

"I suspected this was possible, from the moment Brant first tacked. Space and time are linked; it wasn't much of a leap to conclude we could manipulate one if we were already manipulating the other. I mean, time travel," Owen ruffled his red hair.

"So what all did you see?" Brant shifted in his seat.

Natalie shrugged.

"Not much. I watched myself struggle with Uncle Chris. I didn't find Leo, so I tried to come back here, but then I accidentally time traveled again."

"You did it twice?" Owen gasped. "Could you interact with the timeline? Did any of the theories fit?"

Normally, Natalie could follow Owen's nerdy tangents, but this time he lost her.

"What theories?" Tawney rested her head in her hands. "It's either time travel exists or it doesn't, right?"

"Thanks to SuperNerd," Owen high-fived Natalie, "that question has been blown out of the water. The next question becomes: what kind of timeline does our universe exist within? There are three major theories: fixed, dynamic, or multiple.

"If our timeline is fixed," he continued, "going back in time won't have any effect on the present because those actions have already been taken into account. Think of it like a loop and the present is inevitable."

"But if the timeline is dynamic," Brant leaned in, "any actions in the past can change the present."

Owen twirled his beard stubble.

"That is the most dangerous possibility. If altering situations in the past does change the present, you could create desirable changes. However, you could also create paradoxes and shift the course of the universe towards dissolution."

"What's behind door number three?" Tawney asked apprehensively.

"Alternate realities," Owen nodded. "It's possible that each journey into the past is actually a journey into a different reality, where your actions would only change the events taking place in that reality, not our own."

"Nautilus is counting on the second option," Brant knocked his knuckles on the table. "A dynamic timeline we can change."

"So was Coelacanth," Owen noted. "We're a contingency plan, remember? Meant to rescue humanity from extinction if ever necessary."

"So which is it?" Tawney crossed her arms and turned to Natalie. Brant and Owen followed her lead.

Natalie shrugged.

"I don't know."

"Did anything change after you went back?" Owen asked her.

"I don't think so," Natalie tried to remember, but it was

difficult. "I don't know."

"Was there anything new when you returned to the present?"

"Owen, I don't know!" Natalie was getting frustrated.

"Well, until we know, it isn't safe," he failed to hide his disappointment.

"That's Christopher's biggest concern. I spoke to him briefly outside Ancora II. He warned against using it. He said 'we don't know what happens when you fiddle with the timeline.'"

A long stretch of silence followed her words.

"That means he doesn't know which timeline we fall on either," Owen tapped the table, puzzled.

"Christopher really lied about a lot," Tawney sank into her chair.

"Yeah," Natalie watched the shimmering orb rotate before her, much like the globe hidden away in their parents' office. "He did, didn't he?"

The intertwined pathways were black against the hologram's glowing surface. One of the swirling patterns spun into view with a circle at its center. The white pin bobbed in place atop the sphere, waiting.

"He lied about everything," Natalie breathed.

Wake up, she repeated Christopher's last clue. *I've done nothing but wake up since the bombing. My home was a lie, my parents were a lie, my normal life was a lie. Even tacking was just a lie, a cover-up.*

Natalie watched the dark circle turn past her: the solution to the puzzle.

No, Natalie's mind raced. *The circle is what Christopher told me is the solution.* The orb blurred as she was whisked away on a shiny new train of thought.

Question everything.

No matter how many times the path to the circle didn't work, I kept trying because Christopher said it was the solution.

I had blind faith.

Another swirl rotated into view with a familiar symbol at its center. She had seen it in Christopher's hidden office and again on the globe in her parents' hide out. Three interlocking ellipses formed a knot that circled on forever: never beginning, never ending.

The triquetra.

Natalie hesitated with her finger above the bobbing white pin.

He lied.

She ran her finger over the orb and the pin followed loyally behind her. Nearly halfway to the triquetra, the pathway ended abruptly. The pin floated back to the top of the sphere. Unperturbed, Natalie started again. The pin trailed behind her finger as she traced another black swirl. It led her one entire rotation about the globe and ended on the triquetra.

Holding her breath, Natalie pushed down on the white pin and it slipped easily through the symbol, into the glittering sphere. The orb shattered, projecting a billion pixels across the room. The pin descended vertically towards the table and dissolved into the casing of the logic puzzle. As Natalie watched, the metal retracted in on itself, opening a central compartment. The inner case was lined with purple velvet and housed an aged, cast-iron key. It was heavy and larger than any key she had seen before, spanning the width of her palm. Rough scrapes along its surface showed where it had been used and worn with time. The same mysterious symbol adorned the handle.

"Woah," Owen stared wide-eyed at the key from behind his black-framed glasses. Natalie passed the prize to him.

"Any idea what it opens?" Brant leaned across the table to get a better look.

"Not a clue," Natalie watched Owen meticulously inspect the key.

He ran his thumb along the bit, tracing ridges that turn the pins within its corresponding lock.

"This part seems different," he muttered mostly to himself.

"It's not iron like the rest. It's yellow."

"It looks like the inside of our sparks." Tawney held out her wrist and showed where the golden center of the rock shone near each end, exposed in the holes she had drilled. "What does that mean?"

"That this key doesn't open a normal lock." Owen transferred the key to Natalie with his hands cupped as though he cradled a baby bird. "I didn't see any locks in Ancora or when we were held captive, did you guys?"

"There are too many variables," Natalie bit the inside of her cheek. "Each Ancora, the Nautilus labyrinth, Christopher's office, our parents' office. Even if we knew what we were looking for, there are too many places to check."

"But Christopher must have given this to us for a reason," Brant crossed his arms.

Natalie racked her brain for any clues Christopher gave about a key, but nothing came to mind.

"Whatever it's for, we should keep it safe." She returned the key to its velvet bed and squeezed the sides of the logic puzzle. The metal panels clicked back into place, hiding the key within its shell.

"A more pressing question," Tawney interjected. "Is how are we going to find Leo?"

"I'm going back," Natalie announced. "Maybe if we all go it will be easier."

"I don't think that's such a good idea," Brant adjusted his red cap.

"You want to leave him there?" Tawney accused.

"I agree with Brant," Owen frowned apologetically at Natalie. "It doesn't make sense, Nat. If he got away, we have no idea where to begin looking for him. If he didn't, if he was still in the water…" Owen didn't finish his thought. He didn't have to.

"We could try to travel back in time again," Tawney offered.

"Uncle Chris warned you against this," Owen said quietly. "There may be consequences and the significance of those consequences will multiply the farther we get from the event."

"Which is why we should do it now," Natalie argued. "It's been, what, a few hours at most?"

No one spoke. Tawney shifted in her seat.

"What?" Natalie pressed, sensing their unease.

"We've been here almost two days," Tawney finally admitted.

Natalie blinked.

"Two days?"

Tawney nodded.

"Owen and I searched for Leo while you were sleeping. It's always so dark there! We couldn't see a thing and it was freezing. Literally. We had to abort mission or we were going to drown."

"I was asleep for two days?"

"I said almost," Tawney assessed the sunlight outside the door. "More like a day and a half."

"He saw the photograph of the lighthouse," Brant said, staring out the open archway to the pier. "If he's alive, he'll come back to us. We can stay here a while."

Natalie tried to push past the fact she had lost nearly two days of her life.

"Let's keep training. Did you keep any of Christopher's pistols?"

"All of them," Brant nodded.

"Good," Natalie nodded. "Give me one."

Tawney's jaw dropped. She relinquished one of the handguns in shock.

Natalie tucked the weapon into her waistband. She despised the feeling of it against her skin but she carried it regardless.

A deal's a deal.

"I want to learn how to use this," she held out Chef's bolt. "And where are our Nautilus uniforms?" Natalie asked, noticing they were all back in normal clothes.

"In a pile outside. We plan to burn them," Brant said

pointedly.

"We aren't burning them," Natalie declared.

"What are you thinking?" Owen asked, trying to read her.

"We will never be able to defeat Nautilus in a brute fight. We are outgunned and refuse to compromise. So, let's destroy them from the inside. We're going to infiltrate Nautilus, get to its heart, and neutralize it."

Hopefully before anyone else gets hurt.

"Are you mad?" Brant snorted.

"Yes. Aren't you?" Natalie asked seriously. "An insane group of radicals are manipulating the planet towards a third World War. I was kidnapped and kept in a cellar because I have an ability I didn't ask for. My parents are being held hostage, I had to leave Uncle Chris with two complete strangers, and Leo...Leo...is not here," Natalie managed, her eyes flicking again to the empty chair. "Nautilus gave us the greatest weapon we can use against them. They forced those uniforms on us."

"Christopher would not approve of this," Owen muttered.

"I told you; Christopher's out."

Owen shrugged in surrender.

"Even if Uncle Chris manages a full recovery, he's done. I don't want him involved. No one else dies for us. This is our fight." Natalie blinked away images of Chef's lifeless body lying at the top of the cliff.

Tawney held her gaze for a long moment then grinned.

"Let's get our lives back," Tawney bounced over and took the bolt from Natalie, replacing it with her spark. "You need to get good at this," she tapped Natalie on the head with the middle of the bolt.

Brant squeezed Natalie's shoulder before going back outside.

"Getting back to normal would be nice," Owen admitted. Angie shuffled around his ankles as he followed Brant out onto the beach.

Natalie rested her chin on the mantle and added the Formal

Friday photograph to the many tiny Polaroids in front of her. It was creased and smeared with water damage, but it didn't matter. She studied her mother's face. It was soft and joy-filled. Unbruised, not covered with blood or concern.

Natalie's thoughts drifted to the document hidden in her wardrobe. Her mother was not her mother, but examining the photograph, Natalie yearned for her touch, for her voice.

I think I can love her the same.

Natalie focused in on Leo. His brown hair was cut short, not even a shadow of stubble on his chin.

"Don't be dead," she pleaded quietly. Natalie turned away from the mantle and scratched Enzi's ears, who sat patiently by her side. She shook her head at Owen's parting comment.

Things will never be normal again.

"What a strange world we've found."

Enzi barked excitedly and padded through the arched doorway. Natalie followed his fluffy white tail outside, returning her spark to its rightful place on her wrist.

EPILOGUE

Sunlight shone from beyond his eyelids as warmth replaced the freezing cold that numbed his fingers and toes. His side throbbed. Every heartbeat sent stabbing shards of pain through his abdomen. He groaned, wishing to be numb again, wishing it was night, wishing he was dead. Death would be better than the pain.

"He's dying," a squeaky voice announced next to him.

"Good."

"Oh, come on," someone whined. "He's still a kid."

"So? He's one of them. You think he got that wound pursuing the path of peace?"

"Come on, Lache," one of them pleaded.

A long silence followed.

Dead?

"Fine," the girl conceded. "Get him inside. Call an ambulance. I'm not paying."

Arms lifted him from under his shoulders and around his legs. He cried out as searing pain tore through his side.

Not dead!

"No! No, please!"

They placed him back on the ground. He took quick shallow breaths, willing the pain to stop.

"My friends insist we get you medical attention, which means we have to move you," a firm feminine voice informed him.

Something blocked out the sun.

Dead?

Long silver hair framed rosy cheeks. Bright blue eyes squinted at him with irritation.

Angel. Dead.

"We'll call an ambulance, Lache," another girl said somewhere beyond his sight.

"He'll bleed out before they get here, but go ahead," the silvery angel said. "Tell me, Nautilus scum, why should we bother saving you?"

He shook his head, which made him dizzy.

"Nautilus through and through."

"Not Nautilus," he croaked.

The angel scowled at him.

"Well, if you dress like a Nautilus and act like a Nautilus…" Lache shrugged. "One less of you might help me sleep at night."

He tapped his chest.

"Not...Nautilus."

Lache took hold of his wrist and investigated the bracelet around it.

"What's your name?"

"Leo Merrick," he coughed and dug the back of his head into the sand as blazing hot fire exploded in his side.

"Leonidas Merrick?" the silver angel clarified.

Unable to respond, Leo nodded.

No one calls me Leonidas.

The angel gasped. "Are you calling an ambulance?"

"Yeah," a voice squeaked.

"Get them here now!"

"Die now?" Leo begged.

"No, no," Lache said firmly.

Something soft forced its way beneath the back of his head. "You must stay awake, Leo. Do you hear me? You are not allowed to fall asleep. Talk to me."

Leo shook his head. Talking hurt. Breathing hurt. Not breathing hurt. Death would not hurt. Death would be easy.

"Talk to me! Isn't there something you want to live for? Someone who's searching for you?"

Oh no.

Green eyes, wavy brown hair, and a timid smile swam before him. She leapt off the back of his motorcycle to find her parents, she was nearly shot to save her dog, she was willing to side with the enemy to free her friends from prison. If he didn't arrive at the lighthouse...the freezing cold water...

She'll go back. Die. Reckless. Idiot.

"Nat," Leo croaked, sitting up.

"What?"

"Nat!"

"I hope that ambulance is close, he's imagining bloody bugs," someone grumbled somewhere behind him.

"Lay still," the angel told him. She pressed on his shoulder and held him down. "Everything will be fine, as long as you stay awake. We're with you."

But who's with Natalie?

"Stay awake, Leonidas."

The angel's face became fuzzy. The warmth of the sunlight had bled into the sand. He sank into it. Warm. Still.

"Stay awake."

A siren sounded somewhere far away.

"People are coming to help you."

Help meant more pain. Leo recoiled from it.

"Angel?" he whispered to the silver haired girl. "Find Nat."

"I will," she promised. "As long as you stay awake. Deal?"

Leo feebly lifted his arm and gave her a thumbs-up. The angel toyed for a moment with something on his wrist, then the sirens grew deafening and the world slipped away.

EXTANT

DISCUSSION QUESTIONS

Level 1

- What was your favorite part about this book and why?

- Would you want to be a character in this story? Why or why not?

- Did you learn anything from this story?

- If you had the ability to tack, where would you go and why?

- Do you have a favorite quote or passage from the book? If so, what is it?

- Which places mentioned in the novel would you like to visit?

- Which character do you think is the bravest? The most selfless? The most selfish?

- What do you predict will happen in the sequel?

- What flaws does the protagonist have? Strengths?

- What strengths does the antagonist have? Flaws?

- How do you think Natalie changed throughout the story?

Level 2

- What themes did you notice throughout this novel?

- If you could hear this same story from another character's point of view, which would you choose and why?

- What do you think of the book's title? How do you think it relates to the plot or characters?

- How does the dual timeline structure of the plot affect the flow of the story?

- The author of this story works with animals as a licensed veterinary technician. How did her profession show through in the story?

- Did you come across any words or references you had not heard of before? Did you look them up? If so, what did you find?

- Natalie mentions that the significance of symbols often change with history. Do you have any predictions for what the triquetra symbol may represent?

- At the end of the final chapter, many questions remain unanswered. Which one are you most curious about?

Level 3

- Do you think there are moments in the story where the setting plays an important role in the plot? If so, when?

- Compare and contrast the values of Nautilus and the Coelacanth Project. Which do you feel more aligned with?

- There is some debate throughout the story whether Uncle Christopher is good or bad. What do you think? Did your opinion change throughout the novel?

- What do you think the poem presented at the beginning of the novel is trying to convey? Why do you think Uncle Christopher would name his boat in relation to this poem?

- Are there any pop-culture references in the story that stand out to you? Are there any that you were not familiar with?

- What do the events and clues in the final part of the story lead you to think the rest of the series will cover?